MYSTERIUM

SUSAN FRODERBERG

Mysterium

FARRAR, STRAUS AND GIROUX   New York

Farrar, Straus and Giroux
175 Varick Street, New York 10014

Library of Congress Cataloging-in-Publication Data
Names: Froderberg, Susan, author.
Title: Mysterium / Susan Froderberg.
Description: First edition. | New York : Farrar, Straus and Giroux, 2018.
Identifiers: LCCN 2017058632 | ISBN 9780374217686 (hardcover)
Classification: LCC PS3606.R5827 M97 2018 | DDC 813/.6—dc23
LC record available at https://lccn.loc.gov/2017058632

Designed by Richard Oriolo

Our books may be purchased in bulk for promotional, educational, or
business use. Please contact your local bookseller or the Macmillan
Corporate and Premium Sales Department at 1-800-221-7945, extension
5442, or by e-mail at MacmillanSpecialMarkets@macmillan.com.

www.fsgbooks.com
www.twitter.com/fsgbooks · www.facebook.com/fsgbooks

1   3   5   7   9   10   8   6   4   2

Endpapers map © Jeffrey L. Ward

This book is for Eric

No man is quite sane; each has a vein of folly
in his composition, a slight determination
of blood to the head.

—RALPH WALDO EMERSON, "NATURE"

The mystery which invests every climb
is its necessary uncertainty.

—WILLI UNSOELD

CONTENTS

PART I

1.

ALPINE JOURNAL

SPECTACULAR MOUNTAINS ARE ALIKE IN THEIR CALL TO
the sublime. Dangerous mountains are particularly spectacular,
having the power to startle and bewilder, as well as the means of
being distinguished by remaining improbable to human life. The
way up every daring summit characterizes itself, and a foothold or a
handhold taken, an abseil or belay, a pitch, a bivouac, an anchor
placed, will be imprinted in the body and in the mind of a climber,

thereby becoming part of his or her being. Whether it is Everest with its Icefall, El Capitan with its Ahab, Rainier and its Cadaver Gap, or Mysterium its Sanctuary, it cannot be otherwise: the attempt to reach the top will alter or defeat any woman or man.

THERE WAS more to be written, but the professor closed his notebook. He wanted yet to say that climbing a mountain was like producing a work of art, that not only did one need endurance, perseverance, nerve, strength, and skill, as well as a degree of intelligence, but it was also necessary to be afraid if the accomplishment was to matter. The professor clipped the pen to the notebook and put them back into his rucksack. He switched the headlamp off, then zipped himself into the downy loft of his mummy-shaped bag. He would think more about what he wanted to say later. He needed a good sleep tonight and an early start tomorrow.

WHO WILL *be the first to take? Who will be displaced? These are not simple questions of heights reached or distances achieved, but ways in which the triumphs are attained. The quest is one of danger and desire, this all would agree. Many speak of conquering, be it that of the fear of perishing, or the vanquishing of a given pinnacle. But how are we to live without fear, when the fear within us is the will to exist?*
   One must be afraid to fall.
   One must be willing to fall.

THERE WAS a cry in the dark, a long delirious calling out. It took him time to climb out of the dream and put himself back to here where he was. He opened the tent flap and regarded the silence. The moon was full and had crossed to the other side of the valley since rising, shining sentinel upon the arsenal of gear the professor had racked up before sleep: a silvery chain of carabiners, an array of cams and stoppers and chocks, pulleys and runners and aid slings, coils of rope for haul and belay. There were water jugs huddled in the luminescence, a tin cup lambent alone, a bag of food that hung larval from a tree. There was another tent now, one that wasn't there before the professor had closed his eyes for the night. He had hoped to have the wall to himself for the days ahead. Ridiculous, but still a wish. He switched the headlamp on and looked at the hands that glowed from his watch face. He could beat the sun in its breach over the peaks if he got the stove going right away and water heated up. He shimmied out of his mummy bag, crammed the bulk into its tubular sack, and began to dress before the oncoming dawn.

COURAGE IS esteemed a Platonic ideal in the Western world. To move toward some unknown, to venture, to risk are strivings we are born to. In our willingness to enter the remote or the hidden, the rare, the strange, the alien, we are rendered not only braver but better and more industrious with respect to that which befalls someone unwilling to attempt the seemingly impossible. To strive is to pull away the cotton in our days, those stretches of time that dull the tongue and muffle the spirit.

Just as the climber aspires to feel more alive, so too the climber may climb for immortality. In choosing a course that could lead to death he or she chooses the glory of being remembered. Though there be no such apparent heroism in poetry, is it not for the same honor the truly noble writer writes?

THE PROFESSOR opened a can of Viennese wieners, plucked the pasty little hot dog shapes of uncertain meats from the tin, and sandwiched them into day-old bread. He swallowed the breakfast down with swigs of instant coffee, considering the words written the night prior. Hardly a beginning. There was so much to be said. But how to say it—and what was the *it?*—to say what has not been said? He looked out to the valley beyond. The light of daybreak paled the face of the wall, making the hump of colossal rock shimmer like the flesh of an enormous sea creature. Luster of granite. Igneous mass. Well-formed crystals of feldspar. Resistant to weathering. Ability to take on a polish. Flesh-colored. Block-jointed. Formed by cooling magma. Widely used as ornamental stone. Those who want monuments. *To-tock-ah-noo-lah.* An aggregate of minerals he would have a chance to dance upon. He had studied the way up yesterday, climbing from the base to the crest with his eyes, and now he did so again, reminding himself how to proceed. He would not be going up the easiest route, but instead following the line a drop of water would take on its way down, this for the sake of the purity of the line itself. He would get at least a third of the way up the prow by sundown, averaging at least as much each day after. It would take him three days of steady upward gain to get to the top; could be four if there were weather or some other unforeseeable go-wrong or whipper. There were unknown variables ahead, but with them clear ways as to how to proceed and so a notion of safety. The route had been planned. He had the power of technique and practice, moreover, the intent. It was all a matter of wanting to do it, wanting to do it enough. With such conviction it would then require only the ability to keep on until reaching the zenith, all the while aiming for some intangible point beyond.

Someone inside the tent opposite coughed. The professor looked out to see the shelter bubble and pock. He heard metal of zipper, mumble of voice, rustling from within. He packed his sleeping belongings into the haulbag, stowed the food sack and water jugs into the pig too, adding any miscellaneous gear for what-ifs: space blanket, extra batteries, anorak, bandages, repair kit, ointment, tape. He picked the burden up and heaved it over his shoulder, adding his coils of ropes onto that. He placed the rack of hardware around his neck for now, planning to shift some of this ironmongery to his hip when he arrived to the base of the cloven dome. He slipped the hammer into its holster, filled his chalk pouch with chalk, took a last swig of the instant and tossed the tin cup into the tent. Then he zipped the tent fly closed and was off before the new light.

CLIMBING IS *a matter of style, perhaps more so of social ethos. Above all, it is a subject of ideology and credo.*

HE STARTED up. He hammered and clipped in, ratcheting his way with jumars, using pitons, skyhooks, chockstones, bolts and nuts and cams, and like this he laddered the face of the granite beast. There were stretches of rock where he could climb free, places that felt like play, and he took full advantage of these occasions, securing the etriers to the back of his harness, placing his hands into cracks and fisting to lift himself, laddering up fissures and seams with his feet. The days ahead would be filled with a mix of jamming and edging, stemming and chimneying, fixing hardware, fiddling with riggings, hauling up the unruly pig of a haulbag; all in all, a lot of work. Climbing a big wall is always that, no question. Especially solo. Alone. Lonely. What it could do. Bewildering as a person disappearing on you.

He thought of her again. Amanda. A name that had become an ache. She had been a mirror to him. Now the wall was his mirror; this trace of glacier he hung upon, a polished shield of rock, a revealing glimpse of all that is.

ONE MUST *abandon oneself to the mountain, embracing a doctrine of boldness. One must give all, despite the terror of falling. The way of overcoming foreboding is to remain in fixed contemplation of the object. Do the work, become absorbed by it, and there will be no time to be afraid. One must be aware of the opacity of any emotion that might veil reason. Cease to consider the when, the where, the why of something, and look simply and solely at the what of it. In the doing, one becomes lost in the object. One becomes the object itself.*

ONLY STONE and space and the rope writing scroll in the wind below. The coolness of granite and metal of tool, air that would ruffle his hair and billow his sleeves. A body in motion searching for the lost one. He hammered. He placed an hexentric for aid. He jugged the fixed line, pulled himself farther up the face, cleaned the pitch, set the pulleys, and lifted the pig. He stood in his etriers, one leg bent under him and the other leg straight, dangling on the lip of a bulge, scanning the wall to choose the next piece of rock, repeating the sequence over and again. Then rappelling, cleaning, hauling, moving upward out of instinct and need. Any monotony was broken by a pause to take his jacket off or halt for a long draw of water, to take a chew of jerky or a necessary piss. He rested, penduled in a granite crucible, with towering pines ministering shadows far down in the valley. Throngs of autos moved sluggishly along, some of the motorists pulling over to stop at the side of the road and lumber out of vehicles, pointing, exclaiming, holding binoculars skyward, shifting their weight. The professor wallowed in the glory of being removed, above the pettiness, the trivial, the mundane.

But the smugness was checked as he went back to work, back to pitch after pitch until the end of the day, when finally he reached enough ledge to stretch himself out on.

Night one bivouac. A place to rest. A place to lie against the wall like a tired child. He opened the haulbag, retrieved the mummy bag and the foam pad, and spread them onto the ledge. He unfastened the gear loops from his hip but left the harness on, remaining clipped to a bolt in the rock. He would eat in this rig, sleep in it, live in it, in it answer nature's callings. He took a bag of food and a jug of water out, the headlamp and the notebook and pen, arranging all within the narrow limits of his berth. He looked out to the vastness about him, gobbling almonds, guzzling water. He thought about hot food, cold wine. He imagined Amanda beside him.

He checked the knot at his waist, stowed the food and the water, then opened the notebook to add to what was there. He looked out to the start of the night, the mountains all the greater in their armor of darkness, their backdrop an inky-blue empyrean. He switched the headlamp on, and put pen tip to the page.

EXPOSURE, FATIGUE, *anxiety gripping me. But I cling to the rock and let the days pass as the wall falls slowly away.*

HE KNEW as he wrote that there were truths impossible to articulate, truths that could be realized only in the doing. The poetry was in the climbing.

AS TO *the matter of style: Is one a peak-bagger, or a lover of icy dales and cols? Does he or she climb as an amateur, a mere player, or in the manner of an aristocrat? Is the game bourgeois or professional, an expression of aesthetic or commercial success? Is it sport for sport's sake, or is it striving for an ideal? And as to the ideal? The thing in and of itself.*

MORNING CREPT across the valley and onto the wall in a delicate calligraphy of shadow and light. The professor molted the confines of the mummy bag and sat upright onto his quoin of rock, clinging to a dream in the warm sun. No aperçu. A sleepy mist lingered very low in the vale. There was fruit cocktail for breakfast that he devoured straight from the tin, a hunk of dried meat and hard bread, a ration of water to follow. He watched little cliff swallows dip and swoop as they fed on the wing. They settled on ledges next to him and lifted their feathery scapulars. They panted. They flitted and chittered. They looked in wonder at the man.

ALL HAS *not been told nor all told shall it ever be.*

HE GATHERED food, water, bed, pad, trash, the notebook and pen, and stuffed all the belongings back inside the haulbag. The air was cool and dry, the rock cool and dry, the world of horizontal far below. He looked for a handhold and started up, a way of getting away from the failings he had left on the page. He chalked and sunk fingers into a crack, using grappling-hook hands to pull himself up, fractioning and edging his feet on nubbins of glassy granite. He moved deliberately, lightly, with backstep and cross step, eyeing for holds, transferring weight, not hugging the rock but standing erect, finessing hardware into cracks, manteling onto ledges, crimping and palming and pinching, jamming, smearing, wedging, spidering himself higher. How to describe the tactile delight? The visual delight? He could only consider this later. It was impossible now. Now all he could do was look for the next grip, fit his foot against the roughness, the smoothness, the coolness, and like this ascend the monolith. Where a hand or a foot was placed, this is what determined his life. One step, next step, eye on rock. This was the only truth there was.

AS TO *social ethos: Does one prefer to climb with a crowd or wander uphill alone? Each way up requires a different scheme or tactical ploy. With the former there is mass, with mass comes object, with object the need to conquer by means of assault, with the use of oppression or force. Troops of climbers become a mountain's invaders, with siege tactics requiring quasi-military strategies; loads and relays, depots, supply lines, columns of porters, canisters of oxygen, councils of war, camp upon camp.*

Alpine-style, on the other hand, makes room for the individual. In surroundings of beautiful desolation, one strides not toward mass, but toward anonymity. One moves away from the mob in the direction of spirit, imagination, soul, with the want of the prophet. Alone, one moves in the rhythm of feet and breathing, and in the moment there arises a sense of being and becoming that is not separate from things, but the same. One becomes orbit and poise. One is rock and space and light.

THE PROFESSOR anchored himself at the top point of the pendulum, paid out rope enough to make his way across the granite by swaying himself onto the new crack stratum. He ran forth and back over the rock, increasing his momentum and building to a long series of running swings, coming up short of his aim the first try. He hung on the face, waited for his breath to settle before rejigging the jumar and going at it again. He took off scrambling, leaping like a deer across the wall. And again he was short. It took several more tries for him to finally reach the far crack, but reach it he did. He clipped into an old bolt he found there. The pendulum endeavor had drained him. He took a moment to rest, bending the knee of his uppermost leg, the other leg outstretched in a sling for balancing. The sun was on him, and sweat rolled down the back of his neck. He wanted a drink, but knew he should hold off. He licked his dry lips, sleeved his brow. He could see his long shadow suspended under him, trembling against the cliff. The trees beneath were turned grassy spears, the river a snake through the green. He had come to the most exposed section of the climb, the point where no possibility of retreat existed. He felt very small, no more than a pebble in a crease of the granite mammoth. He leaned into his bent leg more deeply, swallowing drily in the boundlessness that surrounded him, and as he did he heard the dreadful *ping*—that sharp and terrible sound you know too well—and with it the air slapped at his face and he tumbled back into a sudden nothingness, clinging to a bloodcurdling scream that went echoing down through the valley. He dangled like a rag doll, thinking he could still hear the hollow repeat of his horrible wail below. He hung there, oscillating elastically in the stretch of the rope, believing only in the power of the well-placed piton that had arrested him. He bobbed and twirled in a peculiar aftersensation of pleasure, overcome by the weightlessness and spectral light show of his falling. It was a pleasure cut short by the effort to right himself, the thrill dulled too by the irritability he felt for not placing the nut more securely; a feeling made worse by the piece that betrayed when it hit him between the eyes. The nut had slid down the rope to his harness, and he looked at it now with disdain: the aid changed to traitor. He struggled upright, and once more faced the face.

"God," he said, his voice gone oddly tremolo. He took a breath, calming his tone to fatherly. "You're all right," he said, as if he were speaking to his daughter. He rubbed at the bump on his forehead, and moved on to what became steeper yet.

AS TO *the question of conquering.*

KALEIDOSCOPE OF rock, crystal patterns in the mass. "Look," he said, "keep looking." Eyes to the next reach. "Do not forget," the voice sounding alien to his ear, thinking only of the cold hard grain of mineral now against his fingertips. "Feel it," he told himself. He had to, to ease the cold hard fear of falling, with handholds thin as pencil widths, the slipping grip of his shoe on the rock, arteries of magma intruding into the granite, his blood swelling in the veins to bloat the arms, the aorta, his heart pounding a sound of wanting out, the coarseness of nothing giving beneath him, the coarseness of his breath. He felt the hardness in his body as if he were mineralized, as if he were a man of granite, a man willing himself, reaching, his swiftness increasing with the basic sequence repeating, repeating, and no two moves the same. The rock holds all possibilities.

DOES ONE *grant a right to royal blood, or take the stand of the self-made man? When climbing a mountain, one climbs within a society, even when climbing alone. Why should primogeniture be forever a cardinal rule of laying claim? Upon the mountain, the hopes and the aims of the commoners are those of the patricians. For as piracy and war are the beginnings of nobility, so the beginnings of nobility are but an individual's natural superiority; this be true for any woman or man willing to play high for great stakes. Thus mountains are a paradise for those who might become nobles, where every man has a chance to be a baron or a knight, every woman a countess or a queen. At the precipice, one may wander in the kingdom of the possible. Even the names might be taken. Chomolungma yields to Everest as Tahoma does to Rainier; Denali reigns again over McKinley, while Mount Sarasvati remains forever our Mysterium.*

    A climber climbs to name things.

THE TEDIUM. The teeming space. The blazing sun. The incense smell of cedar from the heat off the trees so far down in the valley. The dihedral, the great open book of rock in front of him, hands and feet along the long crack that spines the parts into two and he creeping up and into it, moving forth, duteous, unquestioning. The geometry of the rock, the geodesy; beauty of a perfectly faceted diamond. The mechanical actions, the movements methodical: placing nuts, chocks, slivers of metal, clipping in, rappelling after the pitch, lifting the pig, removing hardware as he moved along, untangling lines, checking the harness knot and buckles too often but instinctively, preparing the next section to repeat the process again, time evaporating like the sweat on his flesh, talking to himself, talking to Amanda. Shadows on the wall across the valley made the shape of a large heart, dark and perfect. His swollen hands pulsed out each beat of his own hollowed muscle; closed-chambered and fisted as it was. He leaned back in the harness, suspicious. He saw her here. She had climbed this face. She had waltzed upon it. Now he pictured her down on the valley floor looking up at him. His Amanda. If only to fall to her. Fall with her. Wonderful. A wonder fall.

    What if?

    Wasn't it the *what if* that made him climb? Made any climber climb?

    It has to be real enough to kill you.

    The final night. The dark slammed down on him. He slept in the hammock beneath the overhang, cradled thousands of feet in the air, a caterpillar in its silken girdle. The rock swelled into a roof that loomed above. He moved from one disagreeable position to another, bent and shifting continuously throughout the night to alleviate the numbness, the spasms and twinges. He was thirsty, but saved what water remained for the heat of tomorrow. He tried to think of pleasant things. If she were here. They could complain together, joke together, manage the night together in their way. He thought of her in her fall. He rarely did this. He wouldn't allow it. But he let himself think of it now, imagining her in the outward arc she drew through empty space. Ten years ago, this day. He pictured the accident for just a minute—no, less—just for the time it took from beginning to end—the mere seconds it takes for a thousand-foot drop. He stopped just before she hit earth, as it happens in a terrifying dream.

He settled into the grateful ache of the need to be with her again.

He drifted into something near sleep.

"Why do the days pass by too quickly, when the nights can be so long?" he had asked her. "The nights are so long because the days pass by too quickly," she had said.

THERE ARE *climbers who climb primarily to enter a deepening mystery. For this woman or man, the long haul up the mountain contains the ecstasy of devotion. No seeker forgoes the slope.*

THE PROFESSOR stood at the top of the mountain, no longer burdened by coils of ropes and racks of pitons and the weight of the haulbag. He was parched and chalked, dirty, thirsty, so very thirsty, his lips blistered, fingers bloated, the skin of his hands worn thin, feet swollen, toes gone numb. He lingered in the strange exhilaration that comes with exhaustion, feeling himself a giant now, with the cliffs and the meadows and the road all so very small below. He looked out to a passing cloud, seeing nature as the manifold, that which bestows and opens. A world of atoms and fire and flux: in it, we are all absorbed.

He turned to what was behind him, feeling suddenly accompanied.

A glove, picked up in a gust, blew past and down off the cliff.

2

SARA TROY

SARASVATI TROY WAS SEVEN YEARS OLD THE DAY HER
mother fell to her death from the face of the cliff. Sara remembers hearing nothing about the accident occurring near to the time that it did, though her father gave her the news only a few days after the tragedy. Professor Troy stood by his daughter at the washbasin as he monitored her climb to the top of the step stool—a fanciful trompe l'oeil platform painted by her

mother to inspire a little Matterhorn—and watched as she was stooped over brushing her teeth, her father explaining the action of up and down rather than of back and forth. Sara was brushed and washed and led to her room, where at the threshold she stopped to gather herself for the nightly leap she made to the foot of her bed, so frightened was she of touching the floor and having hands belonging to who-knows-who the night-sprites were that lived in the down-below grab at her feet. Once she was landed onto the mattress, Sara's father snugged her beneath the quilting, reshaped her pillow, and pulled a chair near to the head of the bed as he usually did. Tonight he had a faraway look in his eyes, with wires of fiery veins in the whites of them, as if he were too tired to read to her at all. She wondered if he would have another spell the way he had yesterday and the day before when he had gone into his room and closed the door and broken into a thunderous weeping. Could it be her mother had done something again to displease him, as she sometimes did being too many weeks away from home? Or might she, Sara, have done something upsetting, demanding more time and tending than what her father was able to give, her needs being the needs of an only child? She smelled the bitterness of coffee on his breath and the woodsmoke in his clothes as he bent forward to palm the hair away from her forehead. She lay still, settled by his touch, hoping for the usual portrayals of fairy-tale beasts and renderings of wild terrain.

Sara recalls nothing of what her father had said when he told of her mother's fatal plummet, his words having dissolved like steam from the recesses of her mind. How would he even have spoken of such a thing? What verbs would he have used to explain: to die, to expire, to perish, to pass or slip away? But he would not have used language that was cliché. Her father was a teacher of philosophy, a man who quoted poets, and if anything he might have told Sara of her mother's demise in terms too abstract for a young girl to understand.

PHENOMENA WITHIN *the form of time we appear, a constant fluctuation of matter, fluid, volatile, fleeting, as are all things in nature. What was becomes that which is. What will be becomes that which was. As a wiser man once said, nothing divine dies.*

SHE WOULD tour the penumbra of her memory. What might have been? Had her father been staring at the play of light on the wall or at the seams of the wood of the floor during his telling? Or had he been gazing out the window at the dark of the night as he spoke of her mother's spectacular ending? And before he switched the lamp off, did he kiss the tip of her nose as he usually did, or was it a tender peck on the eyebrow or lips?

Angel of God, my guardian dear.

There are simple lines from verses learned early that Sara is convinced she will never forget. What she too is certain of always remembering, though the date of the reckoning is unclear, is the very afternoon she discovered, without question, and without her father or anyone else having to announce it: her mother had gone missing for good. The quality of the day, the wistful light of afternoon, the liveliness of the curtains billowing at the window; all this is imprinted in her. Though as to the given day, the month, or even the season—was it barely the beginning of spring, or was it nearly the end of the summer?—that is, as to exactly how much time had passed between her mother's mortal plunge and the occurrence of Sara's startling epiphany, she cannot truly say, for her mother had been an adventuress and was often gone on an outdoor escapade or backcountry feat for stretches of nights and days that kept her a long time away. One cannot always rely on exactitude, this Sara will tell you, for just as one may not be aware of the beginning of a thought before that thought arrives, so why then expect that she be held to apprehending the precise when of her mother's evanescence? Even more puzzling is the amount of time that eventually passed before a second revelation would befall her; that is, her mother was gone bodily—this without a doubt—but she had not completely vanished or been muted. On the contrary, her mother was always and everywhere here these days, despite having decamped from her earthly existence. She was at her daughter's side, or behind and hovering, occasionally ahead, vigilant and guiding, listening to what Sara was saying, studying what Sara was doing, approving, or not, of what and with whom her daughter was playing. She trailed the girl about the house, the yard, the neighborhood, followed her to the park, gave her a push down a slide or a prod on a swing, lifted her to a higher pull-up ring or monkey bar. She accompanied her to school, remindful of mittens in the cold and rubber boots in the rain, patrolling as they crossed the road, endlessly hiving in the foresight of safety and necessity. She peered over her shoulder as Sara sat practicing the scroll of an *M* or an *S* at her desk, and otherwise throughout the day she was encouraging, advising, suggesting, implying, simply mothering the way mothers will do. As the daughter grew older, Sara wished for less maternal proximity, wanting instead more autonomy and privacy. But she understood her mother's deep need to remain close, being so very separate and ghostly alone as she was in that bottomless crevasse of timelessness.

As Sara neared adolescence, she concluded that the constant company of her mother was surely nothing more than her own childish invention, much like a Santa Claus or a guiding saint or an invented playmate. For didn't Sara believe, at least for a period during her earliest years, that all dead people were constantly stirring about in the ether, floating around in the fore and the aft of existence, and so were able to see whatever you did, whenever you did it? Such notions, she realized, are naturally and eventually outgrown. But because she had become used to having her mother so near, and considered this more a blessing than an illness or a hindrance, then why should there be any harm in keeping on with her girlish beliefs? So as Sara grew into her teenage years and soon on to young womanhood, she continued to stay keen to her mother's loving presence, understanding this numinous experience as a wondrous thing. Sara believed she had been bestowed a gift, an awareness of otherworldliness she accepted with utmost care and seriousness. Though of the unusual faculty with which she believed she had been graced, she told not a soul, not even her father. Especially her father. Professor Troy seldom spoke of Amanda, and the daughter learned to honor his wish.

As time went on, Sara heard stories aplenty from the mouths of others, reading too from the pages of magazines and old newspaper clippings of her mother's dramatic passing. For her mother had been an admired climber and a mountain guide, spoken of and written about and photographed often. There was the large framed picture that Sara's father had hung over the mantel, as well as the various journals and specialty books in which Amanda appeared.

Despite the loss of mother and wife, daughter and father carried on in near-perfect serenity. They lived in a Craftsman-style house at the top of a hill surrounded by water, and from this perch they could see mountains all about in the distance. To the east lay the craggy range of the Cascades; the wet forests of the glorious Olympics stretched directly west; Mount

Baker rose a chieftess in the north; and to the south there appeared the glaciered volcanoes of Adams and Rainier, as well as the cloudy plume from St. Helens's brewing fumarole.

Sara could likely find her father at work in the room he called Base Camp, hunched over his desk writing or tipped back in his chair pondering. Behind him were shelves of books, most of these readings on the subject of philosophy, spines embossed with the names of Wittgenstein and Heidegger, Hegel and Kant, Hume and Locke, Heraclitus, Aristotle, Plato. There were also books that went beyond Western thought, some that ventured wildly into theosophy and theology, with authors such as Swedenborg and Milarepa, de Chardin and von Bingen, Professor Troy believing it a good thing to bend one's thinking. Otherwise one could find on the shelves a plenitude of books about climbing, as well as numerous volumes of poetry. For nearness and safekeeping, Troy kept Amanda's favorite books on the topmost shelf closest to his desk: *The Book of Secrets*, *Faith in a Seed*, and *The Divine Comedy* among the few.

Though Professor Troy rarely spoke of his deceased wife, the bedroom he had arranged for his daughter was adorned with climbing relics of all sorts, most all of them Amanda's once-favored equipment. His wife's backpack was doweled on the wall, gravid with a mummy bag stuffed deeply into its middle; her boots laced together and enshrined on a nail beside. Elsewhere covering the walls were various coils of ropes, loops of nylon webbing, brandishings of old crampons and stoppers and chocks. Ice axes and picks hung handsomely aslant.

Amanda's wristwatch and glacier glasses had been placed on a silver tray beneath her photograph on the mantel, along with a necklace of cinnabar beads that had been blessed by a holy man in India.

Sara would poke at the fire, the picture in a molten glow

above, her mother's eyes cast down and glimmering upon those below. She tried to remember her mother as she was when she had been among the living, wanting to add color and lightness to the flickering stream of diminishing memories, and wishing to add warmth and breath and depth to the present company Amanda had become. Sara would watch the fire as it blazed, softening her focus to kindle precious images. She would see her mother out in the yard suspended from the uppermost boughs of one of the old madrone trees; harnessed and asway, a small power tool in hand, Sara's father calling up from down below to *please let me do that, Amanda!* and her mother chortling amid the smooth red branches and oblong leaves. She was often penduled high above the rest of the world; whether in the far reaches of a tree while pruning or up on the tallest rung of a ladder as she painted the house, or up on the very top of the house itself in rubber-soled climbing shoes, armed with hammer and crowbar to pry loose any worn shingles from the roof. "Rock," Amanda would holler when a piece of flashing or gasket or slate might be spilled to the ground. Even at the grocery store, her mother seemed always in need of what would be in the upper recesses of the place. Sara, legs dangling from the child seat of the shopping cart, neck craned back with eyes uplifted, watching as her mother studied the lower and middle shelves for handholds and footholds before proceeding to escalade the racks of cold cereals and condiments. "They always keep the good stuff out of reach," she would say.

Sara clearly recalls too her mother's stories of traveling through India, and loved most the telling of how she had been named. Amanda's eyes would shine as she described her time as a newlywed, when she and Sara's father had trekked through the hills of India. "The Garhwals were a dazzling chain of sparkling peaks, beautiful jeweled tabernacles among the Himalayas," her mother said. "Most unforgettable was the heavenly mountain named for the blessed goddess Sarasvati. She was twin-peaked, sublime in form and pure of line, poised alone in her rise above the other summits. Your father and I stood there in awe and promised that if we should have a daughter someday, we would name her Sarasvati. And so you were invoked, Sarasvati, and soon enough appeared."

IN THE framed photo on the mantel, Amanda stands on a rise of earth poised heavenward with a soffit of cloud overhead, the wind blowing strands of her dark hair wildly about. She has a great swelling of spherical belly, a downy-covered hillock that had been Sara at the time, a mound made grossly noticeable by the harness secured about mother's hips and the backpack strap cinched snug above the breastbone.

Seven years later: *She had not been securely tied in.*

This had been her father's proclamation, heard by Sara just once.

Her father was tall and lean and very strong, though his shoulders had begun to roll slightly inward, as much as his thoughts had—a widower's change in him that his daughter had noticed—a withdrawal and a lessened awareness of her are what she saw. It is true he was often distracted, but he was as conscious and mindful of his daughter as he had been of his wife. Sara embodied her mother, and the girl's presence was a continual and faithful renewal to him.

When not base camped in his study, the professor could be found busy in the kitchen preparing one of his many specialties, usually listening to a favorite piece of music, a clarinet quintet. He played it over and again, never tiring of its unsentimental tenderness and intertwining theme; the melody of cello as out of a cold hollow, the violins a series of rhythmic turns as in snow. The professor hummed to the long-breathed refrains, while Sara cleared away her sketchpad and pencils to set the table for dinner.

It was mountains that Sara loved to draw the most, learned first by copying from books as her mother had taught her. She went on to work from snapshots, and then eventually from memory, drawing a given peak that she and her father had seen on a particular hike or a drive. Lately she worked from imagination, her mountains turning into extraordinary masses of scoria and basalt and tuff. Morning sun in the background. Subalpine lupine in the foreground. A lenticular cloud above.

The mountain she had of course mastered most artfully was that of her namesake, Sarasvati, the pinnacle so titled for the goddess of Hindu and Buddhist myth. Mount Sarasvati, also known as Mysterium.

Its massif was shaped like the letter M. *M* as in mother.

A more secure type of knot has been named in her honor.

Sara drew what she could from descriptions of Mysterium's configuration and from what she had seen in pictures; a double-pinnacled massif with a knife-edged ridge crest and an ominous rock buttress: the mountain for which she had been named. She was captivated by it, and felt it as part of her being. Eventually, renderings would not be enough, and so she made plans to travel with pen and ink, pencils and drawing pad, camera and wide-angle lens, intending to appreciate this home of the gods more deeply, to capture in a glance a mirrored reflection of herself.

Sara would make the trip alone, not counting the faithful spirit of her mother's company. She arrived to Delhi in the fall. From Delhi she journeyed north to Darjeeling and from there ventured northeast to the village of her chosen destination. She spent days moving by train in sweltering heat, the passenger cars packed full with people and chattel. Then, more hours of travel to follow by bus down hot dusty roads clotted with traffic of every type: autos, lorries, motorcycles, ordinary cycles, rickshaws and bullock carts, donkeys and camels and goats pulling loads, monkeys chattering hysterically in the trees. What a surprise to see all of life out on the street in full air: everywhere children begging, turbaned men lounging, women wound among the crowds all in brilliantly colored saris. Crippled limbs, dead eyes, a thrust of hands, the warning of horns, and everywhere cows, cows, cows. Tin collectors and ragpickers gathered trash, pigs and dogs nosed the ground for whatever filth might remain, while buzzards swooped into holy towers to peck offerings of human flesh. Ends converted to new means; whatever might be left aground or afloat had served its purpose to the uttermost.

The bus unloaded at the end of the paved road and Sara traveled the rest of the way by bicycle rickshaw, finally arriving to the guesthouse in the village at the base of the snowy range. She was tired and wilted and grimy, weighed down with an overstuffed backpack, her ears ringing, eyes stinging, throat parched. People everywhere stared at her as if she were a being from some other world entirely, with her turquoise eyes and milky skin and fine light hair. Some of the locals were bold and ventured near her to speak, a few asking if they might touch her hair. Little children, without asking, reached for the hem of her skirt or the tail end of her long braid and, laughing, ran shyly away. An elderly woman from the village approached her and bowed, and Sara allowed the stranger to thumb vermilion on her forehead just above and between her pale eyes. The bindi gave Sara a beatific appearance, and even more were the villagers drawn to her. She was wreathed with necklaces of marigolds, invited into homes for meals, offered cup after cup of spicy milk tea. Sara could feel Amanda encouraging her to volunteer at the village school once she was settled in. Sara, at first, resisted the voice, wanting more time for walks that brought her closer to Mysterium. She also wished for her mother to leave her to her own choices and purposes, as she was now herself a grown woman with a sensible enough head on her shoulders. But within weeks Sara had given in to her mother's counsel and was teaching at the village school, a single room packed with barefoot children seated on a cement floor. Sara was pleased to be there, and the children could see this in her radiant face and in the grace of her gestures. They called her Sunahra-mata: Golden Mother. And in Sara's mothering, she became more a mother to herself.

When her time at the village school came to an end, she could at last make a trip north to have a look at Mysterium, her plan being to get as close to the mountain as was allowed without a government permit and a proper expedition. She hired a guide and two porters to accompany her up to one of the smaller encircling peaks. Their way took them through tropical forest that brought them steeply out of a valley up to a long ridge, and then farther up to the high rim of a magnificent basin. From here they were able to look down into Sarasvati's inner sanctuary, an esplanade of glacier and rock, with hanging valleys of grassy slopes and grazing herds of bharal and tahr, the landscape a fortress that lay between the foot of Sara's namesake and a barrier ring of giant peaks. Anyone wanting to climb the great mountain would have to first pass through this citadel, a steep and forbidding descent from the edge where they stood. From the brink they looked directly ahead at Mysterium, Mount Sarasvati, Goddess of Joy, appearing to them to be rising out of nothing, afloat on a bolster of clouds, levitated, a picture of ascension. The double-peaked massif shimmered in the alpenglow, the lesser eastern summit descendant to the western, the one as guardian and part to the other. "Like mother and child," said Sara, breathless and shivering. A lambent red glowed otherworldly along the curvature of the earth, where rock and snow and ice met sky, and above these palisades and ramparts was spread a rose-colored backscatter, a crepuscular light emitted in prisms and beams. What Sara saw was a picture of eternity, and she was enraptured by it. She had the world ahead of her entirely. To the east lay Nepal, to the north was the high plateau of Tibet, and all around were surrounding glaciers giving way into three main rivers in the valley below, two of the rivers flowing directly southerly into the Ganges. Mother Ganges: ever flowing, ever changing, ever the same; from the threshold they could see where her powers began.

"The fortress below is home of the seven rishis," the guide said. "Hindu sages. The mountain's unrelenting guardians." The porters had bowed their heads and were uttering words to their deities.

Sara looked up, not at the amphitheater of glacier and river beneath her, but at the incite of her christening. "There," she said, pointing to the topmost peak, knowing her mother was listening. "I will stand there someday."

September 7, 1980

Dear Mr. Virgil Adams,

I am Sarasvati Troy, the daughter of Professor Stuart M. Troy and Amanda Laurel Troy, and I introduce myself to you here in the hope of someday making your acquaintance. You're familiar with my parents since many of my father's essays have been published in the American Alpine Journal *while you've been the editor there, and you also wrote a profile about my mother that was printed in A.A.J. only a year before she died. I don't take it as coincidence that the mountain you climbed and made history on just so happens to be my very namesake, but instead feel this as a most important link between us.*

I'm sure you don't need reminding that your success was almost a quarter century ago, the very day coming up next summer. Call it providence (a favorite word of my mother's) that the anniversary of the mountain's crowning also happens to be my twenty-fifth birthday. I was born the day you stood at the top, and I celebrate birthdays by blowing out candles and wishing such an accomplishment true for myself in this lifetime. What memories you must have, and what stories! I hope someday to have a chance to sit and listen to these stories, without sounding too much like just another one of your many admirers. Forgive my clumsiness here, but let me anyway get to the point and say I would absolutely be honored to shake your hand if you might be good enough to give me the opportunity. I'd be happy to fly to Boston for a visit and will promise to keep my stop-by short— maybe just for a few hours of a morning or afternoon? Unless you might happen to be in the Pacific Northwest anytime soon, allowing my father and me to be your welcoming hosts in our home.

Yours most truly, Sara Troy

P.S. Enclosed is a picture I drew of the mountain for you.

"HOW ABOUT I clean up?" Sara said. She was wearing her mother's emerald-colored sweater, and had put the clarinet quintet back on the stereo.

Her father stirred the few remaining embering coals and went to the room he called Base Camp and sat at his desk. Out the window, ominous wavelike shapes with cumulous towers obscured the mountain south. Dashes of rain appeared on the windowpane. A black-tailed deer feeding on the salmonberries and the Himalaya blackberries in the purlieus of the yard bolted off in a leap, leaving behind in the mud its tracks of split hearts.

Professor Troy turned his head to the page and began to write:

Utilitarianism as opposed to the Categorical Imperative: greatest good for the greatest number, or do unto others as you would have them do unto you? As to decision-making in the mountains: argue each and which.

He had left the door open and could hear Sara in the kitchen quietly talking to herself, carrying on the way she used to when conversing with her mother. She had always a natural proclivity for chatter, since she first began to speak. He could not make her words out, and he did not care to eavesdrop, but since her return from India he could hear in her voice a difference, there now being a slightly more musical lilt to it. At his approach, she would stop talking, and always Troy was careful to give a word or a cough, a scuff of a heel, a toss of a key, anything to announce his coming.

He looked up from the page and out to the darkening tent of weather. Tendrils bled like ink from a threatening mass of nimbus. In the distance, a ferryboat sounded a mournful bellow from out on the Sound. What now made him think of his old friend Reddy? Arun Reddy, how was he?

Sara had her hands in soapy water and was sponging the back of a dinner plate when the phenomenon took place; some strange atmospheric shift it was, maybe a warp or a fade or a dilate in the jet stream. A burst of wind flushed sparrows from the trees, jolting the little birds upward and outward erratically in every direction. She raised her head and saw in her reflection in the window a chine of light cleave through the clouds and widen in the sky, a mirrored fiery beam that spread out over her completely.

3.

THE SARASVATI PARTY

THEY MEET AT PROFESSOR STUART TROY'S HOUSE ON AN early spring afternoon. A drizzle outside mounts to downpour, while flames rear to life in the living room fireplace. On the mantel above the fire is the framed photograph of Troy's wife, Amanda, standing on a rocky outcrop at the top of a mountain, eyes focused right at the camera so it appears she scrutinizes those now convened in the room. The eyes take in her husband as he lays copies of an essay out on the coffee table. The gaze includes Wilder and Vida Carson too, seated together on a sofa at one side of the table, and across from them, on the opposing sofa, Doctor Arun Reddy and his son, Devin.

Vida moves restlessly in her seat, shifting from one position to another in an uneasy attempt to settle in. Doctor Reddy, cause of her uneasiness, studies the photograph above the fireplace, conscious of the penetrating look of the flame-lit eyes. He thinks of his own wife. One day, the next day, and like that the world is changed.

The doctor's son, Devin, agreeable mix of father and mother with wavy brown hair and tan-colored skin, picks the pile of papers up and passes a copy to his friend Wilder's wife before handing one to Wilder, keeping an essay for himself, then holding a copy out to his father. The fire crackles and huffs and tongues flames. They lower their heads and read.

Mount Sarasvati, familiar to most as Mysterium, known to the local populace as the bliss-giving goddess, looms 25,845 feet above the surface of the earth. A superbly contoured spectacle rising steeply skyward in the midst of a land recognized as the birthplace of the Hindu religion, she is thereby rich in myth and tradition, inspiring many a holy man, philosopher, and scribe. There is no landscape in the world that incites loftier thoughts than do mountains. Indeed, did God not command Moses to climb Mount Nebo in order to view the Promised Land? The divine career of Jesus was sparked in the once-splendorous hills of Galilee, and his ideas drawn from the altitudinous air. The Tibetan yogi Milarepa wrote his most exquisite poetry on Mount Kailash, where he had made his home in a cave there, and Shelley composed "Mont Blanc" in the Chamonix, overcome with what he described as an overflowing of his soul. Yet even the common man, with little respect for things sacred, has found in the aloofness and majesty of the snowy ranges a reverence beyond compare.

The blessed goddess we call Mysterium is a twin-peaked massif, with a sharp mile-long ridge parting each summit, the eastern summit lower by 745 feet, and recognized as the little goddess, or Mysterium East. A splendid diamond of unearthly proportion, she is set amid a barrier ring of a dozen smaller, but no less precious, gems, none of them under 21,000 feet. These unrelenting guardians, and the impregnability of the mountain's other surroundings, have kept many explorers out of her reach for years. Thus, she remained a supreme temptress, inviolable and eternal, until last year's expedition and our conquest thereof, when, alas, the goddess was overtaken by us. For on August 17, 1956, William W. Hilman and I became the first humans to set foot upon the summit of Mysterium.

The goddess's basin, often referred to as the Sanctuary, is that space amid the foot of the mountain and its ringed fortress. The Sanctuary is itself protected by the Sage's Gorge, a deep, narrow canyon that is known to some as the Valley of the Brahmins, or Valley of the Holy Men; called the Abyss Infested by Devils by yet others. This gorge is a narrow throat of violent river and slick towering walls, making it by far the biggest hindrance to entering the Sanctuary. Nevertheless, it is the single route in.

From Mysterium spring three great rivers, like the many beautiful flowing arms of the goddess Sarasvati herself, two of these rivers emptying directly into the Ganges, the mother river below. Shouldered among the waterways, the Sarasvati range spurs off in outwardly directions to form the letter M. Between the two outermost parallel spurs of the M is carved a shorter stroke, that of the shining pinnacle Mysterium; the longer top and bottom strokes being those of two subsidiary Indo-Tibetan massifs that serve as part of the ring fence of rising sentinels, with secondary ridges branching again from each of these, so in essence forming a fortress

*to the Sanctuary, within which the great Mysterium soars dramat-
ically heavenward.*

Virgil S. Adams
American Alpine Journal, *Spring 1957*

"Adams is a Harvard man," Professor Troy says. "With years
at Oxford mixed in. Hence, his style." He comes back into the
room carrying two pots of something hot that he's brought in
from the kitchen. He is dressed in a pair of fresh denims,
flannel shirt buttoned at the cuffs. "Old Bostonian," he says,
"what they call a Brahmin. A Boston Brahmin. His family
came to this country with the first load of bricks." Troy sets the
containers on the table among a spread of teacups and mugs,
his movements fine and relaxed, precise. "Coffee and/or tea," he
says. "Help yourselves." He takes a seat in one of the armchairs
across from the fire. Watches as Mrs. Carson and his old friend
Reddy continue to read. Watches as they both finish reading.

"Reddy," Troy says. "You're a Brahmin too. Real thing,
aren't you?"

"And I cannot be cast out of my caste, no matter my sins,"
Reddy says. His smile is sharp and quick, his teeth are large
and even and very white. "For all the good it may do me."

"You've all made the how-do-you-dos?"

"Just you left, Professor," Devin says. He gestures to his
friend across the table. "This here's Wilder Carson, buddy I
told you about."

"Brother of Lucas," Troy says. "I see the resemblance."

"You knew my brother?" Wilder says, slumped in his seat,
fists balled in his pockets.

"Lucas was a student in my political philosophy class."

"Yeah, well, we're twins."

"Glad to have you," Troy says, standing to extend a hand, puzzled by his use of present tense. Wilder's handshake is warm enough, but the lack of eye contact lets on a social awkwardness, a peculiarity Troy has seen among other talented climbers, especially those whose style is alpine, even solo at times. Personality types not often of the common persuasion.

"Heard about some of your triumphs even before I'd read your impressive climbing résumé," Troy says. "You've sure nailed a few."

"Make myself into a hammer and go at it. All's there is to it."

"This is Wilder's wife," Devin says.

"Vida. My name's Vida."

"Don't get up." Troy reaches across Wilder and gives Vida's hand a gentle squeeze. "Skip the professor," he says. "Call me Troy."

"Troy." She flushes, smiles nervously. Reddy notices this. Of course he notices. He knows this woman intimately.

"And Wilder, you've met Doctor Reddy?"

"Yeah, me and him just met."

"Yes, he and I have just met," Reddy says. Reddy who has had a long married habit of other women in his life. Reddy who has had Vida.

"Doctor Reddy," she says, "we've actually, he and I already, we were—what was it, last year ago where I was teaching that workshop, wasn't it?"

"Last summer, July it would've been," Wilder says.

"Yes," Reddy says. "July. The lodge out on the peninsula."

"A career boost," Wilder says. "Soon after she got busier teaching."

"What do you teach?" Troy says.

Wilder answers for his wife. "Hindu exercise discipline,"

he says. "Vida's a master of all sorts of tortuous poses. She has people looking like pieces of laundry in a washing machine moving through cycles of tumble and spin."

Reddy and Troy share a quiet laugh.

"How crazy, I mean, how we all ended up here today." Vida hears her voice wavering and thin. But she knew Reddy would be here. Just as he knew she would be. She takes a sip of tea. "Oh," she says, "this is coffee."

"Climbing world is a small world," Troy says.

Reddy says, "You were teaching a yoga retreat that weekend, Mrs. Carson?" As if he has to remind himself of this. As if he has forgotten the long walk they had taken, the loud pound of his heart threatening to give him away every mile of the trail. He had told her to call him Reddy, as everyone did. He had told her he was a doctor, a cancer doctor. He said he had a wife. "And I have a husband," is what Vida said. "And being a yoga teacher, well, you could say healthy people are my ideal too." She had been gathering wild raspberries as they walked along, and she stopped to hold one out to him, the light of late afternoon webbed in her hair. Reddy remembers that light. He remembers opening his mouth to let her drop the berry onto the tip of his tongue. Her fingers, stained from the blood of the fruit, grazed his lips, causing something deeply male from deep within to rush right through him. It was not the first time such a feeling had caused him to move in the direction of another woman. But it had been the last.

"Yoga?" Troy says. "You, Reddy? Tell me you're kidding."

"It was my wife's idea. Maggie's idea. We were taking a weekend. Though somehow we never managed to do any yoga when we were there."

Troy gives his friend a raise of the eyebrows.

Reddy thought to explain. But enough said, and so he did not explain. For to speak of it would be to recall the first hint of Maggie's illness, a part of the weekend he did not wish to conjure, that of the image of his wife mounded over by a downy cover alone in the middle of the bed. The tumulus shape she made. Her hair splayed out across the pillow—when had it become so gray? Gray as the rain that had settled into the valley. Gray as the day. Maggie had not left the bed. Nothing he offered to do could rouse her from her lassitude. She had turned away from him, lay staring out the window. How could he have helped her then, knowing now what he knows? He would not have neglected her. He would not have taken his eyes away, his touch away. He would have listened. But he did not know. She did not know. She had been to the internist. She had been to the psychiatrist. She had been to the naturopath. She had been even to a psychic. She had complained, among many things, of her diminished libido. "You've been married for a considerable amount of time," said the man who delivered her son, Devin, twenty years prior. "Sex with the same person after so many years? Sorry, but we just don't have a pill for that." Reddy's wife had laughed. "You mean yet," she said. She touched the swell of her lower belly, the place just below the solar plexus. Center of sexual drive. Hub of reproduction. She had wondered if this area of tenderness was her sacral chakra or her root chakra. She would ask the yoga teacher at the lodge out on the peninsula over the weekend.

That would have been Vida. Vida Carson. Vida with her ordinary pretty face, but for the one eye that was just slightly askew, a particularity Reddy found immediately appealing. She had a young, muscular body, shoulders rounded and full from repetitive poses, chest held in a position of intention, as if supporting an unreliable weight inside. Vida who now shifts about in her seat. She crosses her legs, uncrosses them, leans forward and takes a sip of the coffee she wishes had been tea.

"Cancer got my mother," Devin says, shaking his head. "Married to a cancer doctor and not a thing in the world he could do about it. He or anyone. Then again, Father was always busy at the clinic doctoring, at least when he wasn't out climbing."

"Medicine is not a perfect science," Reddy says. "And doctors are not gods."

"Right," his son says. "They just too often act like they are."

Reddy lowers his eyes. It is not arrogance, but the neglect his son accuses him of that was his wrongdoing. This is his guilt, his shame. He had forgotten his wife. He had turned away from his son, Maggie's son. And the years too quickly went spinning by.

"I'm sorry, Devin," Vida says. "About your mother. And your wife, Doctor Reddy." But the doctor does not lift his head to look up as she speaks.

Troy goes to the fire, his wife's gaze on all from her perch above. "My husband doesn't care to discuss dead wives," Amanda's eyes are saying. "He prefers quoting poets," say her eyes, "and he will tell you *No poet talks about feelings, only sentimental people do*." He adds another log to the dwindling flames, then puts the wrought-iron screen back to sentinel post and turns to face the group, speaking louder than he needs to. "How about we get on with what we came here to do this afternoon?" He looks at his watch.

"We might wait a little," says Vida. "Aren't we here because of Sara?"

Wilder says, "It's an hour late already."

"Yeah, what's the rush, man?" Devin says. "Have some coffee." He smiles at Wilder, noticing the look on his friend's face, one that's almost always there, a kind of flickering impatience, or else like he's working out calculus equations in his head half the time. But once you get Wilder in the mountains, he's all right. Then it's Wilder at his best. Everyone knows this. Nobody as strong as this guy, nobody as skilled. So he's been a little out of sorts the last year or so, since his brother. But the accident wasn't Wilder's fault. It was just one of those freak things that can happen on a climb. Wilder wouldn't talk about it, but Devin knows being back in the outdoors is his friend's way of working things through. So they get out on the trail a lot, and they train hard. Devin likes the brotherly feeling that comes with being out on the steep together, maybe being an only child and all. And though his father had finally begun to invite him along on some of his climbs, Devin no longer has much interest in being with him. It's too late. Anyway, now he has Wilder, and it's a good thing. They've sat together on punishing summits, looked out to spectacles of snowcapped peaks, looked for different ways up the steepest faces, played the game of naming. They had run up to the top of Apollo with backpacks weighted with cantaloupes. They had talked places, thinking Denali as soon as Devin's semester was over. And then—what luck—chancing into this.

"The photograph," Reddy says, "she would be at the top of where?"

The front door opens and Sara Troy bursts forth in a gust of cool air. She wears a white hooded poncho and is dripping with rain. She pries her rubber boots off, pushes the hood back off her head, shimmies her way out from under the poncho, hangs it on a hook by the door. She is rosy with color, dewy with weather, radiant with smile.

"Everyone's here," she says. "Hooray!" She holds a brown paper bag soaked with rain that has begun to tear away in places.

"You're late," Troy says.

The doctor's son grins at Sara. "You're fine," he says. More than fine. Starting with the first time he set eyes on her, that day on campus, with some rare bird warbling a song from one of the blossoming cherries. Devin had stood at the dorm window looking out into a dazzling light, a light that began to insinuate itself into settled colors and shapes, like a vision of some kind. It was amazing, unbelievable really, seeing all the radiance and shape suddenly becoming a clear and perfect human being. A girl more beautiful than he had ever before seen. He had leaned out the window, hearing the chiming of silvery bracelets as she raised her arms to push the veil of hair away from her face. She had been so near below he could smell the smell of her rising up to him, some sort of cinnamony food is what she smelled of, or buttery, he thought, something totally delicious to eat.

Sara goes over to Troy and kisses him on the brow. She sits on the arm of his armchair, her hair damp and matted against her head. Introductions are made all around. "You look so much like your brother," she says.

"Maybe it's he's the one who looks like me?" says Wilder.

Sara would like to say she's sorry about what happened to Lucas on the Stone Sentinel trip, as everybody in the local mountaineering world has heard about it by now, certainly everyone here in the room, but she can see by the way Wilder holds himself, his head down and looking at nothing in particular, fumbling with something he's got in his pocket, see that it would not be the right thing to talk about at the moment.

"In answer to your question, Reddy," Troy says, "the photograph on the mantel, that's the top of Kilimanjaro. Nothing technical, you know."

"Mother's picture," Sara says. "See her belly? That's me."

"Risky, that altitude at pregnancy," Reddy says.

Troy clears his throat, takes a sip of coffee. "How about we call our meeting to order?" He puts his cup down, sits up straighter. "I suppose I don't need to remind us all of our good fortune at being here with this remarkable opportunity ahead of us, what with a glorious mountain so long closed off to anyone."

"I'll say," says Devin. He nods toward his father. "I'm even willing to put up with this dude day after day."

Wilder snickers.

"We do our best," Reddy says, "is all we can do."

"We're even more fortunate," Troy says, "in having Virgil Adams to lead our expedition."

"Where is he?" Wilder says. "Shouldn't our leader be here?"

"He'll meet with us next time. Mrs. Adams will join us then too. She's offering to manage Base Camp."

"They're not a little over the hill for a climb like this?"

"They're not, Wilder," Troy says. "Rest assured."

"He's superfit for a man of sixty," Sara says. "And his wife, the same. They took me on a hiking trip when I was out visiting them in Boston and, I'm telling you, I was huffing to keep up."

"Truly remarkable that Virgil Adams was right there with William Hilman," Reddy says. "First two to make the summit of Mount Sarasvati. What a feat that was."

"Devin, have we met?" Sara asks. "At school maybe?"

"I've seen you," he says, face reddening. "On your way to class, I guess."

Troy says, "I've looked through everyone's climbing history, and thanks to all of you for getting your info back to me. We've got a strong group here for a self-chosen bunch. A lot of complementary skills among us. We would not do as well one without the other."

Reddy clears his throat. "There is one thing, one troubling matter."

"All concerns are out on the table today," says Troy.

"What troubles me is having married couples on the team."

"Come on, Doctor Reddy," Vida says. "You're joking."

"We can't all be single," Wilder says. "Widowed, or whatever."

"I mean it not against you, Mr. Carson, in particular," Reddy says. "Or your wife." He glances at Vida, that slightly off-center eye making her vulnerable and lovely again.

"Then who in particular are you talking about here?" Vida says. She looks at Reddy now as if she can't really place him. This man who had once been a lover to her. This man she had put her lips to, breathed the words into his mouth: "There is nothing more than this. There is nothing more to want. No other place to be. No one else to be with." Could these words really have been hers?

Sara says, "The Adamses are married too."

"No need to take my concern personally," Reddy says. "But I have seen what can happen. I have seen the dynamics between marital partners, or boyfriend and girlfriend, couples in general, I have seen tendencies that seem to diminish the ability for these people to keep minds straight and to concentrate. I believe, as well, that a couple's allegiance often compromises other team members in that a couple's fidelity is primarily to each other, not to the group itself, nor to the goal itself, which is for all to make it to the top. Be it marital loyalties, or marital disagreements, such things can be absolutely detrimental to an expedition. I have seen it happen, and I have heard many stories too, most all of them with endings not intended."

"Maybe it's a cultural thing you're hung up on," Wilder says. "Being Indian, I mean. With the wife at home doing the cooking and cleaning."

"I am as American as you are, Mr. Carson."

"Disagreements don't just occur between married people," Troy says. "Men and women in close proximity, whether married or not, all can have their problems. I've seen more tempers fly man to man."

"Loyalties shift too," Wilder says. "I've been with guys on a team who double up and care only about the two of them themselves making the summit. Happens all the time. Couple of stronger climbers leaving the rest behind, and not the least bit married."

"Why point your finger at married people, Doctor Reddy?" Vida says.

"It is that, that I . . ." Reddy waggles his head as he speaks, not nodding a yes or shaking a no, but offering some gesture between. "It is, as I am trying to say, have said, it is that oftentimes couples will insist on sticking too closely together, repeatedly to the disservice of others."

Wilder says, "Point's just been made otherwise." He does not explain that sticking too closely together would not be a problem for him and Vida; that he and his wife are rarely aiming for the same thing in the outdoors anymore. He does not tell of the number of times they had tried to get up Rainier before a clear day finally arrived to allow them the summit. He does not say that waiting for the perfect day and predictable conditions takes the splendor and mystery out of a climb. But Vida does not think this way. She is able, but has become too timid above alpine. She needs reliable weather, no surprises. There are arguments every time these days; the mountains too often turned an obstacle between them. Vida shouting, "I cannot be Lucas for you." Vida crying.

"Anyway, Doctor Reddy, you won't need to worry," Vida says. "I'm not on the expedition because I'm trying for the top of Mysterium. My plan's to stay at Base Camp and help Hillary

Adams manage there. She'll be needing help, especially with the equipment and technical stuff."

"Listen, Doc," Wilder says. "Vida and I are happily married and tight as two people can be." He puts an arm around his wife's solidly sculpted shoulder, gives it a squeeze. "But my aim is to get to the summit. Summit is all. No marital strings or quarrels are going to stop me."

"I'd be happier hearing you speak as a member of the team."

"Hey, I'm team, Professor," Wilder says. He straightens himself up in his seat. "All team. Don't worry about my not being team."

"We'll prove how well men and women can work together," Sara says. "We don't need to give in to what was or has been."

"I'm afraid to say you're outvoted on this one, Reddy. I hope this doesn't eliminate you. You're our needed expedition physician, and I don't know of any replacement at this point with your degree of mountaineering expertise."

"Troy, you are my friend. Would I back out on you now?"

"What do we call ourselves," says Devin. "The Adams Party?"

"I think we should call ourselves the Sarasvati Party, as this expedition is really all Sara's idea," Vida says.

"Why do we have to call ourselves something?" Wilder says.

"Everything's in a name," Sara says. "That's why."

"Sarasvati Party—any opposed?" Troy says.

People shake heads.

Wilder shrugs. "Whatever."

"Good," Troy says. "Now all are agreed."

"Now that's settled, let's talk plan of attack," says Devin.

"Alpine-style," Wilder says. "Up fast, down faster."

"Risky," says Reddy. "Not everyone has your speed and strength."

"I agree with Reddy," Troy says. "I'd prefer a traditional approach, a straightforward Himalayan approach. Safer that way." He gives his daughter a stroke on the back.

Wilder makes a face. "Taking the time to umbilical-cord ourselves and supplies up is not necessarily the safer way," he says. "And you know it. The slower we go, the more days on the mountain. More days on the mountain, likelier we are to die on it. Look at your statistics. Simple as that. Especially on Mysterium. Just getting through the Gorge and past the Sanctuary is going to be a bitch. Entire mountain will be a bitch."

"Our style depends on the route we choose," says Troy.

"Professor's right," Devin says. "Route's key. But I'm still for going up with less and getting in and out like lightning."

"An alpine approach, I know, is aesthetically more appealing," Vida says. "But I'd feel safer going expedition-style."

Wilder lets out an audible breath.

"Alpine's easier on the younger of you, for sure," Troy says.

"You're only fifty!" Sara says. "Please."

"We'll speak to Adams, see what approach he votes for," Troy says. "Meanwhile, everyone think more about it. We'll discuss next meeting."

Heads nod.

"Now as to routes. We've got but two to choose from, as I see it."

"I say to take the north route," Wilder says. "It's not been done."

"I would prefer to take the original route," Reddy says. "West Ridge was good enough for Adams and Hilman, and it is good enough for me."

"Not bad footsteps to follow in," Troy says. "Must admit."

"Quick retreat may be difficult on the northern route," Reddy says.

"I'm with Wilder," Devin says. "Doing what hasn't been done."

Troy says, "Any decision awaits Virgil Adams's opinion."

Again a nod of heads.

"Oh," Sara says. "I almost forgot." She hurries into the kitchen, comes back with a large bowl. She puts the bowl on the table and empties the contents of the paper bag into it. "Figs! Big fresh juicy ones. Aren't they perfect?" She holds the bowl up in both hands, proudly, for all to see.

Vida reaches for a fig. "Wow, look at these beauties."

Sara offers the bowl around. Wilder puts a hand up to refuse.

"Whichever route we decide," Troy says, "it will put me and Sara, Adams and Reddy, and Devin and Wilder on the summit slopes for a try to the top. We can break into groups of two, even three, figuring who goes up first and with whom once we're up there." He takes a bite of fig. "Damn, these are good. We've also got the Sherpas to consider. We've got several qualified men in mind, at least one of them intent on reaching the summit too. Any way it goes we're a sufficient number for a team. Or a party, as that's what we intend to call ourselves. Hillary Adams and Vida can manage the appurtenances from Base Camp, and they can direct the porters who'll be relaying food and gear up to us as needed. Adams has already started the colossal job of raising funds. Given his prestigious history, he's our ticket up. But he's got to have a team that looks good on paper to those doling out the cash and equipment."

"I read that William Hilman died just a while ago," Vida says.

Devin nods. "Got butted off a steep trail by a wayward yak."

"He was leading a group of students over a high Tibetan pass," Sara says. "Mr. Adams told me about it. Really sad."

"He'll give us the details around a campfire some night," says Troy.

Reddy takes another fig from the bowl, and bows his head to Sara.

"I've made a list of about a dozen big companies so far who might be potential backers," Vida says. "I could help the Adamses make the inquiries. We need to be thinking publicity too, to bring in more cash and supplies."

"We'll need to file a permit now if we're thinking July," Troy says.

"God, is that lightning?" says Vida.

Everyone looks toward the window. There is a long pause of quiet.

"God does not answer," Reddy says.

Vida recognizes him again, recalls his wit, his attentiveness.

Wilder says, "I'm still thinking about how we're getting up this mother."

Reddy shakes his head. "There are no photographs available, at least that we know of or have seen, taken from the Sanctuary floor. We don't know what we will have above us until we are to arrive."

"Mr. Adams has photographs," Sara says. "He should bring them next time we meet."

"Photos from 1956?" Devin says.

"August 17, 1956," Sara says. "Day that Adams and Hilman made the summit of Mount Sarasvati. My birthday of all days."

"That is really something," Devin says, smiling at her.

"Being named for it, I suppose, you could say I know it by heart."

Wilder laughs an odd laugh. "Sorry to call it a bitch."

"You couldn't of actually been on the mountain," Devin says.

"I've gotten an eyeful of her while trekking," Sara says. "And I've heard stories from Mr. Adams, and have seen his pictures. Anyhow, a lot of what I know is by intuition." She tucks a strand of hair behind her ear.

Wilder says, "We should not be climbing by intuition."

"I've spent a lot of time in India," she says. "And I speak Hindi, and too a bit of Nepalese. I've read everything there is to read about the mountain. It means something to me. I have a feeling, is what I mean."

"You need climbing experience is what you need," says Wilder.

"I've done plenty of trekking in the Himalaya, as well as a lot of technical climbing here, most all of it with my father."

"You've had a most excellent teacher, then," the doctor says. Reddy knows from his years of climbing with Troy, starting back when they were college students. They had beamed their headlamps onto thousand-foot vertical walls together, had placed their spikes into ice of all kinds, hacked away at giant icicle teeth like men in combat, countless times. They had touched a gloved palm one to the other on dozens of summits. Reddy, more than anyone, knows well his friend's excellence.

"Sara and I have climbed Rainier together," Troy says.

"Rainier," Wilder says. "It's just a long slog."

"In the winter it isn't," says Troy. "Going up Cadaver Gap."

"Not so easy," Devin says. "I'm impressed."

"Cascades are not the Himalaya," Wilder says.

"I'm strong," Sara says. "Maybe stronger than you."

Wilder laughs. "Yeah, right."

"Careful," Reddy says. "Easier to choke on words than on a plum."

"Or a fig, Father Doctor," Devin says. "You're not eating a plum."

"Reddy's right. No one knows how any of us will do at altitude," Troy says. "No matter how strong we are now, or will be by the time we're there."

"Sara's time living in India and her ability to speak the language will definitely help us when it comes to Sherpas and porters," Vida says. "You hear so many stories about mix-ups and misunderstandings when you're up there and susceptible and all."

"I promise to do what I can," Sara says. "Not only as a tribute to my mother, most importantly, but to do all I can for all of us, for the party."

Wilder sinks into his seat with a look of soured impatience.

Sara goes to the fireplace, picks her mother's cinnabar beads out from the silver tray on the mantel beneath the photograph. She drapes the beads around her neck.

"You, Sara, need to take full responsibility, you being the instigator and all," Devin says, a big grin on his face.

Sara puts her mother's glacier glasses on, looks around, smiles.

"Take care of yourself, Sara," Wilder says. "We should each of us take responsibility for ourselves and we'll all as a group be better off for it."

"Have a fig, Wilder," Devin says. "They're very sweet. Put something sweet into you, man."

Wilder laughs to himself, reaches into the bowl. "Why not?" He chews the fig slowly, his face softening. He puts the stem in a saucer with the rest of the stems. Then he picks the bowl up from the table and offers it to Reddy with a nod of the head. Reddy nods back, takes a piece of fruit, and passes the bowl across to Vida. Everyone makes noises of relish and pleasure, all in agreement as to the deliciousness of the sweet and fleshy yield of the ficus tree.

Devin holds a fig in the air. "To Sara's yummy offering."

Wilder reaches for the bowl again.

"And to a marvelous idea," Reddy says.

Troy lifts a coffee mug up. "To the Sarasvati Party."

The others in unison raise cups, a fig, a map, a stem.

"To us," they say, "the Sarasvati Party."

"To Mount Mysterium," all say.

PART II

4.

THE GORGE

THEY ARRIVE TO A MODEST GUESTHOUSE WITHIN THE
dusty purlieus of New Delhi, greeted by the blistering weather
of early July and the tonnage of chattel they had freighted
ahead. Surrounding them are mountains of boxes, knolls of
piled rope, the obstacles and toils and quarrels to come. They
work to untangle lines, sort out clothing and tenting, nutri-
ment and equipment, tools and kits for navigation and first

aid. They guzzle sweet bottled drinks beneath a dull aluminum sky. They slap at biting flies, cough and wheeze the soot and fumes of the city, work through moods and lassitude as best they are able; sudoriferous wayfarers, the spent and destined lot of them. Nights they toss restlessly, grateful for a ceiling fan and the last hours upon a mattress for the next few months to come. In dreams they flail beneath monstrous bodies of snow that mute their cries in silence, or they cling desperately to the edges of precipices, struggling for a foothold or a handhold and breath enough. They are cartwheeling. They are falling. They are flying.

They had yesterday boarded the aircraft, spirits high, all laughing and talking easily, ebulliently, calling one to the other as they made their way down the narrow aisle. "Truly more hysteria than humor," said Professor Troy after a particularly bad pun from one of their coterie. They settled into seats and buckled in, music streaming through the earphones, turbines humming in the cowlings, a soft chattering of captain in the loudspeakers overhead. There came the sudden thrust of velocity and weighted press against their chests, the rush of takeoff and thrill of the lift, their hearts propelled, breath quickened, an unconscious clenching of bones and flesh. The jetliner leveled out and was throttled to cruising, and soon pictographs and colored lights signaled safety and release as voices from above spoke of regulations, obligations, duty-free. The seekers closed their eyes and rode the waves of their imaginings, minds in flight, moving through darkening clouds and the vortices of turbulence, veins of lightning rending the black nimbus, their daydreams unsteadied, thoughts disturbed by reflection and questioning. The why was different for every climber; a few answers being reasoned, other rationales myth or easy utterance; some claims blank as a blank page and offering no grounds at all.

Hillary Adams and Vida Carson sat side by side in the middle of the cabin, window and aisle. The bumpier the ride, the more determined they were to converse. They talked old pets and new boots, use of pills for altitude, hygiene while traveling, the perplexities of fashion, the dilemmas of accumulated waste. They spoke of families, upbringings, histories, their ways of seeing, their why-they-are-heres, their beliefs, their wishes, their fears.

In Vida's story the desire to climb was linked to the desire to be with Wilder. "I fell in love," she said, "and was willing to follow him wherever he wanted to go. Learn to do the things he liked to do. I admired his drive, his strength, and his courage. I've never been interested in pessimistic loser types. What can I say?"

"What can you say?" Mrs. Adams said. She sipped her cocktail.

"Who ever thought I'd see the tops of snowy volcanoes, among so many other places I'd never travel to without him as a guide," Vida said. "Amazing, being out there in the middle of all that wildness together. Wilderness, wildness, Wilder, jeez, who knows what it means? I didn't find out he was really a Walter until later." She paused. "Would I have fallen for a Walter?" She smiled, put a few peanuts into her mouth, chewed. "Well, story is I fell in love with the mountains as much as I was with the man who ended up being my husband."

The past tense of Vida's last sentence did not go unnoticed. But Hillary Adams would not speak of the slip, or the mistake, or the hint, or whatever it might have been. Nor did she mention the sway of her own christening, sharing a name with a coeval who happened to be the first person to stand at the top of Everest. Instead the well-mannered Mrs. Adams went on to explain her passion for adventure as it related to her mate as well. "We found a way of being together outside our domestic routine that was akin to lovemaking," she said. "Together we use our bodies and our minds and our instincts. And when we stand at a summit we stand as one." She reached between the seats in front of her to give her husband a poke on the shoulder. Mr. Adams turned to his wife and peered over his reading glasses, only to see her gesturing him back to his book.

Such romantic notions are not shared by everyone, both women agreed. They pushed the attendant light and ordered more peanuts and gin.

Devin Reddy and his father had seats together several rows behind and were ignoring the choppy ride, though both had given up trying to read. Devin had lugged along Shipton's *Mountain Travel Book*, despite his father's pestering him about its bulk and its weight. Reddy had carried with him but a slim volume of the *American Alpine Journal*, edited by their esteemed leader, Virgil S. Adams. The doctor was doing his best to make this trip a restorative treatment of sorts between himself and his son, at the very least a palliative reprieve, the father even going so far as to insist they be seated together. But he could not at times hold back certain harsh remarks, a habit of criticism that had begun soon after his son was born. For Devin had been his wife's wish, no matter Reddy's opposition to having children. She knew this before they had married: Reddy had made clear his ambition to work and to climb. He had begged Maggie to continue her photography, to know life's value in this, but she had at some point decided differently, having realized other aims and needs.

Reddy lectured his son about mountaineering strategies

and routines, unaware of how he sounded now. He left off at anchoring all belays, a dictate he repeated too many times, before going on to speak more generally of historical climbs and famous climbers, about what went right and what didn't; subjects that included neither mother nor wife. If Maggie came up, which sometimes she did, he let her name fall away and quickly got back to the topic. Each, without the other knowing it, had brought a wallet-size photo of Maggie to affix somewhere on the summit. It was too sentimental a gesture to admit to, even for father and son. But if they had cared to discuss it, it would likely have been said that leaving something of Maggie behind was a way of moving on without her, as grown men know they must do.

Nor did Doctor Reddy allow himself to think much of Vida Carson, though here she was and would be in closest proximity until they had mastered the peak and retreated. He could see the top of her head from where he sat. She had cut her long brown hair into a boyish style he found unflattering, and for this he was glad: he did not want to want her again.

The aircraft soared on, rafting through particles of higher atmosphere, the earth's vaporous layers pressing the expanse of wings upward, as flight attendants packed steaming aluminum dishes into the slots of rolling trolleys. A smell of brewed coffee drifted throughout the cabin. Sara's father had fallen asleep in the seat next to her, so she unbuckled and walked the aisle in search of her people, riding through passages of rough air agilely. Stopping to visit with each, she would stand and chat with an elbow planted on the seat ahead, or she would crouch down onto her haunches in the aisle, arms rested on the armrest. Her fingers were ringed with silver rings, her feet were pink and bare, her manner calm, her voice serene as she talked about preferring a turbulent ride as opposed to nothing exciting, and how heartening the talk of the captain was, how she heard the command in him, heard the reassuring certainty in him.

"Yeah, even when the engines bonk out and you're about to plunge into the sea," Devin said. He put on his best airline pilot voice for her: *"Well, hey, folks, looks like we're heading down real quick all of a sudden here. You all might want to reach up and grab one of those yellow plastic masks dangling over your heads. Hope you were paying attention during the demonstration. Only kidding—don't really need to bother with those gadgets anyway, just something to fiddle with to get your minds off the horror of plummeting through the wild blue. May as well just sit back and relax now and make the most of the rest of your life."*

Devin liked making this girl smile. She had a slight buckling of the incisors, one tooth that winged out over the other. He was bewitched, just as he was the first time he saw her striding across campus that spring day so many months ago with all those cherry blossoms snowing down on everyone's heads. She was the call of a bird, is what she was, would always be. He sat smiling and restrained in his seat, his heart ballooning in his chest. He thought of the next few months ahead, how every day he would be with her; whatever happened would happen to them together.

The pilot had cut through the weather, and the ride began to smooth out. Passengers tipped their seats back and struck a variety of poses intended for sleep as they sailed on through the sky. Sara went on talking. She said flying in an airplane made her all the more eager to climb. She said she was aware of herself moving on a rising trajectory, bound by an incredible force beyond one's knowing. "I love the sensation of ascension," she said. "It makes me feel ever more bold and free."

"Bold and free," Devin said. "Who was it said that?"

"My mother," Sara said. "She said that."

"You smell cinnamony."

"Like cinnamon?"

"Like something."

Near the end of the long flight the pilot flew the jumbo jet close to the Himalayan range and announced what was in sight. People tipped heads to their windows. A few from the Sarasvati Party hurried to the rear of the cabin and bent over to peer out the waist-level porthole. They saw before them an unbroken chain of icy pyramids, a thousand or more miles of snow-capped masses, like floating temples they seemed, with valleys of deep blue pooled among the flanks and the crests. And then there she was to behold in all her magnificence: Mysterium, a giantess, splendid, luminescent, at these heights her snowy coating pearly and moist as flesh, with scarves of clouds draped down about her girth. To see her shapely shoulders and head rising to the level of the airplane was astonishing. To know they would walk to a point as high as they now soared, even more mind-boggling: they were staggered by the sight of her. They stared, they coughed, they babbled, they shivered with cold fear in the lakes of their hearts. Sara said she had a sudden crazy urge to weep, but it wasn't fright that brought on her tears. She didn't know what it was.

If you're going to cry, take it outside.

Wilder laughed aloud now at the thought of his brother Lucas's words. People looked at him and went back to their seats, but not Sara, who stayed on her knees to gaze out the porthole. Wilder remained crouched behind her, looking out the window too, watching the airplane's contrails vanish into the icy face behind them. Then he went back to his seat and buckled up. He rested his head against the headrest, fingered the little stone brought from home he carried in his pocket, closed his eyes in the endless drone. He understood why Mrs. Adams and his wife would remain at Base Camp, and was grateful for it. He knew too he had to get to the summit of Mysterium for the sake of his brother. Maybe, in all honesty, for himself, and so for Vida's sake. Whatever. He would let the do-gooders put up their prayer flags where they may; he had brought Lucas's ashes to toss off the top of the mountain.

Why do climbers climb?

"To be somebody," Lucas had said. "Why else?"

THE TWO-STORY guesthouse is an elongated rectangle of tall soot-colored walls. A rusted wrought-iron door yawns open to a dusty inner courtyard with an enfilade of small rooms cubicled into the cinder block on either side inside. Each room has a single bed, a bare light bulb, a chair, a sink, a dusty Shiva seated cross-legged in a dusty niche. The latrines are out-of-doors, as is the wash stall and the shower spigot.

The advantage of the chosen quarters is the outdoor space procured for the party's hundreds of cartons of gear; a narrow confined area along a wall fit into the lee of the guesthouse and enclosed by another soot-colored building that rises beside it. Vultures circle and drift in the vapory char above. Midday there is a smattering of shade from a sad-looking mango tree; otherwise a hot steamy light beams down upon the weary. All day there is a stench of rotting vegetables and sewage, with whiffs of urine and feces from the nearby latrines all mixed with the odor of body essence the work party themselves exude. Hardly a breeze passes through the courtyard; more often squealing pigs, dirt-pecking chickens, roaches, and mice go skittering by.

Hillary Adams has the master list, her husband the task of

the logistics of revising. For several days they will all unbundle, sort and classify, number and order, catalog and allot, then bundle the chattel back up again. The containers will be resorted into no more than sixty-six-pound loads, limits issued for the sake and assent of the porters. Before repacking, clothing and bedding will be sealed in waterproof bags, as will medicine and edible goods.

As to nourishment, their comestibles, their victuals, their eats, there had been arguments aplenty among the group prior to leaving the States as to what should be purchased and hauled. Doctor Reddy argued for relying mostly on local foodstuffs once they had arrived, but others complained that potatoes and cabbages and goat meat and ghee were heavy, adding too much weight to already weighted loads. Professor Troy insisted they keep the menus basic: rice and dal for protein, dates and oatmeal and tea for a day's beginning. Virgil Adams encouraged the addition of luxury items such as chocolate, nuts and dried fruits, biscuits, cheese, a bottle or two of brandy, all of which would boost not only one's energy but one's spirits as well when truly needed. Devin Reddy claimed freeze-dried rations and powdered drink mixes were all that were necessary, supplemented, of course, with plenty of bottles of hot sauce. Vida Carson will bring a special blend of coffee with her, and with it extra jars of peanut butter that she aims to hide among the clothing in several of the still-to-be-sealed loads. Wilder, fiddling with the rock he carries in his pocket, said he would eat whatever, not being as fussy as everybody here has unfortunately turned out to be, and now he tucks into his pack a few special mood-elevating macaroons recently bought on the street, preparing for those more difficult days on the road ahead. Hillary Adams adds to her daypack a tin of biscuits, a package of hard candies, and small envelopes of vitamins K and C for muscle fatigue. Sara carries nothing extra, knowing food and drink will be plenteous enough and that all will be provided for, though she understands the hoarding needs of frightened people.

"All the various supplies are to be apportioned throughout: no particular bundle shall consist of all of any singular good for fear of losing every one of that necessary item," says Adams. "This being a lesson learned on the '56 expedition, in which a precious load holding all the crampons slipped off a narrow path and tumbled like a dumb animal off and over the cliff, then, to explode thousands of feet below. We were thus put into the position of having to cut steps the old-fashioned way."

Taking heed, all go on with the repacking, sorting through piles of wool and mounds of down, struggling to imagine in the sticky heat of Delhi how they will soon be in need of any such wintry garb. Various headlamps and crampons are snugged into bins with water bottles and helmets and goggles, with booties and socks, with iodine pellets and toilet paper, with tampons and mittens. Hats, boots, axes and hammers, rain gear and snow gear are packed among the seam sealant, the batteries, the toothpaste, between layers of underwear and middlewear and outerwear: silk and woolen and fleece. Tent poles and rainflies, oxygen canisters and masks, sleeping bags, bivvy sacks, runners and webbing all get bundled together. They weigh and label and stack completed loads: hundreds of cartons and barrels and duffels the porters will tumpline to Base Camp for this newfangled alpine odyssey.

Devin and Wilder take on the job of untangling and recoiling the six-hundred-foot spools of rope that have split apart during shipment. They face unruly piles, and hours of tedium and slaving: tugging and unknotting, threading, cutting, re-coiling, all the while fighting off snarls of flies as they swab the pour of sweat from their heads. The alpinists among the group argue for less rope; the expedition types want extra for fixed lines. Reddy and Troy add more rope than apportioned to the sixty-six-pound loads; Devin and Wilder only to steal coils back out again: the outcome of this clandestine action to reveal itself seriously once they are up on the mountain. "We've got at least ten thousand feet here," Devin says. "Way too much." He watches Wilder skillfully handling another three-hundred-foot length of nylon stranding, looping it elbow to shoulder, bending the coiled rope into a horseshoe shape, wrapping both loose ends of it about the middle before he squares a knot and cinches it. He tosses the bulk into a duffel.

Devin tips his head in the direction of Reddy. "Some serious pinnacles my old man's compiling," he says.

Doctor Reddy sits cross-legged on the ground surrounded by bottles of analgesics, antibiotics, antidiarrheals, packets of lozenges, rolls of tape, wads of moleskin, bandages, steristrips, tubes of sunscreen and lip balm and superglue. To his right: a scatter of needles and syringes, stethoscope, scalpel, airway, staple kit, tweezers, scissors, safety pins, gloves. On his left: sprays of inhalers and repellents, vials of tinctures, jars of ointments and creams. There are drops for nose, drops for eyes, drops for ears, pills for altitude, pills for malaria, pills for nausea and sleep.

The Sarasvati Party goes on with the packing in the sweltering day. There are few complaints, this being more contest than virtue among the group. Dusty little children make their way around the dung wall and loiter within the courtyard, feet bare, scratching themselves or pulling at their ears, quietly staring at the strange pale people with their curious ways and wealth of belongings. Adams has made everyone in the group agree they will not hand out offerings to beggars of any kind, male or female, baby or elderly, normal or deformed. No candies, no pencils, no toothbrushes, no money. Many of the children flirt and plead. Wilder raises his voice and claps his hands, chasing them away like flies. One grimy little boy ignores him and instead comes closer to Sara. He calls her by name.

"How do you know me?" she says.

The boy takes a finger out of his nose, showing big white teeth when he smiles. He hides behind a taller boy. The taller one offers forth the newspaper rolled up in his hand. "You are the blessed goddess Sarasvati," he says. "You have come to take the others with you up to your mountain."

Devin takes the newspaper and reads from a page of *The Times of India*. "Headline," he says.

A RARE VISIT FROM SARASVATI. An American expedition team has recently received government permission to climb the blessed mountain Sarasvati, called by some Mysterium. Leading the climb will be Mr. Virgil S. Adams, one of the first to reach the summit twenty-five years ago this year. Most interestingly, Miss Sarasvati Troy, a young lady named for the sacred mountain, will be part of the climbing team, as will her father, the legendary Stuart M. Troy.

Below the headline is a photograph of the group taken before they left the States, huddled together, the notches and peaks of shoulders and heads forming a serried ridge among them. There is Sara front row center, the sun a glory of light in her hair. "Check it out, Sara," Devin says. "You're a celebrity."

She fingers her hair back over the crown of her head, smiles her smile.

Troy overhears the talk, shakes his head. "Celebrities," he says.

VIDA LEAVES the lading area and disappears into the guest-house, giving in to the stifling weather and a rush of light-headedness. She cannot dispatch or parcel, label or stack another carton or barrel. She has to put her feet up, close her eyes. She needs relief from the madness of slapping at mean biting flies, relief from the frenzy and noise and odors of the surrounding streets. She goes to her room and lies down on her back on the bed. The ceiling fan stirs above, creaking a worn-out sound. She is weighted, dispirited. She should be elated, she thinks, like Sara, the ever-beaming Sara, even after two days of work and in this miserable heat. Vida tells herself that this trip is a chance that happens only once in a lifetime. So pick yourself up, she thinks. Ponder the opposite. Remember why you said yes to this expedition. You are here to bring life back into your life. She looks at the dusty Shiva seated cross-legged in its dusty niche. Shiva with a look of all-knowing.

Vida closes her eyes, reminds herself that she came here to find her way with Wilder again. Being with him, doing what he most loves to do. To begin again, the two of them. To make it new, as he likes to say. Yes, to make it new. If it might be possible. She rolls onto her side, face toward the cracks and the stains of the rough stucco wall. Why would it not be possible?

She drifts off into the start of a dream, is jerked back fast with a feeling of falling.

She opens her eyes, hearing Reddy outside calling for help with a carry. She stares at the cracks in the wall. Reddy, a decision in her life that had been reckless. She had put herself in jeopardy. She had risked her marriage for a summer of pleasure and a confusing happiness. She had seen herself at the threshold of her life about to change when she said yes to Reddy that day. Her life, with all the predictability and safety built into it, with days thoughtfully and carefully put into place: yes, she had been reckless with it. Impulsive. Unreasonable. But what affair of passion is reasonable? And how does one ever truly explain?

She turns to the deity in the shadowed alcove of the wall.

Shiva with eyes of knowing.

Reddy was a story that had never had a proper ending.

Was it a story still in the telling?

Vida not knowing.

THEY ARE a bedraggled-looking brigade by the end of the third day; sunburned, dirt-caked, sticky with sweat, welted with fly bites, backs and arms and shoulders aching. They line up for tepid showers, soaping grime and dust off with lips tightly sealed to the spray, rinsing mouths with swigs of bottled water, brushing soot and dead insects from their hair. They meet in the common room for dinner, freshly dressed and instantly per-spiring, queuing up buffet-style to pile food onto plates. There are platters of curried vegetables and meats, a heap of wilted bread, bowls of soupy dal, spicy rice, unknown pickled things, swarms of flies alighting over all of it and them. The procession moves half-heartedly along.

"Your head?" Vida says, her one eye endearingly awry.

"I forget to stoop when passing through the doorway of my room," Reddy says, "and like an idiot I hit the beam of the lintel."

For the first time since they were lovers, they offer each other a smile.

They all find places at the table. Troy and Adams take seats at each end. Everyone is quiet in the heat, tired and quiet, sweating quietly. They pick at their food, scoot plates away, ask for more bottled drinks.

Adams clears his throat and pushes his plate aside. "Here," he says, "the photographs I've promised of the mountain." He places the leather-bound album out in front of him and people get up from their chairs and move around to his end of the table as he opens the pages and begins to explain. "Beginning with the Sage's Gorge," Adams says, "one of the finest specimens of powerful water erosion I've ever encountered. This is the abominable moat protecting Mysterium from penetration." He taps a finger to a photograph that shows sheer perpendicular walls ravined thousands of feet high. He turns the page, tilts the album forward to display a picture of steep precipices, dark notches, toothlike ridges, lips of thick ice. "This section here, Hilman and I called Hades," Adams says. He leafs to the next photograph, directing attention to the midsection of the mountain. "And here at this site we were under constant artillery fire as we attempted to pass, with great masses of the glacier breaking free from the icy terrace and thundering down to the valley and any poor soul, such as one of us, below."

"Makes one cringe a bit, doesn't it?" Mrs. Adams says.

"The mountain is angel as well as demon, I assure you," Adams says. "Look here," he says. He flips to the last pages of the album that holds old newspaper clippings; a yellowed photo showing dogs and pigs and cows sprawled dead across the claggy ground, vultures parked on the carcass of a water buffalo, fowl toppled into heaps in the mud. The picture next to it revealing bodies of people shrouded under rugs, their bloated feet exposed. Sara bends closer to read of the havoc:

houses swept away, crops washed out, mothers and babies and old people drowned, some people not found at all.

"So much death on my birthday," she says.

"Yes, it was a most severe monsoon that hit the surrounding villages on the very day we reached Mysterium's summit," Adams says. "I'm sure most of you have by now been told or read of the deadly calamity. Heavy rainfall caused the river to overflow, whereby the waters destroyed everything that lay in the surrounding area. We had angered the goddess, so the Indian newspapers said. Look here. It is written right here." He puts a finger to a place on the page. "'Her sanctuary violated, the goddess had thus been provoked to avenge.'" Adams looks up to the others, their heads bowed toward the page. "And this be in modern times," he says.

"Time to make amends," Sara says. "And balance the Karma."

"If I were to believe in things of that sort. I am, however, not a superstitious man," Adams says. At this he claps the book shut.

People return to their seats. Hillary Adams calls for more tea, and then she passes around added travel permits along with ballpoint pens and a tin of biscuits. After the paperwork is completed, Virgil Adams stands and calls the group to order. All look up to him. He is a solid man, thick shouldered and broad of chest, dense, sturdy, durable. He has a mass of snowy white hair, a nose that is sharp and buttress-like. His flesh is coarsened by weather, lichen dry, speckled over with rust-colored orbicules deposited by sun and time.

"We have a few matters yet to discuss before the truck arrives this evening and the lading and stacking begin," he says. "First, Doctor Reddy will speak a bit on the topic of physical ailments about which we must all be quite conscious. I shall afterwards go over a few logistics of the road trip we have ahead of us for the next, well, who knows how many days it may take, time depending, of course, on travel conditions." Adams takes his seat, folds his speckled hands together in front of him on the table and nods at Reddy.

"Let me begin with infection and prevention," Reddy says. The doctor moves into a mode of practiced lecturing, doing his best to ignore the grunts and the yawns, venturing immediately upon a variety of maladies and complaints, after which he pauses, clears his throat, asks for any questions before going on. His audience swats at flies and remains silent, their attention directed to the open doorway, where a derelict in rags has stopped to peer at them. The raggedy bystander points at Doctor Reddy, says something in garbled Hindi, and begins laughing maniacally. Reddy looks about the room as if for an answer, until a woman enters and slaps the lunatic with a dirty cloth to shoo him away. The man's crazed laughter fades out to the street, out into the din and the throng.

"Going on," Reddy says. He talks of the symptoms of altitude sickness, cerebral and pulmonary edema. He speaks of frostbite, dysentery, hypothermia, snow blindness, bites and stings, trauma of organ and bone, tendon and flesh. He puts forth statistics, risks, emergencies, illness that might turn critical, sickness that may become grave. He talks impending death. He tells of treatment, ways to improvise, means of carrying on. He offers advice. Once again he presses for questions. A woman comes in from the kitchen and goes to Doctor Reddy, asking something in Hindi. "Why keep coming to me?" Reddy says. "I speak no Hindi."

"They think you're still one of them, Father Doctor," Devin says.

Sara says something in the woman's tongue. She speaks softly to her, in clear and simple phrases, aware of the warm light shining down on her head from the naked bulb above.

"Whatever few personal things you want to leave here, please pack them into a duffel with your name and a lock on it, as I intend to do with this heavy leather album, among other things. We shall all collect our belongings here on our return," Adams says, "and thereby have clean clothes and be presentable on our travels home."

People sip their tea, watch women in saris and nose rings clearing dishes away. Bent old men and mangy dogs slink by outside. Across the street, a tamed monkey begs coins and picks lice from the head of a man squat on the ground beside him. A child cries from a back room within the guesthouse somewhere. Hillary collects the paperwork and ballpoint pens. Wilder fumbles with the stone in his pocket. Devin yawns. Sara feels the encouragement of her mother to get people moving, and so breaks the silence and gets up from the table, smiling, always smiling. This is, after all, her party.

THE TRANSPORT truck is a lime-colored military jalopy, an old haulage vehicle painted bright with tropical flowers and a bold sign to HONK PLEASE! blazoned on the tailgate. The driver climbs out of the cab front to greet the expedition team; palms pressed together, he gives a modest tip of the head. He is a big man with a soft paunch, nutmeg-colored skin, hair glossy and stiff as crow wings, appearing to be somewhere around either the far or near side of middle age. He wears a polo shirt imprinted with the name of an Ivy League university, drawstring pajama trousers, plastic sandals, a ring on his pinkie set with a large ruby-colored stone. His lips and teeth are darkened vermilion from the stain of the betel leaf.

A woman thumbs a tilak on each of the passengers' foreheads, and offers words of favor before the journey begins. After her blessing they pile into the haulage vehicle, an assembly of readied troops moving faithfully to duty and call. Virgil and Hillary Adams sit up front with the driver, while the others move into the back of the truck, Devin Reddy climbing up onto a stack of crates, Doctor Reddy, Professor Troy and Sara, Wilder and Vida fitting themselves in with the rest of the tonnage of equipage, tucked and folded among containers and duffels that will serve as seating for the next several nights and days.

The truck *carooms* loudly at the start-up, pouring a thick choke of black smoke into the night. It lumbers out of the lot and onto the potholed road, tottering the riders through the littered streets of the amber-lit city, a hazy shard of moon in the wane above. The travelers pass crumbling hovels, a shantytown of shacks and tents and gutters heaped with sewage and decay. They pass raggedy people spread onto pieces of cardboard or sheets of newspapers, some curled onto plain hard clay or harder pavement; people asleep among the rags and the muck, among the shards of bones and rotted marigolds, the garbage and stench. Rats scamper past innocent dreamers, pigs nibble at the dung, as the riders, guileless too of their visions, list and are jostled along. A pale band of light smokes up from a ragged horizon.

Sara Troy, cross-legged and composed upon a carton marked FRAGILE, closes her eyes and tips her head back against a basket, a bandanna loosely draped about her throat. Her fellow travelers are here because of her, this drowsy towheaded girl; she now the guardian of their destinies, just as mother and father are their daughter's christeners and keepers and will decree destiny to her, and so fate to all: a version and conversion of each into other. How might their story be told?

The group arrives at the Ganges by midafternoon, and here they will follow the holy river with its throngs of devoted for many miles ahead. Upon the river's banks are bathers bathing in the beautifully filthy water, as other souls go about beating their clothes upon stones, and still others drink from the waters or bless themselves with it in their various and curious ways. There are women in colorful saris, brightly veiled and bejeweled with nose hoops and bracelets of gold. There are topknotted sadhus in saffron-colored sheets singing in top voice in strange tongues. There are priests chanting, pilgrims lamenting, families wailing, goats bleating, monkeys screaming, brakes screeching, bells ringing, while everywhere is the smell of sandalwood and camphor, the sting of smoke in the eyes and the nose, the blaze of funeral pyres, a mix of sweet incense and burning dung. They pass a group of men bearing above their heads a stiffened body wrapped in hodden cloth, the corpse posed on a bier of wooden poles and a platform of woven bamboo. The riders begin to notice corpses everywhere along this course: corpses being carted down the road, corpses lined along the banks of the river, corpses piled stiff into flatbeds, all on their way to the flames.

"They say the soul is released through the fontanel," Sara says. "Those who grieve listen for the burst of the head bones. Then comes relief."

The driver puts the brake on and eases out of the line of traffic, the passengers unaware of the sudden blapping of the tire as its fill of air escapes the rubber casing. "Relief," someone says, as the truck rolls to a stop. All trundle out and wander off in separate ways, some ducking behind rocks or dusty shrubbery. Troy finds a flat rock to sit on, and in the minutes of blissful stillness he writes a few of the day's sentences.

A rough climb out of hell at the start. How quickly fatigue can wear one down mentally, morally. Do not allow, especially up on the mountain. Dismiss any doubts or misgivings. This is only the beginning. Turn thinking toward the zenith.

Troy turns to see Vida alone at the side of the road, stooped over and vomiting. Reddy notices this too, goes to her and puts a hand on her back as she gags, her boyishly short hair turned to curls in the wet heat. He offers his handkerchief, some water. He thinks of his wife. He thinks of the hideous disease that snaked its way through her body; Maggie heaving and retching as if she labored to disgorge the evil thing that had lodged itself inside her.

"Vida, there is some medicine if you wish," Reddy says.

Sara goes to her and opens a water bottle and soaks a bandanna. She wrings the wet cloth and Vida takes it and puts it to her forehead and lips. Adams gives Vida his seat in the front of the cab. He climbs into the back with the others and the truck starts up and totters the passengers forward and onto the road, back into a vertigo of diesel fumes and smoke.

The driver stops again toward evening, the pilgrims hungry and weary. They pile out of the truck, arrived at a settlement where dead crows are hung on poles to scare living crows away. Water slurries past in a gray foam. A growling mastiff yanks at its chain. The driver guides them toward a run-down domicile, a shelter appearing more for the keeping of cattle or the storage of tools. He pushes aside a rug that serves as a door, and they enter a dark smoky room. Pupils dilate to calibrate. Candles burn, illuminating the fierce eyes of demons and gods painted on walls: peaceful and wrathful deities alike, lords of death, lords of time. A filthy barefoot man stands before a dung-burning stove stirring something that boils in a pot. He motions them over to a table. They sip at sweet milky tea in the methane smolder of the fire, black ash settling onto their clothes, getting into their noses and throats. They cough. They sneeze. They wipe their weepy eyes. Hardly anyone touches the lumpy mud-colored sludge the cook has served them, but for the driver. Sara takes a bite of it, showing off her courage. Above her head, a mandala of cobweb webbed to the cement, a spider supping on a fly.

The riders return to the truck in silence, climb in and back to the clamor and stagger of the road, leaving the dungeoned clamminess behind, leaving a whirlwind of powdery earth spiraling out into the dissolving world behind.

Dark comes on like a clap of thunder. They are tossed about in the night, reeled in a continual grinding of gears and the miss and surge of the engine, headlights cutting through the dust as the driver steers on, the thick exhaust of piston and cylinder trailing off into the gloom. After a time and to everyone's relief the Delhian pulls off the main road, following a side road to an open strath of scrubby land, and here he puts the brake on. All collect their sleeping pads and makeshift pillows and spread out among the gnashing weeds, sinking to the ground, exhausted, lilting, feeling they are moving still, bounced about by the gouges and the stones in the road, pitched and heaved in the gnarl of clutch and shift. In the trembling air they can still smell the miasma of the pyres and hear the echoing moans and fading laments of the river grievers they have left so many miles behind. Until each of them is seized by slumber. The ghosts of mothers and brothers and wives steal in and veer away in their dreams. Fulgurous clouds gather like prowlers. Lightning flares soundless above.

In the morning they set on their way in a pouring rain, and by noon arrive to another arm of the exalted river. Soon enough they enter the foothills of the Himalaya to begin the endless hairpin turns through a steeply forested gorge, a serpentine journey through a jungle of weeping green, where sharp corners of rock walls are painted brightly in warning to slow the on-coming. The driver tells them it is a perilous road, and only a week ago a trailer filled with men and livestock slipped over the verge of the khud to go crashing down to the raging torrent below. "It is not so unlikely," he says, betel leaf juice puddling in the cleft of his chin. The deity dangling from the rearview mirror jitters and twirls. The windshield wipers groan, the blades barely keeping up with the worsening rain, and how the driver can see the road ahead no one knows, though someone suggests he is driving by braille. The way continues snakelike, riders in the back toppled onto cartons and duffels and one another. Devin has convinced Sara to share the length of the upper crates with him. He holds on to her, she not minding in the least. They pass mudslides, landslides. They maneuver detours, endure delays. They stop to observe a pour of wet earth spilling out over the roadway ahead, watching as it slithers down into the ravine like a slimy breathing thing. The driver gets out of the truck to muscle the boulders out of the way, big guy that he is, a Delhian Hercules in an Ivy League shirt. He leaps back into his seat, eases the wheels through a covering of slick mud, and now the pilgrims are moving forward once more. They pass through tropical woods lush with vegetation, the wet forest im-bued with snarls of primitive trees, with lichens and epiphytes, fronds and boughs and moss and rot, with the hollow calls of alien birds, the shrieks of wild monkeys. They climb high into a thickening mist. The rain continues to fall.

At the end of day three on the road they arrive to a steeply terraced hillside, a huddle of whitewashed abodes and weaving of stone fencing, where women are stooped at the stream beating clothes upon stones. Thousand-foot walls fall sharply away from the hamlet on two sides. Bearded vultures in the slope below glide in pursuit of the day's prey. The riders climb out of the truck, thirsty, grungy, cranky, beat, hearing a final grating and moaning of hinging at the open and close of the tailgate. Goodbye to boister and flog of lime-green vehicle! They arch and flex to work kinks and cramps out of legs and necks, displaying among themselves an array of twists and bends and stretches. They will unload the truck of their tonnage of gear, and before dinner bathe in the icy river. A local cook will make a meal of fresh vegetables, spicy rice, hand-clapped chapatis, thick hot dal, the first honest food any will have eaten since leaving home. After dinner they will blow up the air beds, roll out the sleeping bags, bed down in a family-size tent. Time will pass at random and in swirl, and all will fall into deep slumber in the sound of the ticking rain.

BE BOLD and free. For a lady in heaven cares for thee.

Sara wonders now about her mother's words: Are they her own, or borrowed?

Be bold and free. Carry the thought with you going up the mountain.

Sara recognizes Amanda's motherly need to equip and guide.

Carry the words with you going through life.

What else has her mother to counsel? Tonight she seems to want to go on at length, even knowing Sara's exhaustion from so many long days on the road. But Sara cannot get Amanda's voice out of her head. Foremost are her mother's persuasions as to the better and worse members of the assembly of climbers.

Your father loves having you with him in the mountains.

Sara understands her father's need to keep her close by.

There isn't a more honored climber than Virgil Adams, a real master.

Who would not agree?

Doctor Reddy begrudges his son. As the son does his father.

Yes, Sara sees this too.

The son is resentful. Old wounds. The boy has some growing up to do, though I realize he's recently lost his mother. You alleviate his pain.

Sara likes that she can make Devin feel better.

Sara's mother perceives trouble in the Wilder fellow. He has a deep need to prove something on this expedition. Too deep a need.

But Wilder is their strongest climber.

His wife is fearful. She may fail to act.

Vida might surmount her fears on this trip, Sara believes.

She should work her worries out elsewhere. Not when she's part of a team at twenty-five thousand feet.

Negativity only gets in the way. Sara knows this absolutely.

You need to see what's what, dear Sara. Watch everyone. Be mindful of everything. The goodness in you is often too hard to live with, a goodness too good to be true. You are also in need, don't you see? Too much in need of attention and praise.

Her mother is not being helpful.

Sara rolls to her side, zips the sleeping bag up over her head. I'm on my mountain now: she smiles at the thought of this. She hears Amanda's sigh. "Mother," Sara says, speaking into the depths of the downy cocoon.

But there is nothing more for her mother to say.

. . .

THE SLEEPERS are torn from the conundrum of their dreams as morning begins in a pandemonium of engine din, screeching brakes, blaring horns, bleating goats, bellowing men. Adams and Troy poke their heads out of the tent to see the sudden outpour; the arrival of dozens of mixed Aryan and Mongol types piling out of an old military carrier, men in all manner of dress, their garb a strange array of patched and tattered jungle fatigues mixed with homespun cloaks, tweed vests, camouflage jackets, hooded sweats, silk-ruffled shirts, hand-knit shawls. Headgear is a hodgepodge of worn fedoras or cowboy straws, woolen caps, colorful turbans, embroidered doilies, hair cropped or left long and braided in odd and complicated ways. The barefoot men gather beneath a giant fir tree to umbrella themselves from the drizzle, considering the stacked sixty-plus-pound bundles that await them. Every man is assigned a load and given a number, a headstrap, an advance of a few rupees, a sheet of plastic for the rain. In return each gives a thumbprint and his word to continue the journey beginning to end, from village on through the Gorge and then up to Mysterium's Sanctuary, where Base Camp will be set. The men heft cartons onto their backs to test the weight out, bracing the bundle with a tumpline pressed to the forehead. They walk the loads about, grumble among themselves. They toss the burdens off, point their fingers, wag their heads. Voices pitched, hands waving, they bargain loudly with the overseer.

It is no surprise to Virgil Adams, still no less a delight, that the Sherpa leader, the sirdar in charge of the other Sherpas and the porters, is the firstborn son of the man who had accompanied Hilman and him a quarter century ago to the highest camps of Mysterium. Karma is clearly his father's son, with the same cheekbones, the Eskimo-like nose, the hooded eyes, as well as the small wiry build; a face and body stemmed and leaved from one of the many Tibetan-speaking Buddhist tribes, those arrived from the old land of B'od who have wandered hither over the years. Karma shouts orders in a voice resonant and tenor, making eye contact with the porters that is firm, direct, his stance and gesture clear signs of authority. He wears a turtlenecked sweater, a clean pair of canvas pants, name-brand running shoes, a wristwatch with leather strap— this ensemble many tiers above the subalterns paid to heave the climbers' abundance up to Base Camp. Assisting Karma are two fellow Bhots: Pasang Sherpa and Mingma Sherpa, the two assistant Sherpas looking confusingly alike to the Americans. The two are busy already boiling water for washup and tea for the sahibs, as they will always address those who pay them to tend or carry or wait, though the Sherpas are themselves accomplished climbers. One at a time the sahibs emerge from out of the tent: Virgil and Hillary Adams, Wilder and Vida Carson, Doctor Reddy and son Devin, Professor Troy, all of them bleary-eyed and rumpled. Last comes Sara, even she less spirited than she had been at trip's beginning, her mother's voice too insistent during the night, until nearly dawn, when finally came the silence.

The sahibs mill about as a herd of goats clump in to add to the chaos of daybreak, the nannies and billies saddled with woven panniers needed to carry the porters' staples up the mountain; their pounds of rice, their atta and dal. Soon the shepherds follow; bhakrawallas they are called here, smelling of smoke and dung and grease, hill people of a different strain; a scruffy earth-colored bunch with flat buttery faces and even more antic to their wardrobe than that worn by the porters;

beltless and buttonless, pant zippers left open for the sake of ease. They wear black skullcaps and the dirt they are covered in like a second layer of skin.

The porters and the herders are here for the pay. They are here too for the privilege and reward of accompanying Sarasvati. They are in awe of her, believing her to be the material manifestation of the blessed goddess herself. She, the Virgin. She, the Universe. They want to be of service to this girl. They ask to have photographs taken with her. They watch her; they touch her with their eyes. They call her Didi, meaning big sister. This pleases her, they can see. She speaks to them in Hindi, some Nepalese. She smiles her radiant smile.

Karma Sherpa takes one last group picture, clustering the sahibs into a hillock of shorter to tallest to shorter again, and in a snap of the flash they are set off on their march toward the Gorge. They start up a wide path of pine duff and conifer pollen; black ponchos cowled over their heads and their backpacks, looking like a misshapen troop of ghoulish hunchbacks in a steady rain. A clutch of runny-nosed children run and skip alongside in the mud, soon enough to scream their bye-byes and wave their hoorays. Rodent creatures screech warnings from branches of trees, skittering higher up into limbs or diving down into burrows below. The overhanging boughs are weighted with rain, and doused needles and leaves sprinkle the heads of the crusaders as if to christen and instigate. Sherpas, porters, sahibs: each to be part of the great mountain now.

Adams turns on the path and cheerfully reminds the others of the pleasure of cool weather, even if with it a shower, rather than the merciless heat that can suck the energy from the blood, as was his memory of the trek up a quarter century ago. "Lo, the time-leap," he says, shifting the weight of his pack, water runneling from his poncho and dripping off the tip of his nose. "Yet the way does not change."

His confreres nod their heads, wonder at his diction, return to their pacing. They are relieved, without saying, to be out of the noise and the heave of the rumbling truck, away from the sickening fumes of diesel fuel, cheered to have their feet planted on the ground and to be heading up now into high alpine. They stride through a wooded glen among the flit and chitter of dark-eyed juncos and dull-colored creepers, together lost alone in their thoughts, the difficult terrain ahead of them embosomed by cloud. Each is touched by a familiar landscape and the smell of known aromas, filling them again with the promises and longings of youth. Even the falling rain offers knowable solace. They sense themselves homegoing now.

AS TO *social ethos—more so, ideology and credo—what might be written of the odyssey? As separate climbers we are pairs of arms and legs, eyes and ears. Still, we are also heads and hearts, and together our various parts and aspects constitute the body and soul of the expedition. Then, in our entirety, what values might we take as one to the summit? What lessons might we leave behind? Will our ambitions remain utilitarian, in that we may seek the greatest good for the greatest number of us? At the same time, how do we carry on with each holding to his or her own code of ethics and measure of success? More so, how might our goals be tainted by a need for the limelight, a reliance on public opinion, on an ordinary tendency toward the mean?*

IN THE thrum and patter of rain on hooded capes the corps becomes instruments of percussion slogging along in procession; lug soles slapping into puddles and scraping over stone, heavy boots sucking heavier out of the muck. They travel a footpath sprouted with strange tubular plants rising spirally and dripping like serpentine waterbeasts, and warty amanitas, garish and deadly, glisten and swell in the spongy duff. Lobes of liverwort spore among the conifer, and creeping things rattle in the bracken. The river, in aural pour, moves through the forest as if it were something arboreal.

They hike up and out of the refuge of trees, climbing until they are crested out onto an open ridge where on either side of the path the slope falls steeply away. They pause to get breath, sweat soaking their underclothes. The cold rain drips off the tips of noses and chins, tocks off the hems of their ponchos in a sound of feeble complaints. They nod one to the other and then they toil on again, like an army of insects driven by a remote intelligence. Gray heaps of tumid clouds blacken and shaft above. The muddy traces of their bootsteps sluice away in the rain.

Accumulating cumulonimbus turns raindrops to hailstones that strike like buckshot. They lower their heads, arms raised to shield faces, the stinging pellets making a crackling noise of static that needles the flesh. Adams shouts, signaling downward, as if punching at something menacing in the air, and now all follow, scuttling down the bluff seeking shelter of arbor again. They cross a grassy bald, the ground of the mystifying slick encrusted with lusterless crystals of ice, making the earth look cursed and sown with salt. They hurry off this strange patch of land and enter an enormous burn, the pelleting ice stopping as abruptly as it had begun. They huddle in the blackened forest studying their whereabouts. Surrounding them are dead trees blazed completely of their canopies, charcoaled trunks metallic as armor, fallen branches turned black as gangrenous limbs. They look at one another. They press on.

Each ponders their thoughts, swells of clouds thinning out as they lean into the steep, bootsteps metered to galloping hearts and ballooning lungs. They climb into the meager air of higher country, shed ponchos, drink water, ease up, making guesses at weather and distance, surmising time. The porters and shepherds have stayed at least an hour ahead of the rest of the convoy, the Sherpas having paced themselves between the sahibs; Pasang and Mingma alternating the lead, Karma bringing the rear up, as Hillary Adams keeps post just ahead of him on the trail. She has sauntered along thinking about Thoreau and the word *saunter*, as in *à la Sainte Terre*. Then holy-landers we are, she thinks, *Saint Terrers*, saunterers all. They have sauntered off from the ordinary. They have walked away from the mundane. They have left engines and villages behind, have left life as they know it behind; lives of habit and duty, sales and debt, lives of the common, the hopeless, the mean. They step into form, one behind the other, like iron filings drawn into a single line, their aim being the same, that magnet which draws them upward, though their motives be various and distinct.

Midafternoon they arrive to an alpine meadow in a taper-ing rain. Here they find the porters have cast their loads off, the men now reposed among clumps of heather. The bhakrawallas have nudged their goats to a swale of rich grass on a higher shelf of tundra, where they are crouched on their haunches about a fire drinking their steaming brews, the goats tugging and snapping at the green. The sahibs find a place to settle on the perimeter of the meadow near a small glen of crooked trees. The Sherpas wander about collecting branches and twigs for a fire, pots of water for the tea. Sahibs shuck backpacks and out come binoculars and candy bars, cameras and hats, sheets of plas-tic to flop on. Big woolly rodents, stirred out of their middens, whistle their feral calls. The Sherpas serve the tea and sit among the sahibs and all take in the vast esplanade of steppeland they are settled on. Slow-moving plates of the earth that have heaped and buckled. A spectacle of constant flux stirred by the globe's inferno of core heat. Karma, the sirdar Sherpa, points to the hillside across the valley, to a great scar in the landscape left behind by a massive landslide.

"A tremendous display of the unceasing stirring of nature," Professor Troy says. "The blind, the dumb, the immutable striving in all things."

"Meaning?" Wilder says.

"Meaning what you see before you is the will of all phenomena. As in that which draws the stone to the earth or propels the river to the sea. The same striving that motivates night to overtake the day," Troy says. "Or impels human beings to take risks, you might say."

Sara rolls her neck to relieve the ache of the pack. Devin moves closer, puts his hands on her shoulders. He squeezes and kneads.

"Please," Reddy says. "To show some restraint among company."

Sara tips her head back against Devin's chest. Hillary snaps their photograph. Adams and Karma scan the landscape with binoculars. Reddy sighs and closes his eyes to nap, making use of his backpack as headrest. Sherpa Pasang bellows the fire with his breath to yaw the flame along. Sherpa Mingma prepares the chapatis, patting balls of dough thin and flat between his hands, making the sounds of a happy child clapping. The porters pinch tobacco and roll their smokes, marks from the tumplines furrowed deep into their foreheads, their feet thick with callus and stubbed as clubs, laughing and joking among one another. Despite their hardships, the porters are the most cheerful bunch on the trip, though Sara seems the most pleased. "Alas, this is her party," Adams says, watching her gad about picking starflowers with that smile and those rosy-pomed cheeks. Troy scribbles out another paragraph in his notebook. Wilder stifles a cough that has nagged him throughout the day. Again, Reddy suggests lozenges from the medical kit, but Wilder waves away the offer.

One of the fat marmots delivers another ear-piercing whistle, this followed by a loud shrieking that sends the animals diving back into their holes. People turn to see Vida scrambling from out of the stunted trees, belt dangling from the loops of her khakis, her face drained of color. "Jesus, Jesus, Jesus," she says. "Leeches!" She holds out her blood-covered hands. There are looks of sympathy and disgust from the others. "Revolting beasts," Adams says, shaking his head. Wilder reminds Vida that he warned her. Reddy assures her there can be no harm. He takes a kerchief out of his pocket and begins to swab her fingers clean. "Two I pulled off my legs. One on my backside," she says. She shivers and does a little twitchy jig. Devin says, "Wonder what they feed on when people aren't around?" "Excellent question," says Hillary. The Sherpas, crouched about the cooksite, hold their caps in the smoke of the fire before quickly clapping them back onto their heads; who knows what kind of odd custom this might be? They watch as each of the sahibs quietly moves off into the trees to inspect himself or herself privately.

After lunch they kill the fire and pack up and caravan out of the meadow. The trail soon begins to zigzag up, making for a long grind to a high spur of earth that has everyone pouring sweat again and laboring for breath. Once to the top of the ridge they pause to take deep sucks of the paltry air, hearts booming in their ears. Already the herders and porters are moved far ahead and out of sight. It is windy and cold up here amid these rampages of glaciers, but they wait, wishing enough for a glimpse of Mysterium to withstand a bit of misery. They shed packs, retrieve water bottles. But for the gulping of water and the gurgling of guts, there is undivided silence.

A vision from out of the bands of evanescent light: an enormous bird of some kind, a dark thing riding a vector unseen, flapping its fantastic wings and now approaching so quickly and close they can see the bearded under-beak and the outspread barbs of its talons. The predator lets out a shrill cry and swoops down on its target, sending everyone ducking for cover. The thing tilts wildly, veers, and goes soaring skyward, its wingbeats a helicoptering *whoop, whoop, whoop* above their heads.

"God almighty," Troy says.

"Lamb hawk," says Karma.

"It looked me right in the eyes," Sara says.

They watch the huge bird pilot the valley and disappear into cloud.

"Here this bird common," Karma says. "It feed on marrow. Bird fly with catch of meat bone." Karma grips his hands tightly, holds his fists out. "Then it let bone drop from sky to break on rock." He splays his hands like bird digits. "Now come bird down to feed."

A hard slap of cold air chases them off the ridge. The cadre heads down the declivity, out of the wind and into the valley, over a pellicle of loess and till. Here and there they pass an erratic, those lonely boulders left behind by glacier melt and retreat, weatherworn and alien, some big as houses, all carried great distances; stone foreigners sprung from another time and land. The party follows the path of the porters and herders, arriving to a tarn clear as a mirror where they stop to pause at water's edge. Sara gazes into the pooled looking glass, rafts of clouds and rays of light surrounding her shimmering image. She draws closer to her reflection, tucks loose strands of hair back into her hat. Then the wind picks up to abolish the picture, erasing her eyes, her face, the sky, erasing everything.

They move on through the rugged splendor of the montane, cool wind and cool silence all about. At the end of the vale, at the end of a long day, they are forced to a halt at the verge of a precipice. Ahead of them is a sight wholly strange: a great split in the landscape, the earth appearing clawed apart by something monstrous. The rocky maw opens to tier upon tier of black slabs dropping vertically away, grotesque and exaggerated mineral shapes that can hardly be believed. A gray vapor seeps up among the crags.

"Altogether more frightening from a distance," Adams says.

"As is death," says Troy.

The sahibs step away from the brink. They look at Adams. "I assure you," he says.

"I heard the route is infested with devils," Devin says.

"Don't talk that talk around the porters," says Reddy.

"Believe me," Adams says, "they know their demons better than we."

The herders and porters have, without pause, moved on in an opposite direction with their flocks and their loads. The sahibs turn from the precipice and follow, heading out toward a flat stretch of alpine steppe. They come to a freshet of water, and here the entire party falls out, dropping backpacks and cargo to make camp for the night. The shadowy embrace of the Gorge they will face in the morning. Professor Troy reminds his companions, as he reminds himself, "To worry is to suffer twice."

. . .

THE SAHIBS stake their tents within a shield of wind-bent trees, the Sherpas pitching theirs along the streambank, while the porters and herders shelter among themselves a fair distance away. There is category everywhere here, a bracketing of sorts. Even the goats have their place.

Sherpas Pasang and Mingma—whom the sahibs still have trouble telling apart, so similar in face and manner and dress are they—peel root vegetables, pat chapatis, tend to a pot of boiling rice. The sahibs recline about a crackling fire, watching the day fade away. There is a faint radiant glow in the air, a hint of the blazing light of the universe on the horizon, the hot, dense remnant of energy that has sparked existence.

Wilder stares into the fire, sizzling djinns of red-hot cinders crazing up into the night. He thinks of his brother, their last climb. The Valley of the Pitchforks, Lucas had called their campsite on the Stone Sentinel climb. "The place looks like a basin of devil's tools," he had said. Wilder watches tongues of flames flaring out every which way, his brother's words returning. Night was coming on fast. There was a deep blue atmospheric light in the sky, as there is tonight, and Wilder knew it to be the same blue fire that flamed within him, flamed within him and his twin brother. The earth had smelled of raw and pure elements, of stone and ash, of a cooling luminescence. Wilder smells the smell now in his remembering. Of course he remembers. He remembers all of it.

Lucas, why'd you goddammit take off your boots?

Karma, the sirdar Sherpa, plonks more wood onto the glowing coals. The fire crackles and blazes. Wilder stares into the outburst of flames. Sees the two-man dome he and his brother had pitched. That old thing, set on a bed of ancient craton, faced to open to sunrise. After they had put their tent up, they had to sit and catch their breath, so easily out of breath that first night they were. They panted like old smokers and watched an inferno of clouds dimming out in the twilighting sky. What a sight it was. Who could forget? Their hearts bounded at twice their usual paces. They complained about headaches, drank from their water jugs, praised the alpenglow. Lucas started a fire with one of the army-issue heat tabs he had brought back from training camp in Alaska. Wilder fixed what they liked to call horse ovaries, their jocular take on the word *hors d'oeuvres*. They laughed their breathless laughs. Wilder smiles. He lets out breath. Hears the hum of voices of the others around the fire. He checks his wristwatch, takes a swallow of tea, regards Karma prodding the fire to life.

Wilder and his brother had sat cross-legged, warmed by the fire, watching the simmer of water in the pot, just as Wilder watches the fire before him now. They talked easily, agreed on the why for being all the way out here, though in clumsy phrases that would make no sense to anyone but each other. Above all, they agreed on the pleasure of being far from anything reminding them of everyday chore or obligation. They were alone together, just the two of them, as in a long day of boyhood romp and sport where they could lose track of place and any time given by watch or by clock. He and Lucas understood life in these wild beyonds as something akin to metaphysical parents—so they had tried their best to explain—in that the span of days, with its living creatures and ecosystems, its flora and fauna, its order and flux and its lots and fates—knowing it was all this they were sheltered by, havened by the innate goodness of all these things. Out in the middle of nowhere they could be kids again, feeling cared for without effort, is what they had been trying to say—with some greater thing altogether to father and mother them, and the weeks ahead like another long day of play. The brothers had felt alone together and safe.

Wilder sits with arms rested on raised knees, within the background noise of small talk, the knock of tin spoons against pots. Pyretic sparks arc up and burn out into darkness. He sees Vida looking at him now through the hot glints of the fire. She had been jealous of Lucas, of the closeness between them, the intimacy of twins. She could never, will never, understand it.

"A GOOD sign," Karma says. He raises a thumb skyward. "Tomorrow we have fine day." He is wearing little yellow squares of adhesive cloth outside the corner of each eye. He will adorn his temples in this peculiar way the remainder of the trip, and no one will ask him why, whether out of politeness or superstition.

Sherpas Pasang and Mingma pass around plates of steaming food and pancaked bread to the group, and all sit about staring into the blaze as they supper, their eyes glowing like coals, the night bending in the heat. How wondrously simple and primitive their lives have become. After the meal is finished they drink more tea and contemplate the sky, putting planets into order and story. There is a hint of Mysterium rising and scrimmed in the darkness. Or maybe this vision is just a wish in each seeker.

A long day. Stars to watch, but no stories to tell. No one brings up the task of the Gorge they will have to confront in the morning. No one wishes to worry twice. The decision has been made; the choice is forward and up. In ones and twos they get to their feet, a few to help the Sherpas pick up plates and utensils, the others sooner seeking the warmth of downy beds and the arms of Morpheus.

Occupying one of the tents are Virgil and Hillary Adams, Vida and Wilder Carson, the couples to sleep head to head, feet to feet, accordingly. "The married-people tent," Karma says, pressing the yellow stickers into place at the sides of his eyes. Assigned to the second tent are Doctor Reddy and son Devin, Professor Troy and daughter Sara. "The begetters and the begotten tent," Adams says.

"I never realized the party's beautiful symmetry until now," his wife says. "And I bet Devin and Sara are pleased to be sleeping side by side." She yawns, says, "Anyway, it's time." Hillary watches as Pasang fills a plastic drinking bottle with hot water, and she takes it and thanks him and bids her goodnight. She feels the gnaw of the day in her body, in the pockets and joints of hip bones and knees from the up and down of the steep, an ache in the folds of her shoulders from the weight of the knapsack. She climbs into the tent and shucks her down booties and slides into the warm keep of her sleeping bag. She settles the hot water bottle in the hollow of her low back for a while, and then she maneuvers it into the depths of the bag and welcomes it about her feet. As the others enter the tent she is already fallen into the depths of sleep. Soon enough, all follow her into slumber. The night pulses on.

Wilder's eyes snap open in the dark. He wakes up twisted about in his sleeping bag, choked in windings of clothing, drenched with sweat, his heart pounding like a running animal's. He unzips the mummy bag, works to steady his breath. His eyes adjust to the dark and he searches the tent, looking for remains of the evil callers somewhere near that just were. Images that struck in the night race through his mind, like apparitions creeping in, and now he sees the stranger coming out of the moonscape, the thing gesturing to him and his brother, a demon of stone smiling eerily. They had to run, move quick. *Hurry, man!*

Go! Move your legs, Lucas. Move! But Lucas is slow. Wilder calling and calling in warning, and his panicked cries coming out nothing but a pitiful moaning, like in every horrible dream. He shakes violently in his remembering. And now he sees Lucas running—finally his brother is running—but he is running on bloody stumps.

Wilder jolts upright. He sleeves the sweat from his face. His mouth waters with a sickening taste. He puts his head outside the tent, spits. The fire is dampened to embers, its smolder a quiet rustling in the night. He lies back and zips himself into his mummy bag, works to slow his breath and the wild gallop of his heart. He says his brother's name. He says it again.

MRS. ADAMS peels herself out of the sleeping sack, doing her best not to disturb the others enfolded about her in their feathery confines. She finds the down booties nearby within the pleats of the tent, shoves them onto her socked feet, unzips the flap, and crawls out into the night on hands and knees. Her husband groans. Vida sleeps. Wilder pretends to sleep. Hillary wanders out far away enough from the tent to avoid making noise, pulls her long johns down, and squats against a rock. What pleasure simple relief can bring. And to see now how clear the night is; the sky like a chalkboard filled with geometry problems and eraser swipes. The bright sky replicates the earthly tableau, lighting up the scatter of tents with its pyramids and domes, the camp spread out like a constellation, like a Leo or Cassiopeia or Orion. She breathes in the magnificence that surrounds her: every bit of work to get here worth it for this celestial spectacle alone. It will be etched in her synapses, engrammed in her mind like a sky map drawn by the ancients. She feels as expansive as the universe. She feels safe and very close to her companions, emotionally so. Her scalp and her fingers tingle. Her eyes water up. Her breath feathers vapory afterglows in the cold. She stands and wiggles back into her pants and hurries back to the tent, taking one last look at the display of heroes that rest in the heavens above. And then she is down—fast—like that—flat on her face in the grass. Oh! that stone. Even with eyes on the ground she may not have seen it coming.

SHE HAD not heard a word from her mother since the night before the party had set out, but Sara received plenty of signs from her that were easily recognizable. She had heard her mother's ministrations in the burble and swirl of the stream as the sahibs sat drinking their tea. Not so much the words exactly, Sara will admit, but clearly the waters bore Amanda's reproachful tone. Sara was sent a message first morning out on the trail, a mourning dove turned emissary: *home, home, home*, the bird coo'd. On every tree that Sara passed in the pale aspen grove, there were her mother's almond-shaped eyes intaglio'd into the bark. She felt the brush of her mother's fingers in whisks of chilly air, felt her touch in the sunrays through the cloud-breaks, felt her in the warmth and the itch of the worn emerald-colored sweater.

Sara could see her mother too, see her in her father, in the hunch of her father's shoulders, in the distance in his eyes, in the inwardness of his manner and bearing. Her mother was her father's timbre, his maxims and sighs, his spur and his pause and his grace.

Sara was perched on a rock next to the edge of the cliff looking down into a barren windswept valley. Out of somewhere, or nowhere, there came a feeling of hands on her shoulders: a hint, a portent, a sense of whatever it was threatening to toss her into the abyss. Sara rose and backed away from the brink, shuddering and cold. An outburst of furious birds shot up from the depths below. Light sparked the sky. Weather cracked in the distance.

HILLARY ADAMS spends most of the morning confused as to what to do. She hobbles about using an umbrella as stave, avoiding the aggrieved looks she believes have settled onto the faces of the others. Doctor Reddy examines her and diagnoses a likely broken toe, as well as an ankle sprain. He offers analgesics and to bind the injury. He speaks of elevation, rest, soaking the foot in an icy stream.

"Knitbone," Sara says.

"What, is that a decree?" Reddy says.

"Hell," says Adams. "Why in hell? is all there is to proclaim." He and Reddy help Hillary get up onto the rocks at the side of the stream. Adams makes clucking noises with his tongue. The Sherpas bring hot cups of tea and simple words of concern. The rest of the group stand about, scanning one another's eyes, seeking accord or rejoinder. The water flows icy cold over Mrs. Adams's swollen toe and ankle.

Sara leaves the group and wanders down over the knoll, away from camp and out of sight. Nothing unusual, perhaps a simple need for a few minutes to herself. But she is gone a long time, and now the others begin to wonder. What next? Troy zips his parka up and starts out in Sara's direction, mumbling something about the kind of day it has become, when in an instant his daughter appears from over the crest. She carries a bandanna-wrapped bundle in her hands, a delighted smile on her face, and she ignores the remarks and the questions as she carries on with her mission, all eyes on her, enjoying the flood of attention. She opens the bundle on a flat rock next to where

Mrs. Adams sits, displaying a collection of broad hairy leaves, some of them flowered and filamented.

"You're out collecting posies at a time like this?" Adams says.

"Comfrey," she says. "What my mother called knitbone." She looks around, finds a fist-size rock, and begins to pound the leaves down, making a good pungent mass of the herbs. "Hot water," Sara says. "Or, here, never mind, this tea will do fine." She puts the herb mash into the cup of hot tea and stirs it in with a stick, then spreads the warm paste she has made into a thick layer onto her open bandanna, aware of the power of a good performance. "Now I will need your ankle please." Sara pats herself on the thighs, and Mrs. Adams brings her foot out of the water, dabbing it dry with a sock and settling it gingerly into the hold of the girl's lap. Sara folds the bandanna into itself to keep the poultice together, and now she uses the steaming packet to wrap the ankle, tying the bandage together snug at the ends before giving a final gentle press of intent to the bones and the flesh all around.

"The warmth is good," Hillary says. "If anything."

"The poultice will cool and stiffen," Sara says, "and brace the sprain."

It did just that. Meanwhile, Reddy had splinted the toe with a metal instrument from his medical kit. Mrs. Adams claimed the knitbone poultice to be the better remedy as the tenderness in her ankle was relieved. "But with all due respect to the good doctor, the toe is throbbing and growing more painful." She puts the boot on with difficulty, stands, and looks at the ground. She takes a few limping steps. "It's tight," she says. "The toe is too swelled for the boot." She sits down. She shakes her head, apologizes. She cannot make it through the Gorge walking like a cripple. Adams and Reddy decide between them; the party should remain here at camp until tomorrow. See how Hillary can manage after a day of rest. No one protests, as no one is too eager to face the difficulties of the Gorge.

Late morning the following day, two porters are assigned to be Hillary Adams's escorts back down to the village, acting as crutches, piggybacking her down in places where needed. Sara has made for her a mukluk boot of sorts using a down bootie heeled with a rubber-thonged shoe, and around the whole of it a nylon stuff sack brought to the knee and wrapped in plastic bagging that she binds with lacing and tape. "There," she says. "Padded and waterproofed." Adams has a look of about-to-cry on his face. He declares he must absolutely go back with his wife; Professor Troy would thereby need to take over as expedition leader. Adams says he will not get to the top of Mysterium a second time, it was simply not meant to be. There are immediate protests, loud, all at once, the voices a chorus of pleading. They tell him they disagree. They tell him they need him. He has been through the hardships of the Sage's Gorge before and knows the best line to take. He alone knows the route through the Sanctuary and up to the summit. "At least to go as far as Base Camp and help me to manage there," Vida says. "I can't do it by myself." She is ready to go home too.

"A collective decision must be made," Mrs. Adams says. "Greatest good for the greatest number, as our professor would tell us. You are obligated to stay with the group and remain leader, Ad," she says. "It is your duty, absolutely." She will go back to the village, take her time in the going with the help of the porters and fixed lines, and there should be no arguing. Adams turns about full circle, as if in search of a direction. He raises his arms, looks toward the sky with hands outspread. "A driver will drive me back to Delhi," Hillary says. "There is never a problem finding a man for hire. In Delhi, there will be people to help me gather my things. I am certainly capable of getting help to the airport and from there flying home on my own," she says.

"Quite capable," her husband says.

He looks at her with his stone-colored eyes.

"I am sorry," she says.

"I am not happy," he says.

"You shall get over it," she says.

A WOOLLY mist creeps in from the ravine, spilling up and over the spur of earth the camp is perched on. Sherpa Pasang kneels before last night's fire with bowed head, working to blow life into the dead ashes, but Mingma piles on juniper branches and strikes a match for a quick start. The two Sherpas chuckle between themselves as to the confusion of their identities among the sahibs, knowing their habit of trading hats complicates, though it is a harmless amusement, they agree.

They ready hot water for the sahibs, filling basins up for the morning ablutions. Then to prepare the day's first meal: milky tea and watery porridge that the sahibs will sit and eat in silence, crouched about the fire as they watch the porters load up and head out to follow in the path of the herders with their goats, already far in the lead. Virgil Adams complains of intestinal cramps, certainly a most common ailment on any Himalayan trail, but these pains started immediately after his wife had departed with two of the porters to head back to Delhi and home. He makes frequent trips behind the scrubby trees, keeping the rest of the group waiting for departure, though they are patient enough, as few are cheery about the day's prospects. Doctor Reddy hands Adams a couple of packets of pink tablets from his medical kit. He urges him to drink more tea. "For your mood, I have nothing to offer you," the doctor says.

"Better we should get moving while the weather holds," Troy says. "Sooner we're out of the netherworld the better."

"Who needs to stay in a state of dread any longer than we have to?" Vida says. "My agony junction is already in knots."

"Your agony junction?" Reddy says.

"What?" she says. "You have nothing in your kit for this?"

"No need to work yourself into a tizzy," he says.

"So what if I'm in a tizzy. Is permission needed?"

"Why to be so loud?" Reddy says, noticing her weak eye skewed wild.

"What can I say, Doc?" Wilder says. "She gets this way."

"Screw you," Vida says.

"Should I find something for your nerves?" asks Reddy. Wilder snorts.

"Screw the both of you." She stomps away.

The party prepares to head out; filling water bottles, double-lacing boots, cinching backpacks, zipping jackets to the chin. Karma takes the lead, and the others follow along in the cold air, working out the stiffness and the kinks of the night prior, grappling with questions and dreads, slowing the pace for Adams when he breaks from the line to hurry behind a bush or a rock for an urgent squat. They move through wild rhubarb and crawling juniper, past quartzite rocks encrusted with fluorescent lichen, stepping over clumps of goat droppings freshly steaming along the trail. Stratocumulus clouds tent out in high layers above their heads. They read the sky for signs of bad weather, concerned that rain will complicate the day.

They tramp up an incline following a path along an open shoulder, and after an hour of steady hiking they surmount the ridge. They pause, breathless, and once more face the obsidian jaws of the Gorge: a chasm of jagged rock that strikes like a vicious laugh. In silent defile they move toward it, on into a dampening chill, the clamor from the roaring moat soaring up from below. They follow a precipitous trace that zigzags miles down into the trap of a box canyon, where the moiling waters of the river are hugged by walls cleft and left eerily polished by the glaciers above; black walls that wing sharply up thousands of feet high on either side. Vida works to keep her mind on a single thing, as Wilder had advised when he taught her to climb, that is to lift a leg to plant a foot, putting one foot in front of the other, repeat, repeat, repeat, using the ice axe for stability, breathing rhythmically. Break the task into the smallest pieces. Nothing more. Nothing less.

The route turns more demanding, and soon handholds are necessary as footholds. They clutch at any prop available: roots or shrub, tuber or creeper, rock or vine, whatever they can find to hold themselves to the slope. Someone makes a pathetic joke in a stroke of passing hysteria. No one laughs. No one says anything: every mind only on the next handhold or foothold afforded. The porters stagger ahead under the weight of the loads, bootless and sure-footed, their agility startling. The herders work to keep up with the goats, animals that make play of the steep.

Soon enough the way descends headlong again, only to abruptly seesaw steeply back up. What forged this trail of insanity: Was it fright? Confusion? Misery? Villainy? The necessity of escape? They look for alternate paths, finding no mark, no track, no logic. They look at Adams. He shakes his head. They press on in muted procession, making their way farther into the Gorge's adamantine deeps, moving along a vestige of trail if a trail at all, a trace over thick roots and loose stones forcing them down and up and down once more, through places of dense undergrowth that too often mask dangerous overhangs. The exposed traverse hugs a nightmarish wall of sheer cliff that parallels the turbulent river.

The party is inching ahead, the stony ground widening out and narrowing and widening again when they are struck by a crackling explosion of rock against rock, sending everyone ducking for cover. Porters cling to roots and vines, bowing down to armor themselves with their cartons and duffels, the goats moving in great bounds and leaps. Rocks whistle and hiss as the mineraled artillery goes spinning by, leaving behind a sulfurous stink that ricochets out in a loud bang. Until finally all falls silent. The halt and standstill are abrupt as the onset: a moment of quiet followed by the lonely surrender and clatter of one last stone. A cloud of boulder powder swirls up out of the ravine. They stay hunkered and raise their heads in heed, hearts clobbering rib cages, a tumid pumping in eardrums. Beside them, a swath of earth is swiped raw, the soil gouged out, shrubs crushed flat. There are words of urgency. A call of names. One of the porters is gushing blood from the split flesh of his head, and Reddy scrambles up to reach him, announcing the injury superficial, removing the bandanna from his throat to swab the man's wound. Already the other porters have started to move on, not wanting to linger in this accursed place. The sahibs collect themselves, and with wobbly legs and ringing ears they make their way out of the bedlam and down the steep to the river, a white frothing torrent of monsoon and snow-melt roaring in greeting. Hardly relieved, they face their first crossing.

The goats have found milky pools to drink from, away from the pandemonium of the roil and swell, the bhakrawal-las rocks to sit and smoke on. The porters grab hold of their tumplines, bend deep at the knees to deposit baskets and cartons in the sand. The sharp flanks of the canyon walls tower up dramatically, allowing only a pale band of sky above. Within the mammoth landscape all are made very small. Little Jonahs in the belly of the whale.

Sherpa Karma stands with hands on hips facing the river, the sticky yellow patches of cloth hiding the line that his sight takes. Across the river are clues to a pathway, but how to get there? He puts his hands to his mouth to be heard over the turbulent water, but the words are devoured by its uproar. He points to a natural bridge of sorts: slabs of boulders, a traverse of logs and rocks. Troy nods and finds the porter and the load he is looking for. From out of the porter's basket he withdraws a coil of rope. He unties the cinch knot and flakes the rope out, recoils it and square-knots it to hold, and then hitches the loop of the whole over his shoulder. He unclips the backpack from his waist cinch for safety, and steps out onto one of the river's logs.

He begins to move forward, feeling the powerful din of the river inside his body, the clamor of waters a hard thudding inside his chest. Small voices from behind skip across the water like stones. He cannot look back without losing balance. He cannot ask. The water sploshes over his boots, numbing cold as it seeps over shafts and in through the seaming. He totters on, log to stone to stone, stepping up onto boulders, one to the next, the water leaping at him like a feral animal through a notch in the rock. Halfway across the river he balances on a boulder, an icy slosh walloping him every which way. He pauses now to look back, catching sight of porters and herders and sahibs, all watching him, strung along as they are at the bottom of a fathomless gorge, just little swallowed things. Troy turns and leaps across to another rock. He works his way down to the logjam, the water in a mad cascade. Logs too slippery to pause on. He moves fast, the churning water slamming him, and then he slips. Shit! Wet hip-deep. Climb out. Step up. Leap. Until his feet are planted into the cowbelly sand of the riverbank. "Sweet mother," he says.

He tosses the backpack off, standing erect on the certainty of solid earth. He unknots an end of the coil and half-hitches the rope to a trunk of thick birch. Fingers to his teeth, he lets go a piercing whistle. Wilder raises an open hand to the air. With a strong toss the bulk sails across the water, elegant as an albatross. Wilder snags the tether on the other side, clenches the rope end in his fist.

The sahibs make it over to the other side of the river, one by one with the help of the rope. The porters with their loads are less sure, as are the bhakrawallas with their bleating wall-eyed animals. Wilder navigates the river once again, returning back to ferry loads across for those doubtful. Already the shepherds are cutting wide branches and limbs of trees to lay a wider path across the seething waterway. It will be dusk when the goats are finally hazed over the rickety bridge, and gotten at last across the river.

The Sherpas take the lead, moving upshore in the twilight, finding there a wide sandy bank set back into a copse where they erect the tents and the cook tarp. Porters and herders follow, dropping cartons and barrels, relieving the goats of their panniers. Then the sahibs trail in, unstrapping backpacks, easing their way to the solace of hard ground.

BACKS AND legs aching, minds benumbed with fatigue, the Sherpas keep working. They pitch the tents for the sahibs and find a site upriver for their own abode, the porters and bhakrawallas, as usual, settling with the herd a distance away. Wilder helps the Sherpas pole up a tarpaulin over the cook station, coughing a cough turned hacking, while Vida seeks privacy in the trees, checking herself for leeches routinely. Reddy, curled on a tarp on the ground, dreams aloud in his sleep. Troy takes a place apart from the group to sit with his notebook and pen. His daughter and Devin go out to hunt for firewood, no one but Sara realizing her new love has stuffed a sleeping bag into his pack for them to rest on together. Adams crawls into an empty tent and sprawls out to relax, consoled in knowing his wife has not suffered such a day as today. He imagines her on her way home to safety and ease, home to chicken salad sandwiches, hot lavender baths, the evening news on TV.

None of them is aware of being followed by a large black cat. The panther had been tracking the party during their crossing to her side of the river, a home range she keeps marked dutifully with scrapes of dirt kicked up by her hind feet. No one is alert to the cat's signs; not only have they missed the scrapes, but they also do not notice the trunks of the trees inscribed with her scratches and gouges, nor do they see the staggered line of round paw prints she has augured into the mud. They do not see the cylinders of scat seeded with shards of bone, not a hint of the wads of hair or the bits of pelt, nothing at all that marks her whereabouts.

As reward to the porters for having carried the punishing loads through a most tortuous portion of trail, Adams suggests the sahibs offer to buy a goat from the bhakrawallas to be butchered for dinner. The others agree. Sara considers this a sacrifice of the highest kind, and insists upon being witness to the killing. The herders would prefer to slaughter in their manner, quietly, among themselves, but they allow the girl to stand and watch them slit the goat's throat, taking her observance as blessing, as she is their Sarasvati.

One of the herders comes up from behind the goat and straddles it between withers and hip. Sara sees the glint of the knife blade, sees it like a silvery fish tumbling through a stream. A bright line of blood at the throat yaws open like a bawling mouth. The animal collapses into a mute heap, eyes gaped as the light in the orbs flames out. The shepherds huddle and crouch and begin the work of stripping the hide and sectioning the bones and the flesh, and now Sara can see no more.

From her perch of rock above, the panther scans the human bustle. She vaults boulder to boulder until she is down by the river again. She leaps up onto a limb of a fir tree, and from this place waits for her prey to stray from the flock. She is patient and ready, posed like a sphinx on a pedestal. She breathes contentedly, air vibrating in her glottis, the night dilating as the day begins to constrict. The cat's silky ebony coat conceals her body in the dim light. Her nose ticks to catch a scent: an approaching goat. She flattens her ears back to the sound of the under-hoof cracking of branches. The hair stands in hackles along her spine. She rises onto her haunches, sights before the pounce, and the act is carried out nearly silently. Her razored fangs gouge deep into the animal's neck, piercing the jugular in an instant. She grounds herself with her hind legs, caging the goat with stance and weight as it wrenches and buckles just once, withers to loin to rump, its legs giving a final twitch. Any fleeting deathly frenzy is drowned in the wild laughter of the river and the flurry of slaughter back at the camp. The panther feeds off the flesh hungrily, the goat's heart still beating its useless last beats. What cannot be devoured now will be concealed for later. She uses her forepaws to cover the carcass, scratching up a litter of sticks and leaves. She backs away, studies the cache with clever yellow eyes, her breathing a metered hissing.

Then she turns, and like a dancer exiting the stage, she slinks away back to the cave, to her lair that is hidden there.

Sara lowers her head, recites a blessing before biting into the meat.

"I believe," Professor Troy says, his mouth full of tender brisket, "the custom of prayer before a meal likely originated in animal sacrifice."

"You could well be right," Adams says, reaching for more.

"As Buddhists, we honor all things," says Karma. He tosses his bones into the fire, and holds his empty plate out to the man who sits closest to the roasted goat. "Yes, please," he says.

NEW TENT assignments were made given Hillary's departure, the groupings determined by the party's leader: here on, the Carsons would share a tent with Doctor Reddy and himself. In the second tent would be bedded Professor Troy and daughter Sara and Devin Reddy. This seemed to make perfect sense, and no one, as Adams would say, groused about it.

But worn out as they are after a grueling day, Vida and Reddy have trouble sleeping. They are each too aware of the other, the familiarity of that body next to him or her at rest: the resistance or give of an arm or a hip, the manner of breathing, the scent, the heat, a shift. They lie supine, mindful of what was, of what is and what isn't; their eyes open to the shaded hatches and stipples of the tent in the surrounding dimness. Wilder sleeps on one side of his wife turned away from her, his face toward the nylon wall, his coarse respiring broken by an occasional burst of dry cough. Reddy lies next to Vida on her opposite side. Adams is flat on his back beside Reddy next to the door of the tent, the Bostonian's palate vibrating rhythmically, a commotion broken intermittently by snuffling animal sounds coming from the profundity of his slumber. Reddy pokes Adams with an elbow, provoking him to roll over, his breathing quieting to an even purr. Vida reaches an arm out of her sleeping bag, touches Reddy to thank him and to apologize too for her temper at the start of the day. He takes her hand and squeezes it gently, holds it a moment before letting go. Then they close their eyes to the deepening of the night that binds them, favoring the promise and the bounty of sleep.

THE SHEPHERDS wake before daybreak to decamp without haste, eager to get back across the river again, rattled by the panther's plunder and kill the night prior. The men throw their hands up in blame and resignation, then herd the goats on in a sullen and slow-coming dawn; hooves scraping over stone, satchels of grain flapping over ribs and withers, watery lumps dumped along the pathway. An unearthly light above cleaves through a thin line of overcast sky.

Once the party is safely to the other side of the water all ascend steadily, relieved to be making their way out of this horrible gorge. There is a settling in of pace and deep breathing, the rhythmical clinking of bootsteps in loose stone, the Sanctuary now only a day's foray away; release from this hell within sight. Three hours later they are already a thousand feet above the river, and here the misstep occurs, an off-beat footfall and slide in the talus, a jarring familiar sound, and in an instant one of the porters is calling out, the voice echoing through the vast hollow in his tumble and reel, a terrible wailing scaled and dimmed until it is no longer at all. Gone like a flame blown out. Everyone stands at the brink in the awful silence looking into the gloom below. The other porters release their tumplines and park their loads on the path. Many collapse to the ground, sit with heads cradled in their hands, eyes drawn to the dark earth, to the crawling things beneath their feet.

The sahibs and Sherpas look down over the cliff, jaws hung loose. They look for words. Then Karma claps his hands together and urges the porters to rise. He commands them. He is sirdar. He orders them moving again. There is nothing else here to do.

The party tramps on through a shroud of mist. Everyone feels more heavily laden. The river below turns a crazed churn in the distance, and no wind or air moves through the haze. They labor through a bramble of thorn scrub, a hellish odor of cinder and tar reeking out of the sodden earth, the grade steepening and seeming to cline on endlessly. The porters wear a look of despondency, as does every footslogger, but it is the porters who hold their heads as they weep, the porters who wave their arms about, and now the porters who stop and release their tumplines. They deposit their cartons and bundles right where they stand, along the steep and narrow path. They refuse to go on. They have had enough. The bhakrawallas do their best to scoot the goats along, but even the animals have turned skittish; their horned noggins bob and loll, the rolling orbs of their eyes bulge white.

Adams advises the party to take another line entirely. Best to move lower at this point, not higher. But the porters have parked themselves on the trail, and here they sit and rest against their loads, chary, despaired, layered in their raggedy tweeds and fringed shawls and army fatigues. They moan and whimper and mutter to themselves. One of them begins to wail. Karma presses the heels of his hands to his temples, affixing the yellow tabs. He says he must go ahead, scout out the trail.

Pasang will accompany him on his reconnaissance, but Mingma and the sahibs are to remain with the porters. Pasang follows the sirdar as ordered. The herders stop with their goats on a ledge of grass above the others. They smoke. They talk softly. They watch the head Sherpa and his aide disappear into a congealed mist that clings to the cliff.

The trail the group is perched on is narrow, and no one gets up or moves about much. Adams sits, knees to his chest, gaze fixed on the cliff wall ahead. Professor Troy takes the journal and pen from his pack and begins to scribble his thoughts down; so fastidious is he about the day's entries. Sara sketches the sight she sees across the ravine in her sketchbook, penciling filaments of water cascading from out of the towering walls, an empty aerie of twigs and debris tucked into the rifts between. Wilder fiddles with the rock in his pocket as he talks tactics with Devin. Vida has curled up into herself and sits sideways on the path with her body tipped into a scoop of the cliff, her leg muscles trembling, a taste like rust in her mouth. She will not look down.

Adams sits nearest to Sara. "You must speak to the head porter," he says. "Tell him the most tortuous part of the Gorge has been gotten through. Tell him the porters must believe me. They must trust me. Trust us." She puts her sketchbook back in the pack and gets up and wends her way through the legs asplay on the narrow trail, clinging to the rocky wall. She crouches down to talk to the head porter. She speaks kindly, reassuringly. A few of the other porters put their faces into their hands and shake their heads. They have already decided to go back. They will find a secure place to abandon their loads.

Adams leans out to shout something when Karma's voice cuts him short, the call echoing out loud through the Gorge. "Sahib! Sahib!" The squatters turn to see the sirdar Sherpa moving along the ledge toward the others, Pasang close behind, both approaching with eyes cast toward the ground. Now Adams expects to hear the worst. It is his fault, all of this. They have lost a man. He has lost the way. Weakened in his age, he has forsaken them all.

"Please," Karma says. He touches the yellow patches beside his eyes. "We have seen way from here," he says.

People mutter words of relief. There are heaving sighs, a whimpering, a cough, someone crying.

"Trail difficult only one place. We go down to river once more, but we not cross. The path go up this side river. Not steep to begin." Karma raises a flat hand laterally and cuts the air upwise in front of him. "Way go up straight and we be out. There we place fix lines."

The sahibs nod. Adams and Troy decide the porters must be paid more, despite assurance of the route. Sara appeals to the porters in Hindi. They agree to go on, despite looks of reluctance among them. They stoop, position their tumplines, stand with their loads. Then they follow the sahibs and move on along the ledge. By late afternoon the party is down to the river again, a place where the water rockets out of a sharp notch in the cliff and thunders past. Sara stands transfixed, watching the swell and seethe, following with her eye a foaming white droplet that breaks out from the surge and mass and goes lobbing high into the air, a droplet pitched out into an arc faultless and true. "Only nature performs such acts of perfection," she says, her words swept away in the thunder of the torrent. She keeps her eye on the freed droplet, watching as it lands heavily, silently, without pause, without splash, where it is borne into the rushing waters to become one with the body from which it was sprung.

Karma and Adams walk along the river's banks until they

reach a large overhang in the rock wall, the sand nearly dry in the lee. They agree to make an early camp in the cliff's alcove, far enough away from the boister of the river, better protected from the rain. Eat, sleep, drink tea, make a fire, allow the porters to do their grieving. The loss of the man has shaken everyone, and all could use the rest. The porters and herders move past the sahibs and continue along the river, up through a boulder garden and back into a woods of rhododendron and fir where they stake claim to several small caves.

Wilder brings the hood up over his head and wanders off into a drizzling rain while the others set up and settle into camp. He ducks under the limbs of a dying pine, its core eaten through with ants, entering a copse of thick underbrush and rotting beech. His feet make loud sucking noises in the mud. He pauses, looks about to make certain his privacy, and sees from out of the bushes a creeping army of leeches moving toward his feet, several of the fat worms cobra'ing up out of the mire to reach him. Any need to squat is stifled. He searches for a footpath of some kind, a way around, a way out. Warty toads with spiny crowns jounce about like little horned demons in the leaves. All around are standing snags and fallen logs in various states of rot; fungus erupting on dead stumps like a skin disease; a tar-like resin bubbling out from the scaly bark of a pine. He realizes he is standing amid a microcosm of mysterious plant and animal life in forms grossly primitive. Feed and excrete, growth and decay, life and death: all ends of a single spectrum. He makes a trumpet out of his backside. Then he bends down to examine a piece of dead wood covered over with a slimy-headed mold, the brain-shaped mass expanding and contracting, as if the fungus were breathing.

"It is a living thing."

Wilder bolts up, bawling out loudly as if deranged.

"It is a most simple form of life," the man behind him says.

"You scared the fucking holy bejeezus out of me." Wilder stands with balled fists, knuckles colorless with fright, looking at a bareheaded man wrapped in a crimson robe seated against a tree who smiles at him casually. The man motions with fingers to his lips. Wilder is not sure what the gesture means: Do not speak, or something to eat?

"Where in God's hell did you come from?" Wilder says.

"Hell?" the man says.

"Tibet?"

The man puts a finger back to his lips as if to silence what was said.

"What are you, a monk or something?"

The man smiles his smile again. He reaches beneath his robe and nonchalantly plucks a leech from his shin, flicks the worm off into the leaves. Then he moves from his seat at the base of the tree, picks up his wooden stave, refits the robe over his shoulder, and begins to walk away. He wears Indian army-issue tennis shoes and thick cotton socks. He is bald as the palm of a hand; head shaved and scalp gleaming. Wilder stands watching him as he moves away, thinking the man, without another word, will go on toward wherever it is he is going. India, of course. Probably on his way to see the Dalai Lama.

"Thanks for scaring the shit out of me," Wilder says.

The monk turns to Wilder, nods. "Allow me to make you tea," he says, opening his hand, gesturing toward a lichened block of dark rock within an undercliff. Wilder steps forward, sees an opening grotto'd into the basalt. He stoops and follows the monk inside. The cave is lit by a single candle set into a sill of the rock wall. There is a thin rug spread out on the hard mud floor, a pallet rolled out to serve as bedding and seating.

The monk sinks to his knees onto the pallet, and pats the empty place across from him. Wilder sits. He stifles a cough as he watches the monk light another candle. On the mud floor, within a circle of stone and ash, he prepares a small fire.

"What about the smoke?" Wilder says. This time he can't hold back his cough. The monk points up, and Wilder sees behind and above him a bore of misty light coming through the soffit of rock. The smoke of the fire hugs the wall and goes spiraling up and out the rocky chimney hole. The monk puts a small pot onto the embering coals. He reaches behind him for a metal bottle and pours water out of it into the pot. From a fold in his crimson robe he pulls out a packet, puts his fingers into the packet and brings out a pinch of aromatic leaves. He sprinkles the tea leaves into the water.

"You running away or something?" Wilder says.

The monk shakes his head. "I am going," he says. Smiling, he takes from the copious folds of his robe a small tin can. He reaches back into the crimson pleats and retrieves a folding army knife.

"What else have you got in there?"

"All that I should need," the monk says.

He stabs two holes into the lid of the tin, pours thick milk in the pot.

"Where's your sugar bowl and teacups at?" Wilder says.

The monk reaches into his robe, brings forth a cup. "For you, for me."

"You been in the mountains long?"

"Two months only."

"How do you manage alone?"

"Many kind people. Kind people everywhere."

"Huh," Wilder says. "How come I never meet such people?"

"Your eyes perhaps bad." The monk offers the tea to Wilder.

Wilder takes a sip, and gives it back to the monk. They drink in this manner until the cup is empty, then the monk picks the pot up and pours more tea.

"Where is it you travel to?" the monk says.

"Mount Mysterium."

"Ah, Sarasvati." The monk passes him the teacup again.

"That's right."

"Why? You lose something up there?"

Wilder's laugh erupts into a hacking cough. He clears his throat. "I've got stuff in my pockets too." He pulls out the black stone he has carried from home. "Orgonite," he says. "The real thing." He nods.

The monk takes eyeglasses out of the folds of his robe and examines the stone carefully. He shrugs, hands the thing back to Wilder. "It not real."

"What do you mean, not real?"

"Not real stone."

"There's quartz crystal in it, that's real, and some metal shavings mixed in. The fiberglass resin is just to hold it together."

The monk smiles.

"There's power in it."

The monk looks at him. "Magic power?"

"Metaphysical," he says. He passes the monk the teacup without looking up. "Some very smart people have described it."

The monk takes a sip of tea.

"You put various stones and magnets together and you get powerful reactions. You can capture a part of the energy flow of the universe."

The monk holds the teacup out for Wilder to take.

"Orgone is everywhere about us. It's massless, like ether.

The problem is to gather it and channel its living energy. It can cure diseases."

"You are ill?"

Wilder coughs. "No."

"Then why you need this?" The monk laughs.

"All right, I'll stop trying to convince you." Wilder puts the stone back into his pants pocket. He takes a sip of tea. Then he pulls out from his coat pocket the photograph of Lucas. "This is my brother," Wilder says.

The monk puts the eyeglasses back on and takes the photograph from him. He brings it close to his face and studies it. He looks at it a long time. He cocks his head. "This picture from how many years old?"

"It was," Wilder says. "It . . ." His voice catches again. "Shit."

The monk gives the photograph back. He offers Wilder more tea.

Wilder shakes his head. "My brother. He died is what."

The monk nods. "But why you need picture? Why you need pebble?"

"Who said anything about needing anything?" Wilder decides not to tell of the ashes he has in his backpack. He feels his throat constricting. He blinks.

"Tea," the monk says. "Here, you drink."

IT TAKES little convincing to get the monk to join the others at camp for a meal. The sahibs are astounded to see the man, the Sherpas less so. The porters and bhakrawallas, being Hindu, pretend to take little notice of the stranger who has joined their company; as low as they have been born in caste, the Buddhist's rank is lower. When asked, the monk informs the sahibs he plans to take the path through the Gorge they have journeyed on to get here.

"Then you must be told of the dangers you face if you continue on from the route we came," says Adams. "You should also know there is a big cat slinking around back there. It last night killed one of our goats. Best not to go it alone. Better that you should walk with us."

"He's going the opposite way," Wilder says. "Dharamsala."

"There is an alternate route there," Adams says. "I shall draw it out for you. The way is a bit longer, but much safer. You must climb up out of the Gorge with us, up into the hinterland of the Sanctuary. From there you may turn and go the other way toward your destination, with a bit of traversing."

The monk nods. He is nonchalant about having to retrace his steps. He thanks them for providing him with a safer route to his stopping place. He says he is happy to have their companionship. He sits with his new friends around the crackle and spit of the flames. He reaches into the folds of his robe, brings out a spoon and a bowl and holds the implements out, as beggars do, his bald head gleaming in the light of the fire. He waits patiently for his bowl to be filled.

Sara leaves the campfire to collect the bouquet of valerian she has earlier gathered in the woods. The monk has given her a *kata*, taken from the folds of his robe, and she wears the gift now, draping the white scarf over her head like a veil. She walks upriver to where the porters are lodged, calling to them from a respectful distance. The cave they stay in is lit from within and glows crimson as the monk's robe. One of the men comes out, wrapped in a fringed shawl. "Didi," the man in the shawl says. He says, "Elder sister is here." The other porters come out and all invite her inside to the heat of their fire, but she shakes her head. She stands at the threshold of their crimson domicile, as if by a hearth, and all the men draw closer to see her. She pulls the veil close to her face, speaks to them quietly in Hindi. They cling to her words, to the fire cast in her eyes, to the blaze that reddens her hair and ambers her flesh. This girl, the men will tell you: she is older than the earth itself. She holds a soul reborn and born and born again. In her they take comfort and believe.

For each of the men Sara pinches a white cluster from its stem, handing a floret one by one to all of the porters as they open their hands to her. She speaks in a musical voice, tells them to place this gift of nature inside their caps before sleep tonight. She tells them their dreams will be dreams of enchantment and transport. Their visions will ease the way to a place of perfect rest for their friend. "The waters have taken him," she says. "They are the waters that flow into the Ganges. The waters that flow back to Mother." The porters know this to be true. But to hear Sarasvati speak the words deepens that truth. They take her counsel and her offering as a blessing she bestows upon each of them.

IN A dreary dawn rain they break camp, the river blathering on madly as the troopers turn their backs to take leave of the Gorge. They once again trudge hundreds of feet steeply up, navigating with little technical difficulty, though the labor is great. They climb a staircase of hackly quartz until the way levels out, descending from there to a shelf of lichened rock that brings them to another stretch of cliff ahead. The sahibs take a straight line up, grasping roots and branches along the way, collapsing onto a wide grassy ledge. They rest, wait for the others to come up, watching as the bhakrawallas work a traverse relative to their herd, the goats scrambling forward in wild gambols and bold leaps. The porters, bound to the sixty-plus-pound burdens carapaced to their backs, crawl up the cliff slowly and methodically, like an army of scarab beetles scuttling among the rubble and leaves.

"Now will become difficult," Karma says.

They are gathered at the base of a slab of rock that wings up without shrub or tree for aid in the ascending. The sirdar Sherpa shows the others a narrow chimney holed into a portion of the rock. He opens one of the porter's loads, takes a rope out, carabiners and bolts.

Adams pokes his head inside the rock. "A tight fit."

"I can manage this," Wilder says.

"I am better size," Karma says. He reties the laces of his sneakers and doubles the knots. He pockets the hardware, holsters the hammer, hitches the rope over his shoulder, and then he disappears into the rock cleft. Wedged inside, he begins to shimmy his body up. He presses a foot and a knee on opposite sides of the chimney, reaches for spalls and fins in the mineraled wall and pulls himself higher. He pauses, his hot breath huffing back into his face from off the wall. He is now lodged so deeply into the cranny he is barely able to move at all, his body like an arrowhead that cannot be worked back out again. What now to do? He relies on his father's teachings. He stacks his feet, pushing his way farther up into the body of the rock until he is moved up out of the choke point and the way begins to open up. His hammer has worked its way out of the holster, and is loose on the catch of his thigh. He crimps his fingers into a fissure and with his free hand reaches for the tool, but it is doffed off his leg and goes tumbling into the darkness below. He holds himself to the wall, hearing the clang of metal against stone as the hammer hits bottom. Loud toll of a gong. He settles his breath and looks up into a piercing light, a shining blade that draws him on. With counterforce, with hands and knees and buttocks and feet he moves up, pulled toward the radiant beam. His quickened breath echoes loud all around, a breath larger than he is. The brightness above him bores open as he pushes and pulls his way up, until the light is suddenly on him and flooding down in bestowal and he is reaching up to the lip of the opening, heaving himself up and out of the coal-black hole. He stands breathing hard, sweating, looking down into the narrow chops he was spewed from, seeing himself nearly cocooned in there, perhaps forever, his body fossiled into the chasm of rock for millennia to come.

He shouts out names, waves down to the others. Then he searches for something deeply rooted to the earth. There, a boulder. He secures the rope, tosses the coiled end over the cliff. The anchored assistance Karma places is priceless, especially for the men who are laden. One by one, all come up the face of the cliff with the help of the rope; sahibs, porters, herders, Sherpas, the monk, all toppling over onto the ledge in a splay of poses and shapes and exclamations, the Gorge having spat all of them out at last. Who knows how the goats have managed the way, but the animals appear before them snapping hungrily at the grass.

And now what a sight they behold! At the far end of the hanging valley they are landed upon is a V'd notch, and to this sight all eyes are drawn. For beyond the cleft to dominate the skyline is the glorious mountain herself, Mount Mysterium. A thin veil of cloud at the top of the pinnacle's head spills off into the thin cold air. A diamond choker of ice drapes her throat, and sunglow cloaks her glaciered shoulders. Her flanks are white and soft as ermine. Her base is gowned in cloud. The porters release their loads, fall to their knees, bow their heads. The shepherds raise their arms and chant in praise. The sahibs whoop and holler and take their cameras out. The monk smiles at the spectacle about him.

They gather themselves and shoulder their loads. Renewed and full of rejoice, singing, chanting, laughing, they parade toward the notch. Even the goats bleat and bay as they step through the cleaved rock, moving out of the jaws of the gully and on into the promised land of the Sanctuary. Ahead of them, the blessed goddess, the divine rays of light projected from her heights like arms held out, drawing the holy-landers forward.

5.

THE SANCTUARY

HOW SWEET THE BLOOD FLOWS AFTER THE BODY IS FREED from strain, all senses having been sharpened by danger, awareness honed by abolishing from the mind any triviality otherwise. Do we court circumstances that put us in a state of mortal seriousness, with no room for mistake, purely for the prize of the exhilarating release that follows?

. . .

DAY ONE in the Sanctuary, and the morning star is ablaze when the sojourners wake, a few bright planets and stars shimmering at the pole opposing. Beneath these stellar orbs Mysterium lets go her sable robe, rising forth into a glory of light. The party is settled at her feet in a deep hollow at the end of a valley, their bright red tents set single file in the alpine grass following the line of a meandering stream, shaping Base Camp into the spread of a letter S. The mess tent is pitched within the upper stroke of the colorful S, separating sahib and Sherpa abodes from those of the herders and porters. Inside the mess, eight folding portable chairs surround a folding rectangular table, where here the sahibs will convene and take meals. Far back from the stream a latrine is dug out, with a canvas curtained around tent poles for privacy. A metal washbasin and a bar of soap are settled on a stone; a juniper bough offers prop to a towel. The sahibs wash and dress in daybreak's aubade, the Sherpas collect scrub brush for the fire and put the water to boiling, the bhakrawallas roll their smokes and tend to the goats, while a corps of porters head out to prowl in the dawn on the moraine.

The agony of the Gorge is behind them, the travelers having abandoned all testament to struggle and gladly forgotten the work that brought them to this place. Already sinew and tendon and flesh are mended, the mind without haste erasing past distress. "Not unlike a mother after the labor of birth," is the way Doctor Reddy had put it. Now for the weeks ahead all bodies will do what they must to comply with the altitude: a metabolic recalibrating for each. There will be more breaths taken per minute to draw needed oxygen, triggering blood gases and pressures to shift, with serum diluting and cells amassing, nutrients and minerals and salts all in flux. Hearts pump more stubbornly as rates of respiring climb, while blood acidity and hemoglobin plummet. Sleep and appetite and reason slacken, muscles shrink, body weight falls. Wounds simply fail to heal.

The porters had the night prior celebrated arrival to the Sanctuary in a ritual of chorus and dance. They erected a rock monument modeled in semblance of the avatar Sarasvati; at the foot of it was placed a stone altar and a prasada of chapatis and date sweets. They built an enormous fire in front of the sculpture, luring the others over to gather around in the heat and festivity. The porters sang out loudly to the goddess a melodious air of both joy and lament that was repeated over and again, so that even the sahibs, perched on rocks encircling the fire, could croon along in broken words and waning phrases. The porters chanted. They frapped their feet and waved their arms in harmony, gyrating like red devils in the hot light of the inferno. The bhakrawallas stood about the dancers, enraptured, clapping their hands, intoning in the frenzy and the ecstasy. The sahibs watched the primitive ballet in awe, moving lips or heads or feet to the delirious caroling in their various cadences and ways, each face beaming in the blazing light. Sara looked on with eyes that glowed like coals, her windblown hair turned wild tails of flame, the fire snapping and leaping about her, knowing herself to be the cause of the rapture. The stars above scintillated in the frosty night air, the encircling peaks beneath silent as dutiful sentinels. Mysterium, aloof, loomed huge at the bounds, a somber Buddha pondering in the dim.

FIRST MORNING at Base Camp, and Vida sits on a rock in summer's wintry air warming her hands on a cup of hot cocoa. She looks around in wonderment, her breath literally taken away within the heights and pageantry of the oncoming day. Mysterium is illuminated in dawn, her snowy flanks slowly absorbing the light. A flock of bar-headed geese sail before a wall of snow shouldered high on the glacier: what a rare sight to see them fly in the thin air. Down below, blue sheep forage in the sedges across the stream, as morning light melts night's sprinkling of icy geometry. Vida sips the sweet cocoa, knowing this place will be home for the next month or two to come.

She watches her husband as he laces his boots and snaps his anorak closed. He lifts a chin to her in abbreviated good-bye, then turns to follow a line of porters making their way across the grassy downs. Wilder climbs over a hill of livid-colored boulders, then up through rocky piles of glacial debris, keeping his distance from the men so they won't look back and encourage him to join them. He's had it with all the camaraderie lately, though as he looks to the upper buttress towering a mile overhead he imagines describing what he sees to his brother, telling him what a piece of excellent quartzite that rock is going to be in the climbing, the feeling of Lucas here walking beside him. And hearing his twin agreeing, now both of them noting that the quartzite is sloping downward, you see? And we know down-sloping holds make for hard work and riskier going. He puts the binoculars back into the pouch of his anorak. Best now to take another course up the moraine, a line the porters seem not to have spotted, then to get up quick and over the crest of it to get a look at what might be on the other side. Find the new route to the summit and report it before anyone else does. He picks his pace up, working for breath, lungs hungering in their want for oxygen. A voice skips across the rocks, and he turns his head to see a few of the porters following in his path, one who wears a pink-fringed shawl signaling his way. Wilder speeds up and veers off in another direction, no word or gesture in return. The men turn and push on behind him, and now Wilder pushes all the harder, thankful not to have the weight of a pack on his back today. He won't let the porters get ahead, won't let anyone get ahead; no, not even his brother should beat him. Just as in their days of boyhood together: Who could run or ski the fastest, dive the deepest, jump the farthest, climb the highest? Who might display the greater bravery? The appetites of their youth satisfied most by undertakings strenuous and threatening.

He drives himself on, moving faster, propelled by the challenge. His head throbs, his thighs burn, his calves spasm. He pants like an animal. He knows his own craziness. Maybe more like stupidity, he hears his brother say. No breath to laugh with. He draws everything in, willing his body into a machine, torsional and elastic, legs cranked into rotary motion, muscles of his heart like pistons driven through cylinders, lungs to the point of combusting. He's far in the lead, pouring sweat, soaking in it, with sweat in his eyes, sweat in his ears, his heart in his ears, his legs to the point of crumple and give. Keep on, man, keep on. Do not quit.

Wilder's legs buckle at the top of the moraine. He drops to hands and knees, barking out a spasm of coughing that grabs at his ribs. He hacks. He spits. He sleeves his mouth clean. When finally the coughing settles he stands, legs trembling. "Man alive," he says. He wipes the sweat from his eyes. Straight out ahead of him are massive walls of schist and dolomite wrapped about the mountain's pedestal. He sees the river punching through the snout of the Sage's glacier, the water cut into the depths of the Gorge in a raging impetus to merge with the

Ganges as it heads to the sea. He pulls the binoculars out of his anorak, scans the rock strata for any walk-ups. A porter comes stumbling in behind him.

"Sahib," the porter says. "You strong, Sahib," he says. The man is leaned over, hands on his thighs, the fringe of his shawl dusting the earth as he works to breathe. The porter raises himself up tall and cries a wild animal cry of delight. Wilder grins, pouches the binoculars, and reaches forward, forcing any remaining shaking out of himself with a hard shake of the man's hand.

THE MONK sits cross-legged next to the morning fire running a battery-powered razor over the dome of his head, the dome of the mountain behind him, the bending dome of the day above everything. Virgil Adams, curious, approaches the mendicant in the midst of his morning ablutions.

"Hah! I wondered what the noise was," Adams says. "I thought perhaps we had aggrieved some type of rodent creature in the vicinity." The monk turns the razor off and tucks it back into the folds of his robe. He nods, smoothing a palm over his smooth dome.

"You shall come in and join the plenum for breakfast," Adams says.

The monk follows Adams into the tent where the sahibs are seated around the metal table in wool knit caps, corpulent in their downy parkas. The table is spread with cups of steaming drinks and bowls of cold cereal, and now Pasang carries in a plate of hot chapatis while Mingma replenishes the flask of coffee and hot milk. The monk holds an empty cup out, and nods at the flask of milk. Doctor Reddy puts a bottle of aspirin tablets onto the table between tubs of butter and honey, analgesic for the many suffering from headaches brought on by the heights. Sara reaches in and fingers the depths of her father's coat pocket and retrieves a pen. She picks the aspirin bottle up and adds to the label a *g*.

"Now we have aspiring tablets," she says, setting the bottle back onto the table. Her palms are raw from gripping the hackly rocks during their trek through the Gorge. The pomes of her cheeks are red as the cuts and scrapes of her hands, her nose drippy and roseate in the cold. "For those whose zeal may be fading," she says, shaking the bottle.

Reddy takes a tube out of his kit and puts it in front of Sara. "Apply this ointment to those wounds before you put your gloves back on," he says.

"You have clippers in your kit, Doctor Father?" Devin says.

Reddy sifts through his supplies and produces a pair of tiny scissors.

"Let me trim those flappers for you," says Devin. Sara opens her hands, and he bends over them to snip away the loose skin, his breath a warm steam on her palms.

"Don't overdo it," Reddy says. "Leave skin to protect."

"Know what I'm doing," Devin says. "Had my hands chewed up by gerbil teeth plenty a times."

"Gerbil teeth?" Sara says.

"Those razory handholds we rock climbers sometimes need to cling to." He shows her the fleshy part of his palms, thick as hide. "Your hands are too soft is the problem," Devin says. "They're not broken in." He dabs the ointment onto the cuts.

Wilder tosses aside the tent flap and enters, announcing himself with a sharp cough. "Smells like something that's not for breakfast in here."

Sara smells her hands. "The ointment is odorless."

Her father says, "I say the first order of the day should be, after all the doctoring and nursing and flirting and whiffing, day's first order should be to get out and explore. We should start out sensibly, an unhurried pace until we get acclimated properly. A good week here at fifteen thousand feet should do it."

"When acclimatized, we then ought to begin a search toward the north if we wish to establish a new passage," Adams says. "Otherwise, we could retrace my steps and Hilman's, this, of course, a longer course to take."

"The old way will take us way west," Devin says.

"And I'm here to claim a new route."

"We know, Wilder," Troy says, "so you've said from the beginning."

"Come on," Wilder says. "Make it new or don't bother doing it."

"I'm with Wilder," says Devin. "We should exhaust all possibilities before doing what's already been done."

The monk strokes his head, as if contemplating the debate. He says, "The perfect journey, of course, is that of no need to go."

"Too late for that," Vida says.

"I don't mind retracing Adams and Hilman's steps," Sara says.

Vida clucks her tongue, tired of Sara's constant smile and her sweet replies, tired of the number of overtures she claims. No one could possibly be so sugary nice all the time. Vida reaches for the tub of honey, spoons a gob of it into her tea. "We're all beginning to smell, in case no one has noticed," she says, her spoon clanking against the tin cup as she stirs. She suggests the first order of the day, for those who want to stay and rest, she being one of them, is hot water enough for laundry and baths.

"We've got our work cut out for us establishing camp," Adams says. "We might unpack and check equipment and make lists, sort the food and repack for higher camps. The Sherpas will be happy enough to put up a small shelter for privacy. Heat up some water for a bath. There should be time after the work is done for ambling the slopes. The proper way to accommodate to our beguiling new home, as the professor counsels, is to begin slowly."

"Does everyone from Boston talk like you talk?" Wilder says.

"Why?" Adams says. "How is it you hear me speak?"

Sara reaches for her camera. "I'm going for fresh air and photographs."

Devin bolts up from his chair, zips his coat closed. "Let's do it," he says, following her out of the tent.

"We might any of us have predicted this," Troy says. "Predicted them." He peers into his coffee, realizing he has not before seen his daughter on the brink of a relationship with another man, if she hasn't already slipped off the cliff and fallen for Devin. "Hell," he says. "Such things do happen." He takes a sip of the hot java, feeling the warmth of the liquid cutting a path from throat to chest, the tension in his body subsiding, the stiffness in his back deliquesced.

"The most noteworthy task of a parent would be to bequeath his or her child to another," Adams says. "So I have heard. For how could I really know personally of such matters?"

"We all have to give someone up sometime or another," Reddy says.

Vida feels the remark as a nudge in the ribs. She sits up

straight, lowers her face, unzips her parka. "It's a mushroomy smell is what it is," she says. She puts her nose inside the coat and sniffs.

"Yes, earthy, such as truffles," Adams says.

"Kind of more like wet dog if you ask me," Wilder says.

Troy shrugs, sips his coffee, thinks his thoughts as the others talk on. He turns a spoon on the table, flipping it over again and again. He considers the idea of having to give a daughter away, as people like to put it. But in a sense, can't it be more like a lending, or a sharing, while having someone else to porter the load? He fiddles with the spoon. Maybe it's the sloth in me, he thinks, simple lack of effort, for as life goes on romantic love has become more a burden than a boon, he will confess, and he has relied instead on his daughter for constant company. As for erotic love, as to this he may as well admit a simple failure to act. He knows he's now without plenitude or effort. He hasn't any wish to be overcome again. When work replaces. Climbing replaces. He sees himself as one set on a proper course now, for the labor of concentration forces the mind in a direction that a person can believe in. It's enough to feel the urgency of the task at hand, and for him, this has become enough. Even explaining himself to others is to deviate from what it is that most matters. So, yes, enough. He pushes the spoon aside and sips his coffee, looks to the one now speaking.

"I walked up deeper into the Sanctuary, got up onto the top of the moraine," says Wilder. "There are some variegated cliffs at the base, schist and dolomite looks like. Different slates. I think there'd be a way for us to cut through the cliffs to get up and over and onto the northeast ridge."

"Sooner we find out what is ahead of us the better," Reddy says. "I have no patience for sleeping on it."

"Wilder," Troy says. "How about going out again and scouting around with us tomorrow? Show us what you've seen? See if we can find a breach?"

"I'm wiped, man." He holds a hand up. "Will take your advice to acclimatize."

THE MONK had told a story to the sahibs as they sat about the fire their last night in the Gorge. The story took place on the Crystal Mountain, a vessel of cosmic power known to millions as the center of the metaphysical world. Set high in the middle of the Himalaya between India and China, the mountain forms a spire at the top of the roof of the earth. A most holy site, it is forever protected by the gods from ignorance and illusion, and as if by a magnet, people are drawn to it from near and far.

Several years ago, the monk had said, an American woman of some means joined a small group of travelers to circumambulate the holy mountain. The party, which included two other women, four men, and a guide, set out by jet, and from there they were caravanned to the high plateau region of Tibet. They camped at night in the cold arid desert, each of them sleeping in their own small tent, sharing meals together in a common tent. It was on the second evening on the road, during a modest supper of vegetables and rice, that the American woman announced to the others that she had come on this journey to scatter her daughter's ashes.

"An honor," the guide said.

"What a beautiful gesture," another woman in the party said.

The rest agreed, nodding their heads in assent.

Only one among them remained silent. He was a small good-looking man, of delicate but muscular build. He took a sip of his buttery tea, tasting the rancid taste of it. He gazed into the teacup, uncertain as to whether the woman was being overly forward or was simply self-centered, though she certainly could be either or both. The man did not take her to be a fool, not immediately, though this too he could not be certain of. Perhaps she was slightly deluded. But he was most convinced of the vanity of her act.

She spoke at length about her daughter, a young woman who was certainly beautiful, for the mother had passed a photograph among them. She told of a daughter who had succeeded in the finest schools and was about to begin a fruitful career in family therapy, with a pursuit in circular causation, is what I believed the specialty was called, the monk said. The daughter had exceptional men asking for her hand in marriage, so the mother told her fellow travelers, and surrounding the girl was a bounty of friends everywhere she went. And just at this ripe time of her life, the daughter was riven of all these prizes: a sudden and tragic accident befell her, and she died. What a loss of a beautiful soul, who would say not? The mother lowered her head, and mourned as only a mother can mourn. The others turned her way, reaching a hand out or offering words, a handkerchief, finding perhaps in this grief-stricken woman a sense of what had led them toward this course of sacred pilgrimage they were on. For were they not heartfelt people, turning their attentions as they did to a woman who so deeply lamented?

"Grief," the man said. "Tell me, what is it that grief can teach you?"

They all shook their heads, shunning the man for his callousness.

"It is scene-painting," he said. "It is misleading." He spoke softly.

The others called him a selfish man, a hard and selfish man.

"There is nothing to be gained from the favoring of suffering," he said.

The others went to the woman, embraced her.

"You will find no wisdom in bereavement, only emptiness."

The party turned away from him, and started back upon their journey.

The mother required numerous stop-offs. She would need to shop in the village markets for prayer flags, for a prayer wheel, for incense and beads, for a hat to reflect her sadness, for keepsakes to keep. They would make a visit to each temple along the way so the mother could tell the lamas her story in order that they might bless the ashes she carried.

In every monastery they passed the mother would need to break for tea. The party sat inside painted sanctuaries and caves, surrounded by colorful deities with fingers curved in meaning. The man stood outside waiting, alone, looking up to a vault of ever-changing sky.

There were days the mother's anguish was so great it was impossible for the group to travel at all, and so the journey was often delayed. During these episodes her traveling companions would sit with her. They would bring her tea. They would listen to her speak of her daughter. The mother had many stories of the girl to tell. It would take a lifetime of telling, so many stories there were. They nodded. "It is important to try," they said. "Court your suffering," they said. "You have been cleaved."

They climbed into the caravan and journeyed on, entering territory inhospitable and remote. The man sat in the back of the vehicle alone, packed between bundles of food and luggage, looking out the window to a dun-colored emptiness. Here and there they would pass a scatter of nomads, leathered and dust-covered men tending long-haired bovine, women wandering the desert in tattered and fanciful hats toting children on their backs.

At night, the party camped below star-washed skies, with more stars than the eye could take in. The moon changed from a great white spotlight to a golden floating disc. The man sat in his tent and took his meals alone, for if he were to enter the common tent the others would get up from their seats and leave in protest. He did not mind the solitude of his tent. But it disturbed him that he could not read his book or think his thoughts as the voice of the mother penetrated the canvas walls and spilled into his solitude. He heard tales of the daughter whether he wished to hear them or not. He heard in the mother's voice a tone of great need. He heard around her a chorus of voices meant to comfort her. He thought of Greek tragedies. He thought of costumes and stages, of acts and orations.

After a long week of traveling the party arrived to the base of the Crystal Mountain. They left the caravan and set out through a deep cleft of rock following the way of the pilgrims, most of the pilgrims having traveled from very far away, riding inside the open beds of trucks or on rickety bicycles or sway-backed mules to get to this most holy place. Many of them tethered yaks loaded with provender and belongings, some of them bowed to the ground and moved on hands and knees, prostrating themselves full-length each step of the way. They would endure bitter cold and extreme altitude, though all knew to avoid the dangers of attempting to climb the highest slopes. To defile the sacred mountain by attempting to stand atop it was to violate a most sacred taboo, and for this the punishment was death. The quest was not an attempt to reach a zenith. It was about immersing oneself in an odyssey of eternal circling.

Now the party's guide felt himself entirely necessary to the mother, the monk said. The guide stayed close, carrying her backpack, offering pious words of sympathy and praise, rarely leaving her side, for his duty to her was clear. The mother carried the ashes, her woes, her prayer flags, her hymns and her poems, as well as the succor given by her traveling companions. All gathered at the start of the path around the Crystal Mountain to help her anchor the stringed blocks of colorful cloth, all but the man who could see in the mother's actions not grace but falsity. Knowing himself vanquished, he left the group to join the other pilgrims as they entered the gorge.

At sky burial sites along the way the mother stopped to scatter articles of the daughter's clothing, tossing them among the mounds of discarded raiment that belonged to the dead. The others circled about her as she flung blouses and stockings and skirts to the wind. A few snapped pictures as the mother posed among the heaps of rotted cloth. She paused in many other places along the way, reaching into her hip pouch for handfuls of ashes. She blew the ashes into the thin cold air and watched as they settled into bins and wallows of snow. The others observed her as she crouched to her knees and wept. They squinted, and bowed their heads.

"What happened to the vanquished man?" Reddy said.

"By now the man was far ahead of the rest," said the monk, "as he intended to travel around the entire mountain in a single day. Many of the devout attempt it in this manner."

"So the mother walks around with her entourage in tow," Vida said.

"In the glorification of her ego," Adams said.

"But the mother couldn't have managed the task alone," said Sara.

"She could have managed it differently," Wilder said. "Privately."

"Yes," Troy said. "Less narcissistically."

"It was a way to keep her daughter alive," Sara said. But at this she hung her head to hide the shame on her face, struck by the sudden keen awareness of her own vanity. For she knew she would have acted just as the mother had, presenting her daughter as the heart of the matter: nothing or no one could be more important. Needing to keep the daughter the primary concern, someone born of her and so part of her, was to put herself above the others and their concerns. The daughter required nothing any longer. Only the mother did, demanding the focus of her travel mates, needing to remain in the limelight. Simply put, she was a woman in great want of an audience. Sara wondered if the monk had told this story as a lesson to her.

"A way to keep the daughter alive?" Vida said. "Or herself alive?"

"To lose her motherhood was to lose the person she was," Sara said.

Adams said, "Did the banished man circle the mountain in a day?"

"Could be the man found the famous yogi poet's cave," Troy said. "Maybe he's still there, sitting quietly, spanning time, no longer bothering to abut himself up against the masses, abut himself up against the rest of the world."

"Maybe the man decided to climb to the summit," said Reddy.

"Right," Wilder said. "To hell with the rules."

"And on the way up met his death," Devin said.

The monk sat with his hands open and settled on his knees.

"And so what of the moral?" Reddy said. "Tell us."

The monk laughed. "Moral? Why a moral? It is only a story," he said.

REDDY AND Troy return to Base Camp with the news. "There appears to be no way to the top from the northeast," Troy says. He pulls his wool cap off, tosses it onto the table, and takes a seat next to his daughter.

"Can't be," Wilder says. He drops his task as repackaging assistant. Devin and Sara carry on, the two pouring large containers of orange-drink mix into quart-size plastic bags.

"We'll have to go back around and take the west route, I'm afraid," Troy says. "It's just not possible to get up the escarpment and onto the face any other way. The cliffs are simply impassable. There are no means of traversing. There is no plateau at all. The arête we could see was sharp as a blade of knife in places, and it was bristling with frozen pinnacles."

"The mountain's just showing its teeth is all," Wilder says.

"Below her incisors are walls of icy vertical," Reddy says.

"That's not what I saw, Doc."

"We took the only clear course there was to take," Troy says.

"Sara and I took Wilder's bearings," Devin says. He holds open a container bag as Sara handles the job of ladle and fill. "Climbed up a bluff and onto a saddle. Didn't find a way to get up through the cliffs, but we—"

Sara touches Devin from under the table with her knee as reminder. She has made him promise not to mention the snow leopard, for to tell of it would be to take away the power of what she has seen.

"You two didn't get high enough to really see anything," Wilder says. He coughs, clears his throat, puts his head out of the tent, spits.

"Please," Reddy says. "Hygiene, if you don't mind."

"You don't find ledges and holds until you're up there," Wilder says.

"Let's take the original route," Sara says. "Mr. Adams's line."

"Agree," says Devin. "Going for on-sight at first sight isn't as safe."

Wilder picks up a plastic bag and tosses it back down on the table. Dust powders out in an orange cloud. "What're you saying, man?" he says. "You're doing a one-eighty on me."

Devin explodes in a sneeze.

"Forget it," Wilder says. "Blow your nose. Just don't do it in plain air or you'll be scolded." He and Reddy exchange looks. Wilder gets up from his chair, says, "I'm going back. I'm finding a new route up Mysterium."

DEVIN AND Sara had crossed a rockfall and were walking across a cone of old snow when Sara came to a standstill. She thrust an arm out to stop Devin, and crouched down to take a closer look at the print.

"Looks like a dog paw," Devin said. "But what dog would be way up here?"

Sara looked at him to answer the question, thinking wolf, when right behind him she saw something move at the top of a bulge of rock. Like that—it was quick—the rock, but not a rock, softer than a rock; a frosty head of fur is what it was—

she saw it, so clear it instantly was—the piercing viridescent eyes staring back at her. The creature blinked. Sara felt it like the shutter of a camera, the animal capturing her image in the instant, just as she seized a lasting picture of it. Then the leopard flicked its ears, and in a lavish wave of ample tail it vanished. A shrill cry rang through the cold air, like the wail of a baby. Devin jumped to his feet.

"A cat," Sara said.

"Another cat?" he said.

"Not just another cat."

Devin looked at the ground for pugmarks and scrapes.

"No," she said. "It won't be back to make a second appearance. Not with us here. A snow leopard rarely approaches a human so closely."

WILDER SETS out alone the next day to reconnoiter the upper slopes. He carries in his backpack two bottles of water, a package of beef jerky, a hunk of cheese, a flashlight, an altimeter, a pair of socks, a bivvy sack, his brother's ashes. He is rarely on this trip without his brother's ashes. Wilder has shouldered them most days, will shoulder them every day in safekeeping, until he gets to the top of Mysterium. He sees his own enormity up there standing at the summit. He imagines a feeling of expansiveness and release, a freedom from the bondage of this purgatory, the anguished hold he is stuck in.

He walks on into the silence. The turf of the downs has been colored by summer sun and is scattered with rocks the size and color of headstones. The sky is overcast, and morning fog creeps out of the Gorge far below. He crosses the Sage's river via an avalanche bridge, the water sounding a ghostly sound as it bores its way through the packed snow. He feels the violent tremor of the river beneath his feet. The wind intones an odd song of solitude. Sentinel peaks stand lonely and cold.

He reaches the end of the snowfield and hops back onto the rocks, crossing a slope of limestone boulders. On a patch of blown earth tufted with stiff grass he comes upon a scatter of bones, skeletal shards picked clean by their attacker and the winds. Horns dropped from the skull. A rib cage pursed whole about a hoary forb. Hollowed sockets, a roman nose, a jaw ossified in smile. Long yellowed incisors. Bharal, has to be, probably strayed from the herd and pounced on by a cat. Either that or eaten by a yeti, he thinks. He chuckles, and toes the bones.

He moves straight through the boulder garden of a wide couloir, climbing up and over the broken rocks. A massive wall shoots up into low-hanging clouds, and here Wilder is stopped. No other choice, nowhere else he can see to go. He crawls up through the stony debris, moving onto loose talus that tests his balance, having to sidehill gouge in the slipperiest of places. He moves up and into the snag of clouds, laddering his way through the cobble with blocky holds, until he breaks through the mist and finds himself standing along a dolomite spine, a spur he sees is linked to a farther ravine. He prances along the backbone, boots chinking in the stone, arriving to another slope of boulders. The pitch is steep, but with good cling, and an easy enough traverse takes him up the middle of the corridor. At the top of the coulee he sees little ahead but routine scrambling. He builds cairns along the way, and once he is high enough he spots it; a narrow catwalk of talus through a breach in the cliff: the approach to the upper face. It has to be. He continues up to the catwalk and moves through the rock's chops, breathless, elated, and now he is past the narrow defile and the route seems too obliging to be believed. He crosses a piece of snowfield and mounts the tip of a spur and there it is right in front of him: vertical walls of rock that shoot straight up for miles, the mountain's upper ramparts lobed with snow and streaked with blue ice. From here he sees a way to get onto the rocks on the far side of the ice cliff beneath the upper glacier, and from there up onto the snowy east shoulder, a skyline ridge. Easy enough. Yes, but then the buttress. The buttress, for the toughest. But we have found it, we have found the way. "We'll see," he hears Lucas say.

The wind picks up and wails like a succubus. He turns and rushes down the steep ravine, glissading the slope in the scree, setting off rockfalls and a cloud of spiraling dust in his wake.

WILDER TRUDGES back into camp, announcing his entry with an ear-piercing whistle. Porters and shepherds reposed around their cookfires perk in his direction. The goat herd scatters like a cued break of racked balls. He enters the mess tent, finds Karma and the sahibs solemnly seated about the table like counselors of war, the tent casting a devilish light on their faces.

"Cheer up," Wilder says. He works for his breath. "Guess what? I found it! No kidding. I found the approach for us. Found a place for Advanced Camp too. A place to launch the assault. There's a doable way up the face. You'll see. Whoo-hoo!" he says, coughing.

"There is no break in Mysterium's defense from the north or the east," says Adams. "From reports reported heretofore."

Troy and Reddy nod their heads; give their assessment. They had taken off early in the day, had walked around the prow as Wilder was headed off in his own direction. The two carried with them a rope, hardware, signaling devices, bivvy sacks, food, a stove. They were intent on finding a new line to the summit, even if it should take them several days, determined as they were not to have Wilder prove them unwilling or incapable. After plenty of rough going they finally got around the prow. But at the top of the rise they found themselves standing in front of a bergschrund, where the glacier had spilled dramatically away from the headwall. The deep crevasse was a yawning chasm of wobbly boulders and rubbled-over avalanche debris, with uncertain bridges of old cones of snow spanning the gaps. Above the glacier, glassy towers rose straight up into the clouds. Highly unlikely, technically. Walls terrifying. All of it terrifying. Who knows when those cornices of ice would again break loose and come booming down?

"It would be your life," Reddy said.

Thwarted once more, they had returned to the camp.

"For many in the party it would be impossible climbing," Troy says.

"A death trap, really," Reddy says.

Wilder covers his mouth with a fist, works to stifle the grating in his chest. "Go the other way and have a look. You'll see all anybody'll need is the ability to negotiate some steep terrain. We can skirt to the far left side of the glacier. Though the upper buttress will be tough, I'll admit it. But it's something I know you can do or what are you even doing here?" He looks at Reddy and Troy. They stare back at him, not believing, or not wishing to believe that he has found a new route.

"Things may not always be seen correctly when looking head-on," says Adams.

"We walked around the prow, got up high as one could see and from the best vantage point," Reddy says. "Finding nothing any of us could manage without putting our lives at stake."

"Yeah, and I went up and around the other way," Wilder says.

"We shall all make the west route easily enough," Adams says.

"This we know," Wilder says.

"As leader I am responsible for our party. I must be prudent."

After a long pause, Troy speaks. "I suppose we really ought to have a look and decide if Wilder's route is realizable for everyone here."

"Hey, you've got at least to do that," Wilder says. "Then you'll see."

"Why's it matter so much which way we go?" Sara says, tucking a strand of hair around her ear. "We just want to get to the summit."

"It absolutely does matter," Wilder says. "Who cares if we do what's already been done? Who the hell even wants to do what's been done?"

"I don't need my picture in the newspapers," Sara says.

Vida chuckles. "You don't?"

"I don't need my picture in the newspapers," Wilder says, imitating Sara in a shrill silly voice.

Sara's face turns red as a hard slap on the flesh.

THE MONK will take a vertiginous path away from the party's intended destination, his head aglint in the sun, stave in hand, a robe filled with the party's bestowals. He will ramble the bristly grass to the spur and round the whaleback down to the river, crossing over splinters of bridges, waterfalls spewing along the way. He will move through sun and hail and snow and rain, through swarms of insects and billows of mist, from thin alpine air into thick humidity, traveling pasture into village onto temple, until he comes face-to-face with a brakeless transport truck freighted with melons, never to have the chance, as chance would have it, to stand in this lifetime before the head lama, the reincarnation of the Bodhisattva of Compassion, the great holy man himself, the monk's life having abruptly reached its grand conclusion and come to an end.

Now the mendicant leaves camp accompanied by Adams and Reddy and Troy, the three expeditionists setting out with rations and equipage, this time to have a look at Wilder's gully and the ridge above it. At the base of the moraine the men part ways with their guest.

"I like to give you something for top of sacred mountain," the monk says. His hands are fanned over the gather and spread of his robe, paunched as he is with his provender, his rudiments, and his optionals. "Only best, I believe, to leave there only nothing." He bows and takes his leave.

"Hey," Troy says, giving a holler. "Thanks for the story, by the way."

The monk waves in accord, and walks on. After a few minutes he stops and turns to regard the mountaineers, watching as they scrabble over a sidehill of boulders until they are soon disappeared into the moraine. The monk nods his head. Then he turns toward the path diverging, his toga'd form a darkened cameo in the gloriole of the sun.

Adams and Reddy and Troy hew to the course Wilder has described. They climb the steep gully, following his cairns until they spot the catwalk, moving carefully along the defile through the jaws of the rock, stopping briefly before proceeding up onto a broad ridge of limestone and schist, a level site that provides a clear view of the mountain's north face. A long tumulus of snow lies between the tablet of the highest summit and the lesser peak, Mysterium East. They tip their heads back and gape up at the massive white tabernacle rayed with blue ice, and at the quartzite stanchion that tops it, below the lower east summit.

Adams scans the escarpment with the binoculars. "An easy enough traverse over the rampart there, then under the ice cliff."

"I agree, we can skirt the bottom of the glacier and then move along its far left bank to get up onto the higher rib," Troy says. "That might be the place for Advanced Camp."

"The upper buttress is what will test us," says Reddy.

"But might be doable," Troy says, nodding his head.

"The ridge between the east and the true summit will be no modest romp to the top," says Adams. He regards the mountain as if trying to tame it.

Troy and Reddy look at him, and wait for him to speak, knowing as leader he has to agree.

After a spell of quiet, Adams concedes. "All right," he says, not altering his gaze. "Without further ado, what the hell."

They find a level spot on the soft schist of the broadened crest to stake the tent, safe enough from any rockfall or avalanche debris spilling down the steeply glaciered gully on either side of their new camp. The ridge fish-bones to a needled point that drops off to the river miles below, and above them its spear broadens to meet with a pitch of rock, an abutment hulled in ice rising to sheer cliff.

"Hallelujah," Troy says.

Adams radios down to Karma, advising him to talk to the porters about transporting higher. "This appears to be it," Adams says. "We camp here on the ridge tonight, then make preparations for Advanced Camp. Tell Wilder he was right. Give him the pat on the back he is so in need of." Adams thumbs a button, and Karma's response emits through a scratchy static.

He hits another button. "Yes, fixed lines." A voice crackles back. "No, I descend in the morning. Troy and Reddy will move on ahead." A broken-up over-and-out is twice repeated.

They unpack the food bag and the water bottles, the cook-stove and the kerosene. Troy hauls out tarpaulin, shovel, tent and poles as Reddy levels a swathe in the broken schist, kicking up thin plates of it with his boots. The spall chimes dully, reminding him of the strings of scallop shells his wife had hanging on the eaves, the sound of them clapping in the wind. Reddy takes hold of the shovel and extends the handle, using the tool to plane out a platform. The sun breaks through a cloud, spilling light on the ground in a spread of paling stain. The blade chinks into loose earth. Maggie's ashes were the texture and weight of ground oyster shell. Heavier than expected, and more like tuff than cinder, is what they were. He and his son had stood on the dock and together hefted the receptacle and emptied the contents into the riffled currents of Puget Sound. The calcined remains took on the shape of a body as soon as the particles met the water, a buoyant form that resisted sinking. He and Devin stood and watched the white figure float and drift. They stood for a long time. Then the sky darkened and the rain came down to pock the water over and the tide carried the apparition out to the sway of the sea.

His friend puts a hand on his shoulder, sparking Reddy back to the task at hand. "Altitude getting to you?" Troy says.

"Just moving slowly," Reddy says. "Conserving whatever I've got." He grabs the poles, and together they stake up their nylon dwelling, tossing in the down bags and the sleeping pads.

Adams hunkers over the stove, his nose red and dripping in the cold. He adds a spill of fluid into the spirit cup and pumps the brass tank, making the stove wheeze like a little animal. He takes a matchstick out of its canister, flicks the match with his thumb, touches the fire to the burner head, averting his face as the stove erupts in a whoosh of blue flame. He sets the pot of water onto the top ring for tea, and then again for instant soup, and again for more tea to follow.

The three sit cross-legged on a ground tarp as the water heats only nearly to a boil, watching Mysterium toss off a lenticular cloud she has piked on her platinum helmet. The saucer-like mass drifts out among the encircling mountains, the vapory rotor cloud below it portending turbulent air. They should put the rainfly over the top of the tent tonight, they agree, but for now they recline in the twilight and the whisper of the cook-stove as they drink their hot drinks and dinner on rye crackers and smoked fish, on pemmican and sweet onion and dried figs. The peaks begin to fade out into thick dark cloud, and too soon it begins to sleet: a sudden pestering of ice pellets that smites their coats and their tent and spurs them into activity. They put hoods up, cram a few last bites into their mouths, stuff the rest of the food back into the stuff sack, and launch their packs and themselves into their small nylon abode. Boots come off, head-lamps go on, sleeping pads and down bags are rolled out. Adams settles the cookstove in the tent's vestibule, stokes it to heat water for more tea.

"Almost cozy," Troy says.

"Thou shalt not spill," Adams says.

"Nor eat raw onions again," says Reddy. He takes his cap off and combs his fingers through his thick black hair, scoring it into greasy crevasses. His dark beard is trimmed and the whiskers sprinkled white, as opposed to Troy's reddish beard wiry and grown full, as opposed to the ruts and gullies of Adams's weathered face always daily shaved.

They empty their cups and slide deep into their sleeping bags. Adams takes the spot on the door side of the tent. He pillows his coat into his stuff sack, and curls onto his side and shuts his eyes to the outer dark. In the darkness within he imagines the bed in his house, the pliancy of the mattress, the softness and warmth of his wife, hot milk, cat purring, the furnace on. Wet snow falls softly upon the tent, reminding Adams of the pattering of Hillary's delicate white feet. His breathing turns steady and even, and he falls quickly into a deep sleep. Soon his respiring changes, the pattern altered dramatically, becoming erratic, with a panting that increases in speed and intensity, followed abruptly by a protracted spell of dead quiet. A long pause before the breath finally resets, and the violent huffing begins all over again as the cycle repeats.

"Cheyne-Stoking," Reddy says, his voice hushed.

"I know what it is," Troy says. "Just didn't know what it was called."

"We won't wake him."

"Sleep's too precious. If I have an attack of it do not wake me."

Adams continues his oscillating ventilating, his breathing alternating between crescendo and diminuendo, as he dreams his altitudinous dreams.

"Speaking of sleepmates," Troy whispers, "I wonder if my daughter and your son are behaving themselves in the tent tonight?"

"Please," Reddy says. "I do not wish to picture certain things." He pulls the wool cap down to cover his ears, and rolls onto his side to face the cold wall of the tent. He says his goodnights and closes his eyes, hoping sleep will be kind and overtake his fatigue. His body feels heavy as a magnet weighted to the ground, but his thoughts flurry about like flakes of snow. He thinks of his son, the youth and vitality that are lost on him;

Devin not wise enough to really know what love is. As if I should know it myself, he thinks. Reddy heaves a breath of weariness. He has resigned himself to forgetting about romance and affairs past; what is any of it now but abandoned fancy and piddling story? But at times during the night he is helpless, as images and scents of what he had once so desired come to him unbidden. When yearnings would wake him he would touch himself. He would wonder, how many years before the hardness in me is gone? At the moment, he thinks, I long only for a decent night's sleep.

THE SUN'S morning rays lamp and warm the men as they ready themselves for the day's earthly endeavors. The three breakfast on instant coffee and smoky jerky, tabled on a promontory below the thrones of the gods, their minds trained on a single thing: Victory, a good of which they need not speak.

After the meal, Adams prepares for Base Camp. He will head back down alone, keeping his mind occupied by composing a letter to Hillary, then to write and hand the missive off to one of the bhakrawallas sent back to the village where mail can be posted.

Reddy and Troy pack up for the push ahead. They set out each with a spool of rope over a shoulder, armored with anchors and wands, slings and hammers, intending to place fixed lines on any menacing stretches of the ravine. They drop spools and hardware and packs at the top of the first disobliging pitch, and plant into the ground a tall fluorescent wand. Troy brings forth the metal spikes and the hammer. He drives the first piton into an outcrop of cross-bedded rock, his labor pealing out like a dull bell, the rock exhaling whiffs of sulfurous dust at its puncture. Reddy figure-eights a loop of tubular webbing to the anchor, as Troy picks up a piece of limestone come loose from the bed. He studies it, then hands the shard over to Reddy.

"Crustacean?"

"Or some arthropod that walked the ocean floor." Troy zips the find into the inner pouch of his parka. "Further scrutiny at teatime."

They get back to the job, down-climbing to a natural resting place that makes for an intermediate site, securing and tying off this time with a carabiner clove-hitched to the kernmantle line. At the bottom of the steep pitch they place another anchor, and here at the start of the rope up they plant a second wand. Then they move on to the next difficult incline and repeat their routine, working together with a practiced efficiency.

With efforts complete they lunch in full sun, squinting into the radiance, the dazzling light imbuing the rare atmosphere a cerulean blue. Deep-sky blue. A blue truer than blue. The surrounding peaks glitter like jewels, and small iridescent clouds roam the sky. Down below in the amphitheater of the Sanctuary, a thin spire of smoke twines up among their scarlet-colored S'ing of tents. They can see Adams nearly back to Base Camp now, a tiny black spider creeping across the moraine.

Troy takes the fossil from his pocket, examines it more closely. "Might be a shell-less mollusk. Though these look like tentacles, don't they?"

Reddy takes the rock, slowly turns it over in his hand. He gives it back to Troy. "Appendages of some kind," he says. "Imagine these things should crawl into your tent at night."

"Imagine the great plates of earth that once were."

"Imagine the drift," Reddy says. "The collision."

"All the crumpling."

"All the warp and contort of it."

"Carrying these creatures from the sea."

"The Tethys, I believe."

"What magnitudinous drama," Troy says.

"And yet so many people will ask why we climb."

"What else but for all this," Troy says. "For this heavenly spectacle." He tosses the rock, arcing it out into the peerless blue. "And to triumph, of course."

Base Camp, 15,000 feet

July 24, 1981

My Dearest Hillary,

I am now settled back down in the foothold of the Sanctuary with at last a few moments to write to you, having just returned from a night spent with Professor Troy and Doctor Reddy on a lofty ridge 2,000 feet higher upon the mountain's shins. We three had the day prior set forth to explore the possibility of an alternative approach to Mysterium's summit, the prod toward a new route brought about by Wilder Carson's preliminary survey of the mountain's upper reaches. The accomplished young man's insistence that the party make it new, so to speak, put us more mature fellows in the position of feeling rather moth-eaten and dull. Well, ha! and pshaw to this, our trio agreed.

As we elders were already betaken toward the snowy collets and furbelows of the bliss-giving goddess and were, by this time, properly acclimatized after a week at 15,000 feet, we thereby moved upward and on with little hesitation to inspect what we had yet to know of her. We hereby came to an unfamiliar place that bestowed to us a view of Sarasvati's face never before seen. Yes, Carson was indeed correct in his reconnaissance report, and has since been given the credit that is due him.

On this untried part of the peak, the professor and the doctor and I found a broad ridge on which to make camp for the night, and from the crest we could see above us a most excellent site where an Advanced Base Camp might be established. Such a position will put us at a greater advantage in our aim to instill our party at yet higher camps among the icy flounces and sky-woven pleats of Saras-vati, as we make our way up to the mount's precious crown.

Which brings me only to the thought of you my darling, and with it a wish to run my fingers through your silken hair. Ah, the thought of pressing my lips to your tender lips! How might I even begin to tell you how much I miss you, sweet Hillary? Take my promise to strive toward more precise and ardent wording, so that I might be a wiser lover to you in our days ahead.

Yours and always,
Ad

DOWN IN the Sanctuary, Wilder leaves the confines of his sleeping bag and exits the tent. He zips the flap closed, and now Vida begins to dress in the cold. It has to be Mingma who sets the morning's basin of warm water outside the tent; she hears him muttering, as he often does, maybe as a way of announcing himself, though could be he prays. She pulls her down parka out of the stuff sack it is pillowcased in and puts the coat on, then stuffs her sleeping bag into the casing. Finds her boots, shoves them on. Locates her gloves and tin cup, toothpaste and toothbrush. She crawls out of the tent and looks up to a sky thronged with snow-boding clouds.

She fills her tin cup with water from the water jug, puts a plug of paste onto her toothbrush, and begins to scrub her teeth. Wilder is over on the other side of the mess tent, waving his arms about as he wrangles with the porters, the unruly beard on his face making him appear a burlier man than he really is. Vida doesn't like the feel of her husband's thick whiskers, and because he knows this he is considerate enough to keep his face away from hers. She sees him pointing up to the summit, and she gets that sinking feeling in her gut; *sinking*, there is no better word for it. She knows they have traveled far and hard to climb the mountain, not just camp and play at its feet in the thrilling scenery, like children. But how will it be to be alone for weeks with only a Sherpa and a few porters as companions in the Sanctuary? She takes the toothbrush out of her mouth. Will Adams stay at Base Camp? Probably not. She takes a mouthful of water and rinses, the swishing noise a crazed jangling inside her brain. She spits, and now she hears another sound, realizing it comes from inside the other tent. The sound of Devin and Sara lingering in their sleeping bags. Her stomach grumbles. She takes a swallow of water, hearing the happiness and intimacy between them. She tosses the water out of her cup. Looks up to see Mysterium shimmering in a pour of morning light, dominating everything, the way a goddess does.

AS PARTY leader it is up to Adams to determine the hardiest porters willing to transport provisions to higher settlements on the mountain. The other porters he will pay and discharge, as too will the bhakrawallas be relieved, the goats saddling back only the food needed to get the herders to hearth and kin again.

"The men want to go home," Wilder says. "Every last one."

"Leave it to me," Adams says. "I am practiced at such matters." He looks into the mess tent. "Where is our translator?" he says.

"Over there she is," Vida says, pointing toward the stream where Sara and Devin stand holding each other, looking out across the grassy downs at the wild bharal sheep that are feeding. "And to think Reddy was worried about married couples on this trip," she says.

Adams marches out toward the stream, stomping carelessly over the heads of wild lilies and hairy vetch. Dalliance in the heights, he thinks. Altitudinous lusts and seductions. Perhaps the mountains themselves inspire it, as a person is caught up and carried away in the rapture of landscape and circumstance. His mind goes this way and that. Adams understands why Sara would be drawn to Devin's pluck and skill, his splendidly youthful body and obliging mind. He sees too how Sara's joyful smile easily captured the boy, her serene being carrying him away into some blissful delirium. The first time he and his wife had met the girl, they saw her fruitful as the earth with her golden hair and flushed cheeks, agreeing between them the name Heidi would have been perfectly fitting. In the startling blue of her eyes they saw that she was too good to be true, and both were at once smitten with her. Yet now Adams sees less a Heidi, and more a Beatrice. Yes, a Beatrice, she is. Incarnation of beatific love, an inspiration and guide. A means of transference, inscrutable, unknowable, anything we wish her to be. He sighs deeply, working for breath in the covetous air. He works to focus his mind. "Lovely Sara," he calls out, "I need your assistance."

The couple let go their embrace, turn to their distinguished leader, the man the Sherpas have come to call Bhalu Sahib, with great affection. Virgil Adams, their Lord Bear, is still very broad in shoulders and chest, but he has become hollow-cheeked and leaner during the passing weeks of their odyssey, though his step and gait are still quick and deliberate, the look in his eyes sharp as a metal spike.

"See you back at mess tent," Devin says. He gives a tug to the plaited ties of Sara's ski cap hanging beneath her chin.

The porters get up from about their cookfire, welcoming sahib and little sister, please, to take hot tea and chapatis and to sit with them. Adams politely declines. The men are still attired in every item of clothing each of them owns. They are wearing rubber shoes, perhaps more likely plastic, or some sort of polymer of dubious quality; in any case, shoes they have carried all this way to be worn now as if a reward for having arrived at their intended destination. The men gather around Sara and Adams, and the head porter says in a few words of peculiar English that tomorrow they plan all to return home. Sara speaks to him in Hindi, asking that some of the men be invited to stay and help carry to higher camps. The head porter looks up to the darkening sky, snugging the pink-fringed shawl around him. He points to the mountain, looming like a massive sepulchre in the thickening mist. He gives a shake of the head. "No, Didi," he says. "We cannot do, dear sister."

"Tell them we will double their pay," Adams says.

There is a curmurring among the porters, who seem to have understood Adams's words clearly enough. Sara speaks for Adams again, telling the head porter they will leave him with his crew to decide.

"But not to dither." Adams raises a finger in emphasis.

They are turned and headed back to the mess tent when the head porter calls out. "Sahib," he says, nodding to Adams. He turns to Sara, explains in Hindi that he believes some of the porters will agree to stay if they are paid twice what they are owed, but they must be paid right away.

"On that, we shall have to get back to you," Adams says.

Once back inside the mess tent he grumbles about not trusting them. "They could take double the money and leave as they might," he says. "There would be no stopping them."

Karma suggests paying the porters all that is owed them up until today, as well as paying them now half of the total they have asked to carry to Advanced Camp, the remaining half to be paid at arrival to Advanced. "I believe we will have much help," Karma says. He presses the sticky yellow patches firmly against his temples.

But now it is Vida who resists. "This is a perfect campsite," she says. "Why go higher?"

"There is too much distance between here and the summit," Adams says. "It is better for all of us to have a base set farther up."

"I don't have a good feeling about going up there."

Wilder looks at her. "You don't go and you'll hold us all back."

"Troy and Reddy will have set fixed lines," Adams says. "The route will be safe. Certainly, if porters with heavy bundles can manage it . . ."

"It looks steep," she says. "It looks cold and barren up there."

"What're you doing here, Vida?" Wilder says. "Why did you come?"

She turns away, feeling lost, as if her compass is off, the needle wagging unreliably. "I don't know," she says, her words coming out hard as stones.

EXPLORING. RISK-TAKING. What is it but a matter of character, appetite, heart or might or eye, that which leads one on toward any such endeavor? Call it a calling. Call it a summoning, bound as we

are by a law of universal striving, this dictate being the only truth
that governs: a truth simply writ in a seed.

REDDY AND Troy pack up food, the stove, and the tent, and start for the base of the northern glacier, intending to traverse the far side of this river of snow and ice; from there to gain the farther ridge and determine Advanced Camp. They march beneath a vault of gray sky, across tiers of gravel and spall, coming to a milky stream that dribbles out of the glacier's ducts, stopping to fill their plastic bottles. They take long drinks, and fill the bottles again. They climb on through loose talus up onto a rampart of protalus, a slope of detrital accrual angled in repose, the tension between friction and gravity a point of delicacy where holding on meets letting go. From the top of the rampart they can see the icy snout of the glacier scarred by past avalanche, its base a littoral of grit and rocky flotsam. They will cross at the point where the throat narrows, aware of the perils here of icefall and snowslide.

Troy is the first to span the danger zone, and he does so as quickly as heart and lungs will allow, feeling himself tethered and weighted into slow motion and arriving to the other side too many minutes later, heaving breathlessly. Reddy pushes himself to follow in Troy's tracks, the quarter mile of uncertainty seeming to go on endlessly, knowing this undertaking a gambling game of spinning beads and numbers they play. Once to the other side of the couloir they pause to gulp oxygen, letting their hearts settle before heading up a stratum of crumbling black schist. Straight up the two move, topping a rock staircase that brings them onto a lofty perch of earth, the plateau a skyscraper world of glacial block and fold, a world bare of insect or animal or plant of any kind. They stake the tent and, here, within the vastness of radiant silence, they spend the night.

SARA WAKES and exits the tent at nature's calling, stumbling out into a campsite mantled in white, last night's pregnant air having turned to snow. She avoids the latrine to pee behind it instead, preferring the freshness of the air to the stench inside. She squats and admires the dawn flushing her namesake in color, the purity of the snow adding even more grace and substance to the mountain's corpus. To imagine that she will soon enough stand tall at the pinnacle seems impossible. Her throat aches at the thought of it. She thinks about her mother, her silence now, her persistent distance. But with only a slight shift of cognition, Sara senses her mother everywhere about her, audible and palpable, really so very close. She shivers in the cold, hurries back to the tent, seeing fresh tracks that have since crossed her path. There is the broad slippery imprint of her down bootie, and over this the snow leopard's print embossed onto her own.

KARMA AND Adams round the porters up as the others begin to reorganize Base Camp. Half of the porters agree to carry to a higher camp for the extra pay. Of these, only seven are asked to stay; the men selected, Adams and Karma have decided, the least indolent and the most fit. The remaining porters, disgruntled at having been rebuffed, are discharged home to their villages, as too are all the bhakrawallas told to go home. Adams assures the men a safe passage back through the Gorge with the aid of fixed ropes left in place. He offers the herders tender for the butchering of two goats before they depart. After plenty of bargaining, it is agreed.

Adams too decides it best for Vida to remain in the Sanctuary at Base Camp. "In the old days I might have told you to buck up," he says. "But I have learned that to push someone higher when it is against that person's will is only to invite distress. Besides, the weather has changed," he says, "with wet snow inviting difficulty." Adams says Mingma Sherpa will remain with Vida here and assist in the dispatch of porters up to Advanced Camp. Pasang Sherpa will manage Advanced, forwarding the cache of supplies as needed to higher sights on the mountain. Karma, the sirdar Sherpa, will accompany the sahibs as far as he can, intending to stand with them at the summit.

Adams and the Sherpas begin the mammoth task of recoiling rope and reorganizing gear. Chaotic piles of equipment and provisions are scattered everywhere about camp. Sara and Devin and Vida are assigned to the mess tent to tackle the job of repackaging the rations, measuring out of large containers various foodstuffs that need to be packed into day-unit piles intended to feed parties of four. The job is colossal. They must think through noodles and lentils, quinoa and couscous, oatmeal and cornmeal, instant potatoes and puddings and soups, sorting out the precooked, the freeze-dried, the dehydrated. They need to tube the tubs of peanut butter, slab the wheels of cheese, rebag bags of almonds and corn nuts, raisins and figs. They quota the drink mixes, the coffee and tea and dry milk, then allocate the jello, the jerkied meats, the smoked fish, the pickled greens.

All the while, Sara and Devin work side by side, both of them besotted. It is impossible to ignore. Others try politely not to see, averting their eyes, pretending they have not seen, but see they do, and with it comes an avalanche of feelings for at least a few.

"That's it," Vida says when Sara and Devin come lip-to-lip with a twist of licorice between them. Vida tosses a package of sour lemon drops onto the table, announces she's going out for some breaths of thin air. She is light-headed, unsettled. To have new love around her reminds her of what she no longer has. She feels sadness, envy, anger, self-pity—why not admit it, it's true. The days of wanting, not planning, days of having, not thinking, seem altogether past her now. All of it gone, as if the person she remembers being never was. She is thinner, harder, colder, and suddenly thirty feels old. She sits on the canvas seat of a folding aluminum stool outside the mess tent watching the snow coming down. Big soft flakes land on her lips, thatch in her eyelashes. She pulls the hood of her anorak up over her hat, zips herself in up to the chin.

"Sauce-making," the porters call it. They had pointed at the tent Sara and Devin were in, the men standing about giggling like children.

For Sherpas Mingma and Pasang, any *jiggy-jiggy* upon a sacred mountain is strictly forbidden and so foretokens punishment, especially among the unmarried. They gather stones and build a stupa to appease the goddess Sarasvati, decorating the mound with juniper boughs and colorful prayer flags. In front of the stupa they assemble a small altar, and here they place sticks of burning incense, asking the goddess to ensure safe passage for all to her summit. Though the most exalted virtue for the sahibs is victory, the highest good for the porters and Sherpas forever remains the blessing.

Wilder watches Vida settling into her huff. He scratches his beard, looks up to the sky for signs of the impending. He feels nettled too at the sight of Sara and Devin all lovey-dovey together, feels it like a tussis, like something not properly healed. Devin had offered him a lone and steady friendship this trip, and now this comrade in arms is lost to him, with Sara the sole object of Devin's scrutiny and care. Irony, I guess you would call it, Wilder thinks, for isn't it a kind of leaving that Lucas had accused me of when Vida came into the picture? Didn't I leave my twin brother for a new other half, as he called her? He looks up to the sky, blinks the snow from his eyes. Or did I partway leave my wife after Lucas died? He sees Vida sitting outside in the snow looking like a wing-tucked insect nabbed in a vast white net. He goes to her, stands there as if he has words of truth to speak, maybe something he has not been able to say. He covers his mouth to stifle a cough. She looks at him, squinting to keep the snow from striking her eyes.

THE SEVEN porters stand around moaning about their loads, though the weight of the carry is repacked to half of what each man has this far hauled. Wilder stoops to pick one of the bundles up to prove the task manageable, strapping the bulk onto his back and charging off in the lead. The porters grudgingly fix tumplines to their foreheads, lift the burdens, following Wilder. He leads them across the river over an old avalanche cone of snow and begins the climb up into the ravine.

When the porters arrive to the fixed line at the steepest pitch in the gully all draw to a halt. They loosen headstraps and drop cargo without further ado, refusing now to carry any farther. The scree is loose and slippery, made worse with the cover of fresh snow. Adams encounters the frightened men as they are turned to head back to Base Camp, their loads abandoned. "Where is Sara?" he says.

"Right behind," Wilder says. "Likely right ahead of Devin."

Adams quickens his pace to her.

"Sixteen thousand feet," Sara says, heaving breath. "Feeling it."

"A thousand more to the ridge," Devin says. "Halfway there."

"Wait," Sara says. "To catch air." She pauses for her

breathing to settle, looking far below to tents turned vermilion dots in the hollow, bright as pricks of blood. "Wow, we've walked all the way up here from down there."

"Sara," Adams says, intercepting the girl. "Talk to the porters," he says. "They are transporters, not climbers or Sherpas, understood. But tell them the way is safe. Look, a rope is fixed for them to make it up the couloir. If I can do it, sexagenarian that I now am, so can they. Tell them we will not only double their pay, but triple it."

Sara makes clear to the men the offer. The porters turn to one another and opine among themselves. Two break from the group. They go to Sara, lower their heads, say they are sorry. No, they cannot do it. They have families who depend on them to return home. They bring hands together in prayer, and wait for her to speak. She hesitates, but gestures in return, giving them her blessing. The men thank her, both reaching out to touch the sleeve of her anorak. They turn to head down the ravine, back to Base Camp to collect their things.

Wilder volunteers to get the other five porters up the ridge, assisting them into their waist harnesses, attaching to each harness a safety tether and mechanical ascender. With Sara as template, he shows the men where to clip the carabiner onto the static line above the device. Now tackled and coupled, Sara takes the lead, scrabbling up the cliff, sliding the metal link up on the rope as she proceeds, the long rope of her braided hair swaying side to side from beneath her knitted cap. Those below move out of line of the fall of loose rock, their necks craned and mouths hung open, gazing up at Sara's ascension, as though the world of the vertical were most natural to her. She reaches the wand at the top of the line, plants her feet, and waves down to those who will follow, clouds of cumulus billowing above her head. "Come up," she says, breathless. "Come up." She stands at the top upright and proud, her arms held akimbo.

One by one, each of the porters hefts his load, clips in, and jumars up the steep pitch. Animated by Sara, and delighted with their newly spawned mountaineering skills, they are nearly enthusiastic when they come to the next fixed line. Wilder and Devin go back to retrieve the abandoned cargo. Sara, trailed by Adams, leads the porters to the tent at the top of the ridge.

"THIS COULD not be a more inspiring place," Sara says. Her father has just marched back to Ridge Camp, and Sara embraces him, both of them squashy and plump with down. "Aspiring," she says, "I should say."

Troy points to the higher crest out across the glacier. "There," he says, "is where we were. That's where we've planted Advanced Camp."

"The new snow on the slope to getting there is unappealing," Adams says.

Reddy and Troy agree. "Avalanches began tumbling down last evening," Reddy says. "We tested those wet slabs a little nervously coming back across. Best to wait until morning to make the crossing again. Before daybreak," he says, "when the snow is good and hard."

The porters settle their hauls for stockpiling before the next shuttle up. Adams insists they return to the ridge early tomorrow with more carries. Sherpa Pasang opens up several of the cartons, humming a tune as he sorts through food and gear. He finds the snow shovel, and begins to expand Ridge Camp.

"Fixed lines are in place," Reddy says. "Pasang and I should go down to Base Camp and help the porters carry up supplies tomorrow. As it is, we will be back-and-forthing for the next many days. Professor, I leave you with the others tonight at this magnificent site."

"I should be up at Advanced again by the time you're back," Troy says. "I'll start ferrying cargo from here to there before dawn."

"And from there we begin the assault," Wilder says.

"If the mountain does not first assault us," Adams says. "Having to make tomorrow's crossing beneath that steep snow chute makes me rather uneasy, I must once again admit."

"You'll need to move fast, old man," Wilder says with a grin.

"If the weather lets up we'll be fine," Troy says. "Most of the new stuff will be shed from the mountain with temps warming during the day. It will freeze tonight. Be crusted over by morning."

"Then let us pray the mountain will play for us today a concerto of sloughing snow," says Adams. "And be done with it."

By evening the surrounding mountains have snagged the clouds, a canopy that closes up over them like an infant's skull. They crawl into their tents for the night and are barely settled in when the terrifying boom hits. All bolt upright in their sleeping bags. The avalanche is farther away than it sounds, but all night long they hear the grating of closer snowslides heaving down the narrow defiles on both sides of their campsite, making everyone jittery about tomorrow's crossing. All night long it snows a wet and heavy snow. At sunrise, it is still snowing, making it too dangerous to cross the chute. All agree retreating back to Base Camp would be iffy with the trail through the gully erased by the fresh cover, and the fixed lines certain to be buried. What to do but wait it out?

"We have supplies enough," Troy says. "Just need patience enough."

"The Himalaya can test one's staying power," Adams says.

Karma presses the sticky yellow tabs in place on the side of his face. Still no one asks him about this practice, not because of any kind of manners, but because the sirdar's habit no longer seems odd.

"I'm going to the ladies' room," Sara says.

"Tie in," her father says.

She hooks the rope into the coupling link on her harness, trudges through the snow to a place that slants down the ridge. How much more difficult it is for a woman. Having to get the cumbersome rain pants down over the heavy wool pants, and beneath this there is still long underwear and another layer of regular underwear to manage, and all of it you have to get around the harness without peeing on it. She squats and catches her breath. Feels the warm dribble in the cold. Her backside must be red as a monk's robe, she thinks. She reaches for a handful of snow to clean herself, and sees the drops of blood she has left in the white. But she knows it's not the right time of the moon's cycle, and the spotting isn't enough spill to even call it the usual.

She heaves a breathless breath, returns to her companions.

Devin takes from out of his backpack Shipton's book, *Mountain Travel*.

"You kidding?" Wilder says. "What's that thing weigh?"

"You're sounding like my old man," Devin says.

Troy pulls out notebook and pen from his backpack.

"I've got a deck of cards," Sara says.

People moan.

Adams takes a pencil and pad out and begins a letter to Hillary, expecting mail to go down with the two porters on their way back to the village. Sara volunteers Devin to assist her in making couscous and goat stew. Troy scribbles in his journal. Wilder grabs the shovel and heads out to scout for a latrine, coughing his dogged cough. Karma puts up a cook tarp, leveling a spot upside of the ridge, anchoring the plastic cover with stakes. The six of them will spend the next five days at Ridge Camp, sleeping, or trying to sleep, melting snow for water, cooking, eating, drinking, reading, writing, sketching, woolgathering, storytelling, all the while waiting for the sky to clear. Mornings will be clouded over and cold, and by the time breakfast is finished it will have begun to snow again, and so on through the afternoons. The waiting becomes shapeless, the hours of constant white and drift without width or breadth, with the silently falling snow blotting everything about them out. The days tock past like a watch face missing the hour hand.

Ridge Camp, 17,000 feet

July 28, 1981

My Darling Hillary,

We are many of us in the party now moved up beyond the mountain's ankles and toes, to be perched upon her lovely knees. All but Doctor Reddy and Mrs. Carson and two of the Sherpas are situated with us here on the higher ridge; the aforementioned party members down at Sanctuary Base Camp with porters and shepherds. We have gotten a handful of porters who remain with the expedition to carry thus far, and we hope to convince them to assist us with transport at least to Advanced Camp, which we plan soon to establish. We should have done so by now, but constant wet snowfall has been a nuisance; thereby we remain camped on the ridge and wait out the weather so to avoid unnecessary objective dangers, in particular, those of the meddlesome avalanche. Inclement conditions are surely to lessen, and we plan then to begin the arduous task of conveying cargo loads up from the Sanctuary to Ridge Camp here, stopping to pause before going beyond to Advanced Camp, all of us then to serve as beasts of burden. Once most or all supplies are delivered to Advanced, we are set to take serious possession of Mysterium. Ah, how she beckons.

Logistics have been set and camps are planned to be roughly situated as follows: Advanced Camp at 19,200 feet; Camp I on a high rib just beyond the eastern glacier at 21,800 feet; Camp II on the skyline crest of the east ridge at the top of the glacier, putting us at 23,600 feet. From there we follow the snowy shoulder to the buttress, hoping to make some headway up the rock and find ledge and protection enough for Camp III. The buttress, undoubtedly, will be the crux. If all goes as expected, depending, as you well know, on weather and lay of the land, we thereby will have installed our last camp and so achieved a height of over 24,500 feet: alas, we shall there be clinging to the lovely throat of Sarasvati. From this point we make our summit approach, the last thrust via Mysterium East at 25,100 feet, from there upward to 25,845 feet, where we shall stand atop the mountain's precious summit, and there be handed our crown.

Most all are feeling well, even so for the usual headaches, stomach upsets that manifest in each direction, sleeplessness, and the fearful nuisance of weather. The loss of a porter in the Gorge has affected us all profoundly. Still, morale is good as we remain quite hopeful, and none complain much of adversity.

However, I, my darling, must protest your absence all the while, if protest only in silence to myself. I realize I am one of the few of the core of this party fortunate to have a precious one left to write home to. Aside from Mrs. Carson, though even she has lost a brother-in-law, each has lost someone most close to them: a mother, a wife, a brother. On this expedition many must walk with their ghosts, perhaps as do I, being so acutely aware of my climbing partner Hilman with me here again these days. Yet, my dearest Hillary, I hold more than ever to thoughts of you. I think of you as I fall into sleep at night, and again as soon as I wake. The amber of our memories is ever more cherished as I see budding love now about me on the mountain. The gods do in truth send down to earth the glory of youth, and youth shall forever avail itself in delicious flesh and beguiling anatomy. And so always the lovers are seized, are they not? Caught in the rapturous arms of the other. No longer are they left to wander up and down in search of a higher place or a better world, for they find the entire world right where they are, there in the eyes of the beloved.

And is this not, my darling, that which has carried the two of us along these many years, despite our trespasses and errors?

Thou art not gone being gone.

Always your devoted husband,
Ad

THERE IS no sitting around a campfire as they wait the weather out, but they huddle around portable stoves melting water and drinking tea as Virgil Adams tells of William Hilman's last adventure, the details told to him by one of the youths in the group the revered climber was with at the time.

Adams says, "Bill simply got a bit too close to a yak along a narrow path as he was trying to sidle by."

"He got butted down the steep, right?" Devin says.

"Yaks can get temperamental," says Wilder.

Adams nods, takes a sip of tea. "Those who saw the yak butt quickly down-climbed the slope and hauled Hilman back up. His head was bleeding badly, but he was still alive. Fortunately, there was a nursing student among the group who had a first-aid kit that included needle and thread and scissor, and she stitched up the split flesh of Bill's head."

"That was a blessing," Sara says.

"Evidently, once stitched and bandaged, he was capable of walking without assistance," says Adams. "He made it down to the village, where the group checked into a hostel and Bill took to a bunk to rest. Though he soon thereafter fell into a state of fevered bewilderment. They say he lay in bed for several days after the accident before succumbing to his injuries, when the dark thence clapped down on him with disinterested finality."

"Everyone gets their turn," Troy says.

Adams puts a spoonful of milk powder into his tea, stirs, and goes on with his story. "The young woman who had sutured his wounds sat by his bedside during his last hours, making notes of the gibberish he spoke in his delirium, hoping to decipher any thoughts or wishes that might be passed on to his family. Yet no sense could be made of the garble. *Be told and fly? Dig hold of thee? Too cold for me?* Alas, it shall be anyone's guess."

"Simple nonsense, I suppose," Troy says. "A head injury."

"*Buy gold and flee?*" Adams says.

Wilder snorts a laugh.

Adams swallows his tea. "To conclude, then, Bill Hilman was bathed and dressed in woolens and fresh denims, hair and boots brushed clean, mustache waxed, ice axe tucked into the stiffened crook of his arm, and his body was thuswise neatly parceled into his sleeping bag and flown back home. He was given an impressive memorial service," he says. "In attendance were a former United States president, a Nobel Prize–winning scientist, and several Hollywood box office stars. Eulogies were voiced and wreaths arranged for a man whose future had indeed been annihilated, though his past, as was said, could not be nullified of its particular significance. A statue of him with rope coiled over his shoulder was raised in the park by the lake."

Devin scoops up a pot of snow, puts the pot to the flame.

"What was it like at the top of Mysterium?" Sara says.

"Mount Sarasvati," Adams says.

"Mount Sarasvati," Sara repeats, ever pleased at the sound of her name.

"What do I recollect?" Adams says. "There were definite words repeated between us, words meant to mark synapse and history. I will tell you that Hilman and I stood at the summit for many minutes longer than we should have stayed—this, you see, an attempt to take the whole of it in, wishing, as we did, to retain every speck and whit of our experience. We shook hands in a gesture of camaraderie. We shook hands again, to fix the time forever in memory."

People sip their tea. Wait for their leader to go on.

"Lord, it was cold," says Adams. He raises his shoulders and rubs his hands together. "The cold seeped in through the seams and weaving of our clothing, a maligning iciness that moved toes to spine to nape. We shivered in the wind, and agreed to head down. And just at this moment, we should be startled by the most incredible passing sight."

"Sight of what?" says Sara.

"A swan," Adams says, "is what we thought it was. There

was before us, of all things, a large white bird winging across the desolate space, an expanse that fell away like forgotten time over the rapturous depths of the frozen cliffs. I shall never forget the sight of it."

"A bird that high up?" Devin says. "No way."

Adams raises an arm and passes a gloved hand through the air. "As though it be the spirit of Sarasvati herself, this is what Hilman said. I remember his words exactly. I remember we stood watching the bird until it had glided completely from our vision. Then the sun disappeared suddenly behind a thick cloud, dimming the vista, filching our heat, making us altogether colder. We turned and quickly began the long and perilous descent."

"Have some more tea," Wilder says, engrossed by the story. He holds the thermos forth.

"Oddly enough," Adams says, "we would later see the white bird everywhere. It went flying past us as we trudged down the mountain. Later, at camp, we opened the tent flap to see it dabbling on roots beside a tarn."

"Imagine," Sara says. "Just imagine."

"The same bird was waiting for us in Darjeeling," Adams says. "And then we would see it again in Paris. Yes, just imagine." He peers into his cup of tea. "I even saw the white bird when I arrived in Boston. I still, to this day, see the flutter of its wings in my sleep."

THE ENCAMPMENT at the Sanctuary had been stilled into an icy purity. The colony was nearly deserted now, with only a nylon four-man left standing for the porters, another tent for the Sherpas, both A-frames weathered into graupeled triangles. On the opposite side of the mess tent was left a single dome pitched for the sahibs, mammiform and flawless in the new-fallen snow.

Snow-sculpted boulders cast shadows of plump cherubim, and juniper boughs were furled over into frosty embryos. The world was hushed to new. To Vida it seemed a starting over. A different time, a different place entirely.

Reddy arrived back down to Base Camp midday from up on the ridge, finding the outpost a ghost town with the horde of shepherds gone and their goats gone, and all but a tentful of porters departed. For those who were still here there would be a soaring fire tonight, curried goat meat and falafel for dinner, hot water for washup before bed for any who wished.

Within the flurry of camp work and evening routine there was too the occurrence of an odd phenomenon. It was when Vida was setting the table for mess, mingling a hand among the forks, when the words *What are you doing?* were abruptly spewed from among the tangle of metal tines. It was a message truly startling in its clarity. She dropped the utensils and peered at them. Glyphs of light played upon the walls of the tent in the flickering wick of the lantern. She turned to Reddy, who was seated at the table making lists of provisions, wondering if he had heard what she had heard. His head was kept bent to the task, his serious forehead illumined, his elongated earlobes and warrior nose cast in golden light. His face startled her, for he was suddenly evinced to her differently, strangely. The tent flaps riffled, the wind carrying in an incense smell of burning juniper. Reddy looked up, his eyes glassy nuggets of blackest sapphire. Vida saw him turbaned and necklaced with marigolds, the smoke of incense nimbused about his head, an aura of the mystical about him. He cleared his throat, making Vida suddenly aware of her staring and turning himself back to the familiar Reddy again. No more aura, no more marigolds. She returned to her task. She rustled the forks again, hearing only the ordinary, now just the sound of forks.

When dinner was finished the Sherpas retired for the night, leaving the two sahibs alone. Vida put a headlamp on, announced she was going out, "To do my toilette." Reddy filled a flask with hot tea, and headed straight for the tent. He took his boots off, crawled inside, peeled off layers of wool and fleece, leaving his long johns on, his hat on, his headlamp on. He wormed into his sleeping bag, stuffed his parka in the stuff sack, pillowed his neck with it. When Vida entered he had his light beamed on pages of the *American Alpine Journal*. She scooted into the narrow space beside him. "That little book gets around," she said.

"After this I'll only have food labels to read."

"You left your boots outside," she said. "I put them in the vestibule."

Reddy sat up. "Thank you. But I did remember the tea."

She wiped the toothpaste off the rim of her tin cup, and Reddy poured steaming milky tea from the flask. She put her hand in a position of salute to cover her eyes. "You mind redirecting your light?" she said.

"Sorry." He tipped the headlamp and torched the ceiling.

"This is pretty weird," she said. She warmed her hands on the tin cup.

"Everything is weird up here in the wilds of altitude."

"Sleeping together is what I mean. Alone is what I mean."

Vida's boyish haircut had grown out, and long wisps of it escaped about her face from out of her wool hat. Reddy put a finger to one of the curls to move it away from her eye. "Have some more tea."

She held her cup out. "Tower of Babel seems long ago."

"I recall the feeling of being horribly responsible for you."

"Horribly?" she said.

"We were not wearing helmets, if you recall."

"There weren't any climbers above us."

"That, we did not really know."

"It was late in the day."

"It was my fault," he said. "We had stayed far too long in bed."

"We were not thinking loose rockfall, I guess."

"We were thinking summits of another kind."

Vida looked at him with her soft brown off-kilter eyes.

"I was thinking only about you falling, and me falling along with you," Reddy said.

"Listen to us talking like this."

"Well, our circumstances did carry a good deal of risk," he said. "If you or I had been grimly injured what would the other of us have done? Mountain rescue would have been called. A report would have been filed. There would have been hospital documents to sign. Family to call. My wife. Your husband. There would have been explaining. Confessing. Apologies. Pleading. Remorse. Wounds that would not heal."

"You told me the category was pretty-easy," she said. "But of course why should I have trusted you on top of a mountain, just because I trusted you on top of me?"

Reddy reached a hand to her.

Vida flinched. "Is that thunder?" she said.

IT WAS mostly because she dreaded the many weeks of solitude, but also she knew she wanted to try to climb with Reddy again, just the two of them. This time, she would do it. She would erase her Tower of Babel defeat. She would revise the story; tell it new.

The snowfall had finally stopped. After five long days,

Reddy had to go on ahead. He needed to get the porters started with the shuttling of loads, get them to the ridge before the others were completely out of food up there, deliver oxygen and medicine to them. He wanted to be back on the mountain, help Troy push to Advanced Camp. The mountain's base of snow was packed and cold again, making the climb through the gully easier in many ways. Reddy would dig out the fixed lines. "The way is safe," he told Vida. He told her she would get lonely if she stayed behind.

She is properly clothed and prepared to start out long before dawn. In the grim cold hour of three in the morning she moves through her dressing and washing routine. Then a quick breakfast of hot cocoa and stale fig bars. Now she fits her headlamp around her knit cap, switches the light on, starts out behind Reddy. They head up and over the moraine. It is not exactly the two of them. Behind Vida are the five porters who remain with the expedition, and trailing the porters, Sherpa Mingma. Here in the pitch-dark of a stark frozen world there are no human comforts, aside from what they give one another, no more and no less than being in the same place at the same time. She once again feels close to Reddy, alone with their secret together.

Mingma and the porters hadn't any inkling of the couple's love play during the night. There was no second stupa built for either portent or penance; no prayer flags, no altar, no offerings. No one would know that Reddy had reached into Vida's sleeping bag for the hand she had tucked beneath her chin, kissing her fingers to wake her. And no one would know that it was Vida who earlier had first put a hand out to him, and when she did he unzipped his sleeping bag, and then he opened hers, and soon one was inside the other, entirely, completely, falling together in a paroxysm of sensation and snowballed emotion.

Avalanche rubble had been spewed out across the natural snow bridge covering the Sage's river, a lathery white outpour that filled in and covered over the passageway. The former route is turned an imbroglio of heaping blocks of snow and toppled boulders, a frozen spill creating a colossal lingua they will have to detour a mile or more to get around. They trod along, the sluice and leak of subterranean meltwater from the glacier crooning melancholy harmonies beneath their feet. All about them the cold rings out in distance and in space. The going is trying, especially for the porters with their burdens tumped to foreheads and weighted onto backs. Reddy paces himself to ease the men's labor, with Vida right behind him keeping space enough between them to allow herself her thoughts. And he, his. There is no talk, only walking and breathing. She keeps her eyes on the ground ahead of her, heeding her footing, stepping deliberately, paying attention, for there is nothing more important than paying attention. She considers it the single golden rule.

Wilder's gully is filled with crusty deep snow. Reddy hinges at the knees, swinging his legs to cut bootsteps in the deep. Still it is strenuous uphill work for those following behind. Vida falls into a silent intoning, letting the mantra repeat as she sets her respiring and her ice axe and her boot stride into a definite rhythm: step, step, plant, breath, step, step, plant, breath, and on and on repeating, her heart adding its own metered variation to the theme. The sun edges up behind Mysterium's darkened profile. Flesh-colored clouds open like hands in the paling sky.

Vida struggles on, breathlessly, gravity pulling at her bones. In the vast and barren landscape she is small and insignificant and alone. How little even lovemaking does to erase the aloneness that confronts you up here. You look loneliness in the eye. It looks you in the eye. No, it's more that you are the eye, you are the loneliness itself. Ironic, she thinks, that she climbs primarily for the romance of it, so she has always said. And just what is romance anyway but an ideal, a mystery, a transcendence, a lifting? A glance exchanged, an affinity, a coming together, a longing for harmony, is what she believes. This man or that man has been her reply to why climb, whenever she might be asked to explain. Who knows why she always felt she had to have an answer.

There is more searching and more work still when they get up to the middle of the gully and finally find the fluorescent wand that signals the start of the buried rope. Reddy and Mingma dig on hands and knees trying to locate the fixed line while Vida stomps her feet and claps her hands to keep her heat inside. After more than an hour the first rope is exposed and freed, and they all harness up and clip in, lining up behind Reddy one by one as he again kicks out big steps, making a staircase of snow for the others to follow him in. But now the slope is rinded in ice, and even with the aid of the rope Vida begins to question the soundness of the ground beneath her feet. She knows the porters are only getting colder as she hesitates. Reddy shouts out from above, "Do not look down!" And then he has a hand out and is reaching for her, and she is pulled up with determined force, dragged up and plopped down in the snow, backpack and all, attaching herself to as much of the earth as possible. She sits up, tries to slow her breathing. She sees Base Camp diminished to small puddles of color far below, the spiral of river beside it, the great ocean of sky circumscribing everything.

Reddy reaches a hand out and pulls her up to standing.

"You are fine," he says. "And very beautiful." He brushes the snow off her chest.

"Let me ask you," she says, her voice thin and quivery in the cold. "Why do you climb?"

He studies the look on her face, realizing the question is no joke. "I suppose," he says, "for the boyish feeling that nothing can stop me."

She nods. "I like that about you."

It's true what Reddy says about the rest of the ascent being easier. Though steep, there are good handholds and footholds. She goes back to paying attention, does not look down until she gets to the top of the ridge.

People put their tasks and their cups of tea down, turn heads, stand up, say their heys and their namastes and their what-do-you-knows when they see Vida coming up over the crest behind Reddy. Wilder sits, regarding her as if she were someone unfamiliar to him. Then he goes into a fit of coughing that has him up and lurching about.

Out of admiration or obligation or an unusual bout of rivalry, her husband says he will stay with his wife at Ridge Camp. Tomorrow he will let Doctor Reddy go in his place with Karma and Troy up to Advanced Camp. As if Reddy would have it be otherwise. As if Wilder had seen something new in the wandering vulnerability of Vida's eyes.

IN HIS brother's face, Wilder had seen a horrifying emptiness, a look that would not be forgotten.

No, don't you ever forget.

They had left the tent behind, planning a rapid alpine-style ascent to the top of Stone Sentinel, expecting better weather. But the wind slowed them, and then conditions turned worse.

He and Lucas had plodded on. They knew they should stop and light the stove, melt snow, drink tea, feed themselves, but their fingers were numb and both were too exhausted to bother; a failing they recognized as they trudged on. It was hours before they finally found a rocky outcrop to protect them from the icy wind for the night. Their feet were stone cold and painfully distended, and they realized they would never get their boots back on if they were to take them off. Wilder's feet ache just to remember it.

He will remember it.

The last leg to the summit was no more than a hike ahead of them the next day. They could make it, but now they absolutely had to drink. "We need to force it," Wilder had said, and as he lighted the stove he saw Lucas doing what he never should have done. He cried his brother's name out, but Lucas had already gotten his boots off. His feet were mottled and grossly swollen, the toes a dark purplish color, like those of sick old folks or people you see homeless on the street. Wilder wrapped his brother's bloated feet in layers of fleece and wool, told him not to worry, said they'd be to safety soon enough. He'd carry him to the top and all the way down if he had to. They were sure to find trekkers on the other side of the summit, find help by noon the next day.

Wilder prepared the last meal they would share on the mountain. He was afraid for his brother; afraid Lucas might lose his feet. But Wilder had to think. He had to think sharp for the both of them. He felt the lonely pauses of the skipped beats of his heart. He melted snow and they drank tea and then they bundled themselves into their mummy bags and waited for dawn to come. The wind shrieked in loud she-devil pronouncements. The brothers shivered through the long night.

By morning the wind had died, but Lucas's feet were worse, the raw flesh starting to eviscerate in places. Wilder broke down and sobbed. He tried to get his brother to stand, but Lucas could not, and when Wilder helped him to sit, he collapsed to his back. Wilder propped him up once more to stay. "Leave me alone," Lucas said. "Just leave me alone." And at this Wilder gave his brother a hard punch on the shoulder, slumping Lucas back onto the ground. "Don't say that to me," Wilder said, blood searing through his veins with each unruly systole. "Don't you ever say that to me ever." He got Lucas deeper into his sleeping bag and zipped him in. "Stay here. I need to go on ahead. You have all the food and all the water I am melting for you for tomorrow, you see, do you see? Melting water, here, look, for you to drink. You need to drink. Promise me you'll drink. Say it, you sonofabitch! Say it! Don't laugh at me." But now Wilder was laughing too. Suddenly nothing seemed more hilarious, more ridiculous, more perfectly stupid than the situation they had put themselves in. They laughed and laughed. They laughed until their jaws ached, laughed until they could laugh no more.

To forget is to suffer the loss twice.

He will remember it all.

Wilder sees himself the following morning zipping Lucas into the sleeping bag up to his chin. He wrapped the other mummy sack tightly around his brother's head and his shoulders. He coiled the rope about this chrysalis that was his brother, and anchored him to a rock. Then Wilder was off. He would be at the top in roughly six hours. He would find help in the hut just off the other side of the summit, and he would be back to Lucas only a few hours later.

Two hours after Wilder left his brother the notorious white

wind began its assault again, this time with a staggering ferocity. Over and over the gale force knocked Wilder off his feet.
He clung to boulders to keep from being blown off the ridge. He
struggled on, lurching forward with outstretched arms. He tottered and fell, tottered and fell again. He crawled on hands and
knees. Like this, and more than a day later, Wilder reached the
top of Stone Sentinel. Without his brother.

He hates to remember it.

He will always remember it.

IN THE gloom of another predawn dark the upper camp begins
to stir. There are muffled voices, the hiss and poof of a stove lit,
a clattering of tin cups and cutlery. Professor Troy, Doctor
Reddy, and Sherpa Karma down a quick breakfast of tinned
fish and yesterday's chapatis, and then the men's accoutrement
commences. First the wool shirts and wool pants over the wool
long johns, and over all of this wool sweaters and jackets of
fleece. Over the fleece the down parkas, and over the parkas
the anoraks. Hats on. Next, the struggle of cold boots and cold
fingers and frozen lacings, followed by pairings and lacings of
gaiters. Headlamps over hats. Harnesses buckled up. Crampons
fitted onto rubber-lugged soles and strapped and clasped.
Glacier glasses in pocket. Ice axes in hand. Outer mittens on,
gloves and liners beneath. They shoulder their loads, their
regalia governing their movement and mien, their apparatus
prescribing a way of looking at things.

Barrows of clouds have cleared in the night, and the moon
waxes gibbous. The men move along in the rasp and the chink
of their bootsteps and axe plants, in a clanking of hardware
from inside their duffeled loads, the beams of their headlamps
boring a path in the dark, the boot tracks of so many days ago

erased. Their muscles are stiff in the bitter cold, their eyes sting in the freeze, and though they are three, it is dark and lonely going.

It feels a long time before the sun begins to candle the path. Mysterium's darkened gendarmes color and stand taller in the light. When the men arrive to the base of the glacier they find it a different place than it had been, the path that crosses the steep couloir obliterated since with the pile and cleave of avalanche: the mountain staving off her intruders. The men realize the peril they face: no longer is it a simple gamble of spinning wheels and beads, but instead a lethal game of revolver and bullets, with muzzle set to the temple.

Troy is first to cross the chute. Behind him, loose chunks of snow roll down the slope like guillotined heads. Once he is to the other side and safe, Karma follows quickly in his tracks. Reddy is the last to cross. They wait. Reddy hesitates, his heart pounding in alarm. He looks up to Mysterium's icy fundus, all the hardness covered over and softened by snow. He sees the mountain pouring forth during his passage, her sloughing miscarrying him to a cold and smothering death. His head aches as if his skull were being chiseled. He cannot think. Troy and Karma wait, shivering, losing patience, but they know not to call out, fearing the oscillating waves that might set everything above them to rampage. Reddy's legs are frigid stiff, his mouth sour and dry. He cannot move, cannot even swallow. How long will he make them wait? And how could he turn back? He orders himself to move. *Go forward now.* He stands paralyzed. The wind gusts up and peals deliriously down the length of the glacier, and in it he hears his wife's laughter. Her laugh exactly. *Move, why don't you?* The sound of her mocking him. *Why suddenly now the coward?* He stabs his ice axe into the slope's rimy skin, takes a step, and now finally he is walking, slanting into the wind, staggering into Maggie's wintry laugh.

ALL NIGHT avalanches crack and slither past, and bursts of wind from their mass and tumble lash at the tent in their passing. The men lie in fear in the dark and the cold, trembling as the mountain loudly purges herself, expecting at any moment a suffocating load of snow to burst forth into the tent, an evil visitant entering viciously to swallow them alive and whole.

To be interred with one's heart beating and with the mind still lit with thought, to be frozen and entombed in snow, is altogether more horrifying than falling from the top of a cliff, Troy believes. He has come to see falling as being polar to ascending, both passages defined by laws of motion and gravity. And just as ascension is circumscribed by laws of boundlessness and liberty, so it follows that plummeting can be realized as a release, a letting go, a magnificent deliverance. Troy speaks rarely of his wife, but he has imagined her in her falling, imagined her cascading down the mountain like a droplet of water, as if it had been for Amanda not terrifying, but rapturous, spilled into the arms of death in glorious velocity without time enough for craze or fear or pain, those last moments of worldly excess become an ecstasy. A wonder fall.

But to die interred is a nightmare. Burial offers no more a solace in its opposite than that of exhuming. To inter and to unearth are occurrences of stagnancy and fixity, the matter contained in the ossuaries and reliquaries of that which is covered or dug up just material turned static, inert, useless, like a thing tilled out and tossed from a garden that hinders the sprouting of seeds and the tubering of roots, whether a rock clogged in the soil or a bone chewed to a nub.

Reddy could not bear to have his wife's remains put into

the ground at all. At least to throw her ashes to the wind was to see her aloft before the particles settled on the water like snow afloat, a contoured white mass set adrift in the tug of the moon and borne out to the cradling of the sea. The doctor pictures his wife's essence moving continually, gyrating through time, wheeling like blood cells through arteries.

Karma believes death, by whatever measure—whether it be a snuffing or a stamping out, a toppling to a final landing, a heart failed or an organ withered—that mortality, by any means, is to be seen simply as a first step outwardly. He knows that one should acknowledge life's sufferings, but not live in fear or dread and so relinquish one's mind and soul to the torment of that which cannot be swayed. He knows it is necessary to turn thoughts away from the worry of future sorrow and demise, to contemplate instead the clemency that death brings. For Karma sees the movement through the posthumous intervals before one's next rebirth as an opportunity for liberty most profound. One is offered guidance through the state of the in-between of birth and death, guidance handed down in ancient teachings, lessons incorporated into a knowing while one is still alive. It then comes naturally to see the between-life, the interim time that comes after death, as akin to being guided up a mountain, and so an ascension most divine.

THE THREE men get little sleep with loud snow vipers sliding by in the night, and by two in the morning they are sitting up to light the stove for hot water. They gear up, zip the tent closed, leave Advanced Camp, and start back down to the ridge. After a long night of rumbling and quaking, Mysterium has finally settled into a cold slumber of her own. Her icebound tors stand guard in the distance as the men move toward the couloir. The wind mewls through cleavers and rifts. This time it is Reddy who takes the lead when it comes time to traverse the avalanche chute. He cannot bear the hideous shriek of the wind and in it the sound of his wife laughing at him. He does not look up, does not look down, but instead he keeps his headlamp aimed straight ahead and does not hesitate, knowing the line across the jumbled plot of rock and snow better on the return. Troy follows, hungry for breath in Reddy's tracks. Then Karma, yellow patches in place on his face, and almost nonchalant in his bearing as he crosses the snow-crudded gully. His comrades watch the sirdar Sherpa's traverse as he approaches, nervously wishing him more quickly to safety, and barely has he gotten across the icy quandary when the mountain erupts and a terrible blast of snow shoots off the snout of the glacier. The two look back to see Karma launched like a missile, a seething mass sliding past beneath him. The frozen expulsion lands the Sherpa near Troy and Reddy's feet. They help him up and all scramble on, Karma unaware that one of the yellow patches has been brushed from his face and is left behind, embedded deep in the snow.

FOR THE next many days they will carry. Any plan for alpine methods quick and light are by now amended to Himalayan enterprise. They will manage logistics in the manner of a traditional siege-style expedition. They will freight loads from lower Base Camp up to the small camp at the ridge throughout the day repeatedly, building up the cache there, and from the cache pile they will ferry the stockpiles up to Advanced Camp, heavily laden and slowed to a plod as they try to move swiftly across the avalanche path. They will lug up sustenance and safety, heave implements for shelter, for comfort and necessity, emergency and undertaking. They will bear the hardships of weather, the difficulties of fatigue, the torment of fright, the numbness of denial and dismay, all the while urging the porters along with encouraging words and smiling faces as Mysterium awaits them.

"Please God don't let avalanches fall on us," Sara said before making the first of many traverses to Advanced Camp.

And none did.

ADVANCED CAMP is set in the snow on the broad spine of a humped ridge, a 19,200-foot promontory wide enough for a scattering of people and a strewing of equipment. The party's stakes and poles, axes and ropes, appear a tangle of lines and lances and barbs stuck onto the back of an albino seagoing beast. Fish-shaped clouds bleed red into an eventide sky.

The porters build walls of boxed loads to fix a wind-protected scullery on the ridge's prow. They cover the shelter over with a large tarpaulin and bunker themselves in. Plenty of juniper brush has been hauled up from the Sanctuary, and the Sherpas fetch stones from the undercliff below to encompass a fire pit. The party's settlement soon turns an alpine sprawl safe enough from avalanche, with runoffs ravined on either side.

"Safe enough, unless she should toss us clean off," Adams says, reaching to a billet of wood and affecting to knock it. Wilder, hand in pocket, fiddles with his nugget of orgonite. Karma presses the lone adhesive tab on the side of his face. Reddy searches among the strewn gear for his medical kit and the remedies within, believing he alone on the expedition shuns superstition. Sherpa Pasang hums as he scatters rice blessed by a village lama around the perimeter of the camp. The porters turn their noses up at Pasang's Buddhist practice of grain sprinkling, instead asking their Didi to keep them safe from harm by performing the ceremony of *Raksha Bandhan*, a service typically carried out by a sister for her brother, in which the sister secures a colorful thread to his wrist and vows prayers of love to him.

The mountain releases a full moon from out of its darkness, like an ovum spewed from an ovary. The celestial light transforms the encampment into a residence of alabaster. Soon the sacred ritual begins. One by one the porters come forward and hold an arm out to Sara, who wears the kata over her head like a veil again. She loops and binds the wristlet to a wrist, promising a bond of protection. Each devotee gazes at her wide-eyed, feeling the piety that travels through her fingers as a gesture toward the infinite. There is a collective breath of tenderness among the faithful at the end of the sacrament. Sherpa Pasang strikes a match to a bough, humming one of his melodies as he waits for the blaze. The wind chorals up and down the ravine. The stars brim with significance.

SHE IS coming down the slope through a swirling mist, the sun dimmed behind her, when she sees it. The body is an odd triangular shape, magnified and enormous, the towering figure surrounded in an aureole of rainbow, the head gloried in shimmering rings. She wings her arms up and down, knowing the phenomenon of the specter ahead is she, Sarasvati.

ALL NIGHT long the mountain convulses feverishly as Sara lies in her lover's arms feeling the world in its tumble and spin. Her skin is colorless as the landscape surrounding them, the surface veins in her face like the blue striae of glacial ice, her eyes pale and hollow as thaw holes. Her breasts are tender, her lips parched and fissured, the sores on her hands slow to heal. Vertigo sours her mouth with a taste of curdled milk, and her stomach turns at the hint of food. She has toted provisions for days with little appetite, but today she awakes at Ridge Camp without vitality; even standing upright is an undertaking. Devin urges her to drink, refusing to shuttle again until Sara is well enough to accompany him.

Vida locates the radio, puts in the call, and Reddy is there with Mingma and two porters by midday. Sara has her head out of the tent and is vomiting a clear ichorous-looking liquid when the doctor arrives. He goes to her and opens his medical kit.

Vida, having done her share of shuttling for the past week, has packed her backpack, prepared to head back to lower Base Camp, the banging of high avalanches encouraging her down. Mingma accompanies her and leads on the descent, a porter trailing behind her, the sun a gloomy dimness in the clouds. Vida's thoughts drift and whorl about like loose snow as she heads down the gully toward the Sanctuary. She muses about love as she trudges along, what it is, or was, or wasn't. Concluding only that happiness is forever for those in love, because love, she sees, is truly aspiring. She knows love is never low, but always a looking up, being ceaselessly above. And now that she has been with Reddy again, she sees clearly that her marriage to Wilder has tumbled down to its end.

It is finished.

She will tell Wilder just as soon as she is off the mountain.

Vida's eyes water and her nose drips in the biting air. The wind whimpers through the gully. She plods on, trying to think of the kindest words there might be to tell Wilder she is leaving. She sinks up to the knees, cursing the deep and wet snow of midday. Aspiring tablets, she thinks, must be what I need.

DOCTOR REDDY gives Sara a pill to melt under her tongue, medicine that relieves the queasiness and makes her sleepy. Sherpa Pasang prepares cup after cup of hot instant orange drink for her to drink. Once she can take in no more, Reddy prescribes oxygen. He puts the canister next to her, handling it gently as a baby, covering the tank with a down parka to keep the cold of its metal away from the patient. He puts the mask on Sara's face, pulls the elastic ties snug at the sides, adjusts the regulator. She is soon asleep in the susurrus hum of pressured gas.

In her sleep Sara sees a woman roaming up and down the mountain. The woman has dark hair, her mother's color, and a furrowed brow. The woman is not lost, but something has gone wrong. Sara follows and sees that the ice is suffused with blooms of blood. The woman works to wash the blood away, sploshing each spot with water from her water bottle, the water turning the rime a pale pinkish color, like an oozing. But as soon as the woman has doused one part of the icy slope, she finds a trail leading to another section seeped by the bleeding. The task seems endless, hopeless, yet there is no choice but to carry on. So she waters and she waters. She soaks, sops, rinses, thins, wanting to purify, to rectify.

Late afternoon Sara wakes, finding Devin still in the tent beside her. The doctor's remedies bring relief, and by evening she is herself again, her cheeks restored to a rosy glow, her eyes lively and bright. By evening, she is baking apples for dinner, infusing the air with cinnamon, the warm desert and her good health restoring the lull in the party's morale once more.

"AND YOUR father and I saw the splendid mountain and said one day we will have a daughter just as splendid and we will christen her Sarasvati."

"What was I then?" Sara said. "Before I wasn't?"

"Well, let's say we are each of us pieces of fleshy fruit."

Sara watched her mother's lips moving as she spoke.

"Yes, and inside each of us there are hollow stone ovaries."

"What's ovaries?"

"An ovary stone is like a peach pit, sweetie."

"Oh."

"Children have little stones, and adults have big ones."

"They grow in us, the stones?"

"In girls the stone grows in the uterus. Here, down in here."

Sara looked into her mother's eyes. "Then what?"

"That's all there is to it," Amanda said. "You are born with the stone and you carry it all through your life. This is what your dying is. It is just something you have in you from the very beginning. It is part of you."

"You carry it?"

"Men are especially proud of it."

"Why?"

"Because without it they wouldn't be here at all. And they are honored because women carry stones for them in their uteruses, so they can make more stones and more boys and men and make more of all of us."

"Then we are lucky?"

"Very, for our fruit is double that of a man's. Our fruit is twofold. Women carry a new life and they carry dying at the same time."

"Is there a stone in the baby inside?"

"There is, so the mother has two stones inside her, you see."

"You mean two dyings in her?"

"Two deaths. Yes. She holds her own and also the child's."

"Where does my stone go when I die?"

"It goes back into the garden."

"In the dirt?"

"How else can a stone grow into a peach tree? Of course, in the dirt."

Sara nodded her head. "What if I were a peach?"

"Then you would be the most perfect peach there ever could be, sweet Sarasvati."

THERE ARE more days of bad weather, more days of waiting it out; a festerfest, as Devin likes to call these layovers, as they all fester about in layers of wool and fleece in their tents. People are bored, weary of being sedentary, and tensions begin to rankle like blisters. The mountain shakes off wave upon wave of new downfall, and though Adams considers Advanced Camp a relatively secure location, nerves are taut. On the next cold morning of cloudless sky, Wilder and Devin gear up in readiness to set out, aiming to reckon a course to Camp I safe enough for everyone.

Devin wants Sara to come along, but it is another day of stomach trouble and so she stays back to rest up for the more difficult days ahead. Reddy riffles through his kit and brings her a bottle of pills. "Take one capsule three times a day until all the capsules are gone. Follow each with plenty of water. We've all been through these disturbances of the gastrointestinal tract, a common problem on every expedition," he says.

"If you say so, Doctor," Devin says, looking at Sara as he speaks. He squeezes her hand.

"Go on, Devin," she says. "Go with Wilder."

And Devin does. He and Wilder pack up their harnesses, their hardware and rope, both eager to begin some real climbing after so many weeks on the trail. Wilder is pleased to have his friend once again at his side and all to himself. The two are paced together the way they used to be back in the days of their training jaunts, and little to no conversation is all right by both of them. They revel in the glorious morning, filled with camaraderie, with brilliant sunshine and an ultramarine sky. They tromp up toward the middle of a col, the snowy ground radiant as the sea, their glacier glasses necessities against the intensity of the glare. Both are content and lost in thought as they make their way through heavy drifts in the steep of a waning slope. But the sudden rasp of a snowslide shakes them from their silence. The earth quivers beneath their feet. Wilder feels it like the church bells ringing forlorn as he and his brother started out toward Stone Sentinel; when the bells stopped the sound still resonated from the ground, seeping deep into his boot soles. Wilder feels an omen in the tremoring.

But there is no time to call out.

Wilder and Devin leap into the air, jumping for cover under an outcrop of rock, clinging to ice axes sunk deep, heads ducked, bodies clenched like fists. A flue of wind spews past. When the trembling earth settles they lift their heads to see a tranquil slope. They hear the perfect silence again.

"Thought it for sure the big guy in the white suit coming for us."

"It was the next couloir over."

They shake the snow off, refit their packs, plant their axes, and start back up the scarp. They are hardly back into a rhythm when *kaboom!* the shock resounds like a launched bomb, and when they look up they see a roaring torrent charging at them. Wilder vaults back to the outcrop of rocks, but the thing already has Devin in its maw and he is flailing down the mountain, tumbling over and over like a piece of seaweed tossed onto a surf-beaten beach, the weight of the demon carrying him under and pounding down on him so hard he feels his neck about to snap. But now he is suddenly back on the surface, moving his arms as if swimming, his body bobbing along on a great tide of snow, a long sledless ride of snow, until finally the slide finds its point of repose as gravity gives way to friction and the steamrolling stops. Devin is buried, punched onto his side by the clobbering mass, like a small animal pinned into submission by an angry master. His hands are cupped over his head like a wrestler in defense. He takes in a breath, sucking in snow, coughing the snow out, only to suck it back in again, and coughing, choking, sucking, and now he knows he is drowning is what's happening, he's drowning. He struggles to move a hand to his face, and he fingers the snow away, carving a pocket of air out to breathe in. *God, can this be? God, oh God, oh God can this be?* The only response a deathly pocket of silence. His heart beating fast enough to kill him. His warm breath freezing the air pocket, icing a mask on his face. There is no air, no sound, no light, no weight, no cold, no breath. Then there is no fear. There is no thought at all.

Like out of an anesthesia he wakes. Someone calling his name. *Let me sleep.* Wilder calling his name. *Leave me be.* Wilder's face above his face, digging him out of the frozen concrete, screaming, "Say something, would you! Speak, man, would you speak!" Wilder gets a grip under an armpit and pulls Devin's torso out and upright, then grabs both of his arms and drags his friend out of the frozen tomb. Devin is flopped on his back, face splintered with ice, the skin beneath a deathly blue. "Sit up, man. Try to sit up. Sit up would you goddamn you!" But Devin doesn't move and now Wilder is pummeling him, yelling again and again to wake up goddamn you wake up.

Devin opens his eyes.

"Where's my sunglasses at?" he says. "My friggin' gloves?"

THE POWDERY tail of the avalanche scattered everyone about camp like an army of insects come out from under an upturned rock. Its buffeting wind flattened two of the tents, and sent the third one over the cliff along with several toppled cartons of supplies that had been the walls of the makeshift kitchen. Who knows where the tarp was lofted off to.

When Devin and Wilder straggled in they found people stunned and completely encrusted with snow, all lurching about like mummies. Adams looked especially spooked, having just seen Sara arise from out of a mound of white powder, as though she were being hatched from an egg.

The whirlwind and barrage of spindrift left snow in everything. Snow was wedged inside boots, caked into underwear, frozen into frozen layers within every layer of their clothing. Snow pelleted their hair, was clogged into ears and up nostrils, seeped beneath eyelids. They swiped at their veiled faces, slapped at themselves. They circled about as if lost. Then, as if abruptly finding a trail sign pointing the way, they snapped to and all started digging into the flattened tents, searching frantically for dry clothing before they iced up completely.

After a change of clothes, Adams surveyed the shambles, collecting broken poles and stakes. Troy and Reddy uncovered a coil of rope and used it to downclimb the scarp in search of the lost tent. Karma ordered Pasang to take charge of the porters, directing them to gather and shuttle and resettle the camp beside the shelter of a rock wall several hundred yards away. The sirdar Sherpa pressed his temples, feeling only the cold flesh of his fingertips against the cold flesh of his face, the single yellow tab he had left to him now lost in the blast of snow.

Down at Base Camp, Vida and Mingma and the few porters with them had burst out of their tents when they heard the explosion. They looked up to see a colossal white cloud balloon and volute down the mountain, a discharge ending in a fabulous display of cannonading ballistics, leaving a funnel of snow dust in the wake, like a great plume of cold breath.

"Come in, Advanced Camp," Vida said.

Reddy's voice sputtered through the scratch and the static. "Oscar Kilo," he said. "All okay."

AS WE *are, so is* Mysterium. *For that which fires all is no more and no less than restiveness and insatiety. Gravity, petrology, orogeny, performance, attainment, acquirement: none of it flamed by content. Mountains will court and pursue; men will let themselves be wooed and tempted afresh. For the stars, for the mountains, for the seas, for humankind, there is only will, only drive.*

Nature cares not for the being, only for the species.

The world is a sublimely callous place.

6.

THE SUMMIT

NO ONE WANTED TO TALK ABOUT IT. FOR IF THEY WERE TO talk about it they would need to call upon logic and reason. They would have to tally the risk, reckon the drawbacks, rethink the reward. And all would necessarily conclude that there was only one intelligent choice and only one thing to do: Leave. Call it quits. Get off the mountain. Go down now.

But no one would speak of retreat.

A threshold crossed, they cast their gazes to the zenith.

THE MORNING is without cloud-form or wind-blow or portent of any kind as the crusaders ready themselves for the climb up the couloir and on to Camp I. Adams and Karma, Wilder and Devin and Sara gather their equipage. They clip on, buckle in, gird up, declare their goodbyes, leaving the porters and embers of the morning cookfire behind. The first steep stretch of the hump they now call the Bobsled, a moniker in honor of Devin Reddy's calamitous ride down the masticating declivity. They laugh as they cant up the alabaster bank, entitled now to wise-crack about it.

Troy and Reddy had the day prior set out ahead to establish the higher camp, aiming for the crest of one of the mountain's prominent white bones so as to settle them at a roost of twenty-one-thousand-plus feet in altitude, a site they would name in tribute to their leader: Camp I now christened Adams' Rib. The two had passed through the snow-shed funnel of the Bob-sled and from there had made their way up and over the berg-schrund, walking with fanatical care and prayerful delicacy across the frozen ocean of broken waves and gaping ice that had severed from the head of the glacier. They sidetracked cat-aracts of seracs and skirted fathomless crevasses in a world without code or plumb or plane. They punched through a pas-ture of snow rollers and finger drifts in crust knee-deep that brought them to the base of the thousand-foot slope. They tip-toed up the precipitous rib on the front points of crampons, hammering the picks of their ice axes into deep turquoise ice, Reddy leading the first seventy-degree pitch, anchoring pick-ets and flukes along the way, belaying Troy up to lead the next section of vertical. Blood surged through their arteries and veins in hard-won joy. They were doing some real climbing now.

Adams had over the past week talked about the options for the various summit teams. It was agreed that Reddy and Troy should try for the top in tandem, Adams then joining forces with them to make it a trio. Wilder and Devin and Sara would triplet up and form the other team. This would have left Karma to choose between which of the two groups he would accompany, going with the vigor of youth or with the wisdom of the elders, if the sirdar Sherpa hadn't decided to say nay to the summit either way. Without the squares of yellow to affix to his face, he would assist the others only to the highest camp. The single question remaining was which team would have the first chance to make it to the top of Mysterium, a thought lingering in the minds of Reddy and Troy as they rested on the crest of Adams' Rib, taking hungry sucks of the miserly air.

The pair stood high upon a glimmering white scimitar two thousand feet below the northeast shoulder. Not far ahead was a tranche of snowy ground wide enough to erect two small high-altitude tents, the platform safe from any kind of snowy barrage, so high were they perched and away from possible avalanche. Past what would be the campsite, the crest thinned out to a long precarious knife-edge, this stretch a test they would face in order to get onto the farmost glacier and up onto the cold bald slopes of the mountain's formidable collarbones.

They laid the ground sheet out and spread the sack of tent over it, assembled the poles and slipped the skeleton through the nylon sleeving, then raised the whole of the body and pulled out the guy ropes and planted the stakes to taut it all in place. They worked together in their usual mode of practiced efficiency, knowing without speaking the next step of the routine, knowing too, without speaking, the progress made toward their vainglorious aim. What speaks to them is ahead of them. And once they have reached the zenith there will be a new search for the next wreath of laurels, another crown yet to be taken, the men's linear goals turned a circling. The way of absurd heroes, you may say, rolling a mythical stone.

A CRYSTAL cold morning turns into the scorching bake of midday. The sun's incinerating beams reflected off snow hinder them all, but especially trouble their leader. Karma urges him to make use of the oxygen, despite Adams's resistance to expending precious supplies of it. "A few might need this crutch only as we near the apogee," he said. "Or for spells of serious illness. However, most of us should likely not require it at all."

Eschew bottled oxygen as aid to the top; all in the party had agreed.

But now it is otherwise.

"We need you sharp as you can be," says Troy.

Adams, admitting responsibility to the expedition, fits the canister onto his back, snugs the mask over his face. Karma adjusts the regulator, and Adams starts out once again, his crampons sounding like grinding teeth as he proceeds across the icy derm. Breathing in the gas does bring relief from the dizzying altitude and insufferable fatigue, but still the furnace of sun slows his progress. He remains at the tail of the cordée the entire day.

As Adams trudges up the toilsome field of hip-deep snow he realizes the measure of his fervor has diminished over the years, as he supposes is the case for his general lack of inclination toward many other things. He is not certain, or perhaps he simply cannot too well recollect, what lure has led him thus far today, other than having been charmed by Miss Sarasvati

Troy, though he has a vague notion it may have to do with wanting something back he once had. Ardor, could be, or simply gaiety. Or perhaps, and more seriously, a deep wish to achieve some lasting state of grace.

He misses his wife terribly. Of this, there is no doubt.

Adams raises his head and looks up to the line of climbers crawling along the steep ridge in the clear and deathly air. They are, if you will, but mites on a lioness, fleas on a grizzly, lice on a great white whale. He sees them toiling upward. Before them is a white cross, a pillared patch of light beside the sun that meets the curvature of pure earth. What is this phenomenon called? He no longer summons nouns without effort.

Deep breaths of the bottled oxygen.

Step, breath, step, breath, plant, step, breath. Rest.

He knows he is slow. He senses he is no longer needed.

Parhelion.

Hooray! Rest. He would laugh if there were air enough.

He looks in wonder at the vastness of his environs, at the delirious emptiness that encompasses him: a frigid and limitless sky, barren pastures of slick white. Is it the place, or something within himself that besets him with a sense of utter loneliness? Some nameless anxiety has tempered the future. In the scale of his surroundings, he is reduced. Or is it time that has demoted him? His heart rattles like a cheap prize inside the skeletal coffers of his chest. He cannot remember the gulf of such moods when he stepped upon these ridges and cols a quarter century ago.

Not so.

There was a palpable sadness or, perhaps, more a remorse that dampened some of the grandeur he and Hilman had captured when standing at the top of Mysterium. Once home, he had tried to describe the regret to his wife. Hillary was in the kitchen pouring kibble into a dog bowl; he remembers this like yesterday. He explained to her that what he had come up against at the summit might be akin to the contrition experienced by elephant hunters. Despite the thrill, the arduous chase, the necessary strength and endurance, the marksmanship needed, the bounty of the ivory that awaits, there is a feeling of sacrilege as one watches the great bulk shudder and collapse in a huff of dust. Hillary stood hugging the dog bowl, the dog prancing about her feet as she studied her husband's eyes.

He and Hilman had started down the slippery ridge, frostbitten, exhausted, oxygen depleted, and despite some odd letdown, ravenous for more adventure. It was the heyday of climbing, no doubt about it, and both were caught in the thrill of further record-breaking undertakings. Men had time again after another big war and were once more out eagerly claiming virgin summits, poking their flags into the icy skins of the world's most onerous prominences, for want of other things to master. Some would be heroes again for their countries. A few, better loved.

The world, of course, had changed, what with aluminum ladders and fixed lines de rigueur, and with all the highly paid guides for those clients eager to climb just about anything that might add to image and name. Alas, the earth has long since been ravaged and befouled. Clients! Are we not all of us doomed by such terms? Base Camp at Everest, so it's been said, is now a motley city of nylon-domed abodes surrounded by piles of empty oxygen cylinders and heaps of frozen excrement. What was the word for the latter? Wait. It will come. Adams plants his axe, as if to loosen the peculiar curlicues of his worn brain. He checks the gauge of his oxygen tank, refits the mask. *Frozen fecaloma?* Close, but not it. At least Mysterium has kept a measure of purity, barely touched as she is. Yet what heroism will there be for anyone on this expedition? Doing what has already been done.

Coprolith? Or something near it.

How the mind wanders for the wanderer.

Adams looks up to see the line of roped climbers tilted into the wind, twines of white dust ghosting about them. If Sara is roped in the middle with Wilder in the lead, surely Reddy's son will be tied in right behind her. She and Devin are obviously ready to take the plunge. "Be bold and free," Adams heard Sara say to her beau, words that would surely turn a young man's doubts and fears to a promontory of certainty and desire, given a loveful girl like herself. Is such sweetness and light in a human to be believed? Why not? And as to her words, yes, and absolutely: be bold and free. For those who work to forge and form know the longing to push into worlds unexplored, and so discover something new, if only about themselves. In that lies the detonating spark.

Meltwater inside the body of the glacier travels subterranean paths beneath his feet, emitting an eerie harmonic sound. There is a word for this melancholic resonance, he is sure of it. He refits his goggles.

Skirl!

Yes. He is getting quicker.

Snow particles sparkle and waft about him like angelic dust, stellars of icy crystals becoming tiny mirrors of the miracle of existence. Sun spokes fan out from the core of hot star in which they are born, piercing the figures up on the ridge with a singular radiant shaft, burning the entire line of climbers away in a flaming light. Adams foreheads his goggles, wipes his eyes. The group reappears, yet he sees they are hardly moving. Perhaps they have stopped to drink, or stopped for breath. Then he sees one of them rising balloon-like above the others, hovering there in the air, as if with wings. How is such a trick accomplished? He pulls the binoculars out of his jacket pocket to sharpen and zoom what he sees. Sara is in the lead, she the bright patch in the snow at the start of the line, Devin roped directly behind her as expected, and then, lastly, Wilder. They are clearly together with feet solidly planted upon the frozen ground. But Karma? Where is Karma? Adams scans the slope. He must radio Vida back at Base Camp this evening; inquire as to whether the Sherpa has made the higher camp. He shall tell her too of the image of one of the party levitating, so to amuse her. There have been crazier tricks of the retina reported at these heights. He feels the delicate wobble of the earth on its axis, his boot soles giving beneath his feet. He digs a heel in. Plants the axe. Squints in the prismed light. He breathes. There are, he knows, many ways for the story to go, possibilities spiraling out this way and that in a burst of dumb chance. There will be a birthday this trip, an anniversary, guaranteed. With any luck, no serious injury or further fatality. He is here to see the story through. Fate shuffles, we play. Who can say? Buy gold and flee?

Be bold and free!

"Hilman, my friend, I have got it!"

SARA LEADS the way across the frozen plateau, Devin roped behind her, Wilder at the tail of the line, the mountain a marmoreal palace rising beside them. Wending their way up the outer edge of a glacial corrie, the climbers are decelerated and diminished within the immensity of the landscape, their long-humped shadows clinging ancient and reptilian to their clawed feet, the icy firma beneath making a brittle sound like the crackling of branches, or a snapping of frangible bones. They move through a numbing wonderland of tottering blocks and shattered slab, seracs erratic and titanic as buildings, any of them boding to any moment topple their icy tonnage and come crashing down as the glacier courses seaward in actual measure each day. Fangs of icicles threaten to bite a rope or sever a limb in two, and funnels of frozen holes, moulins unforgiving of any slip, alert a simple willingness to swallow any or all of the careless. A bristling maze of crevasses appears through a swirl of ice dust, some of the vertical fissures narrow enough to step across, others gaping like gangrenous wounds, black and hellishly deep, a few insidious, like cancerous ulcers hidden beneath a thin gauzing. All about are the ghastly and the ravishing, the horrible and the beautiful, the fascinens, the tremendum, all of that which appalls and is sublime, and none of any of it lost to them as they move through the tors of this purgatorial world.

Little snow whirls auger about at their feet. The sun is high and ringing, the blood singing in their ears. They stop to drink, shedding down coats and layers of wool and fleece as the heat becomes more stifling. They wrap their necks with balaclavas, concealing flesh with hoods and gloves, eyes covered with mirrored glasses and attached leather patches that shield the sides, noses and lips painted thick with zinc paste, cheeks lubed with a shielding grease. They slog on with their sap boiling steadily away, their tongues swelling in the scorched and waterless air. A glacial tributary below gurgles and purls in the deep.

Following the route where the fathers had gone before them, the trio arrives to the roping-up place at the base of the operose rib. A path of small steps has been chopped out of the ice from the bottom to the top of the thousand-foot incline, a place to stape their front points. Fixed lines have been planted along the way. They stand in a pyramid of shade cast off by the steep rise, suddenly shivering in their freezing sweat, quickly combing through backpacks and adding back layers of clothing

before they start up the cold blue wall. Tightening their cram-
pon straps, cinching their packs snug to shoulders and backs,
the climbers one at a time clip their etriers and jumars to the
fixed line and rung their bodies up, adjusting the cam, top-
stepping and pulling up with hardened arms, muscles biting,
lungs on fire. There are stretches where they need to detour the
vertical and traverse the rib instead, avoiding with tremendous
care the bayonets of ice that promise to slice the nylon line or
them. Laboring on, one by one laddering themselves up to the
top of the crest until they are emerged up and over the verge,
and then all lie sprawled in the wondrous light. Mysterium, a
towering priestess of velvety-white geometry, beckons from
above.

Devin's father comes forward and looms over his son, casting the younger man into a puddle of shadow. Reddy reaches a
hand down to offer him a lift up, but Devin rolls onto his
knees and gets himself to his feet.

"Welcome to Adams' Rib," Troy says. He slaps Wilder and
Devin on a shoulder each in reward as they stand. His daughter
he embraces wholeheartedly, and she clings to her father's
downy corpulence for a long time, both knowing they are closer
to something unspeakable now.

Reddy looks over the cliff for the other two to appear, but
sees only Karma below at the roping-up place. The Sherpa
paces and shuffles about, clapping his hands and stomping his
feet to keep from freezing in the shade as he waits for Adams,
who must still be very far behind as he is nowhere in sight.
Karma, losing patience in the cold, retraces his steps back into
the raging sun until finally he sees their leader come out from
around an edifice of ice. Adams stops, tugs a kerchief from out
of his pocket, wipes the fog from his goggles. He looks up at
the other climbers gathered far ahead of him, little dots they

are up high on the rib, and he cups his hands together, calling out loudly to them in his familiar trebled yodel. Someone on the crest raises an ice axe in answer. Then Karma appears directly in front of him, seeming from out of nowhere, like an apparition out of a cloud. The Sherpa's form dilates and fades in the squint-white light as he approaches. He holds a water bottle out to his leader, but Adams just stands fixed with a spooked look on his face, sweat pouring off his brow.

"Sahib."

Adams nods, his throat scoured raw from calling out in the vaporless air, his mouth parched, his lips cracked and blistered.

"Drink, Sahib."

Adams takes the bottle. With trembling hands he puts the rim to his swollen lips, spilling most of the water down the front of his jacket. He coughs. He takes gulps of air, takes another drink of water. He heaves. "Shall go back," he says, his voice a sandpapered whisper. Karma pushes the bottle forward, and Adams takes another swig, their shadows pools of melted anatomy beneath their feet.

"Poorly acclimatized, I am." Adams hands the bottle back.

"Camp One is very small camp," Karma says. He raises the water bottle toward the top of the rib. "Very crowded if we go up and make seven. Best for Sahib and me that we drop loads at roping-up place and go down to low camp. Please, you rest two days there and be good."

Adams looks up to the crest. He huffs out a speck of dry laugh. "I would swear that I saw one of them levitating up there."

UP ON Adams' Rib, nothing is more paramount than keeping one's feet reliably on the ground. Though Camp I is spectacularly placed, it is anything but spacious, the crest broadening out only wide enough to accommodate two small tents, allowing little clearance and heart-stopping drop-offs on either side. Devin and Sara and Wilder had intended to let go their loads and return to Advanced Camp the same day to lessen the population. But since Adams and Karma have retreated, the three toss out the ground cover, plant the second A-frame, and begin to settle in for the night. With cliff edges but a few feet away from the outside of each tent, the party designates east and west crest for specific purposes: the upside to be snow source for meltwater, downside of the tents now decreed the latrine.

The sun dips behind the western peaks and hurls the camp into shadow and below-zero cold. The threesome roll out sleeping pads and down-filled bags, and they huddle inside their shelter; Reddy and Troy settle in for the night inside the A-frame pitched beside. They light cookstoves, melt snow, boil the meal, drink tea. In one tent there is talk of esteemed climbers, talk of other summits, the meaning of success. Next door, they chew over movies and music and first meals of choosing as soon as they're back home to the States. All make plans for the next day, exchanging information with staccato'd shouts out the mouths of the tent flaps. Come first light they will one by one rappel down the splintery blue-glass of Adams' Rib and together make their way back across the bergschrund, glissading down the Bobsled and back to Advanced Camp. Then begins the routine of shuttling provisions and equipment higher onto the mountain, caching much of the cargo at the roping-up place, an undertaking that will take many all-day forays without porter assistance. Through the unpersuadable landscape they will each be laden and traipse.

ADAMS SITS cross-legged in the shaded cover of an abutment of rock, arms outstretched and rested upon his knees, examining bands of seared flesh. Pasang, crouched beside the firepit, blows at the dead ash as he watches his leader. The ash comes alive in a pulsing glow, and the Sherpa adds twigs to the embers. When there are flames enough he adds more brush to blaze the fire, then gets up to attend Adams, who has been sitting in the same position staring at the burns on his arms for too long.

"Bhalu Sahib," Pasang says.

Adams shifts his gaze to look up to the one who is speaking. The Sherpa sees the man's eyes gone strange beneath the shaggy white brows.

"You wear gloves in sun, but shirt not more long at sleeves."

Adams squints at the Sherpa as if he were looking into a blinding snow. Then he goes back to studying his forearms.

"Sahib," Pasang says. He puts his hand on the man's bear-like shoulder. "Bhalu Sahib," he says.

VIDA AND two of the porters head out from Base Camp carrying pack loads of extra rations and oxygen canisters at Karma's radio'd request. They climb up into the gully and out of the thick mist of the Sanctuary; swelling clouds passing above like a tote of slow-moving cargo. It will be a full day's journey to Advanced Camp, but the going is easier this time, with the glacier's steep gutter now innocent of fresh downfall, and a path hard-packed enough for them to troop across. They stop midday to rest at the ridge and make tea. It is nearly evening when they enter Advanced, where the tents and the makeshift kitchen are now positioned within a lee of solid rock. There is a smoky fire burning, and salty buttery tea when they arrive. But Reddy has yet to return down from Camp I on Adams' Rib.

Vida looks in on Adams and finds him asleep in his tent. They say he has complained of a severe headache and extreme fatigue, but so has most everyone at some point during this trip. She closes the tent flap to leave him to his dreams, but when he hears the zipper finish Adams opens his eyes and goes back to gazing at his wife, whom he believes he sees lying here next to him. He reaches out to touch the long hair spilled out about her pillow, breathes in her scent perfused throughout their nylon room. She carries the home smell of lavender soap and mahogany polish, of potting humus and of something medicinal, like camphor or menthol. She has her home sweater on, which is odd, but he believes there must be good reason for it, for Hillary does nothing without thinking matters through. He reaches out and takes her in his arms, holding on to her as if she were tethered and keeping him afloat. He bobs and drifts along in the soft even rhythm of her breathing. It is a fine thing being married for a long time, no longer having to say what the other already knows you will say.

But she speaks, stealing away the silence between them. She wishes to ask him a question. Perhaps, he thinks, she wonders about my having missed a day of shaving. But the query is otherwise, taking him by surprise.

"Why?" Adams says. "After all our years you shall ask me why?"

His wife looks into his mica-colored eyes.

"There are no words, really, to constitute a rational reply," he says. "What we cannot speak about we must pass over in silence, so it is said in the *Tractatus*; the last line, mind you."

"Don't give me Wittgenstein," she says. "Try."

"I know only that my nature must be utterance enough. My entire being would be the answer I give to you."

She regards him with a tender ferocity.

"Stop listening to the professor's philosophy talk," she says.

MIDAFTERNOON VIDA goes back to check on Adams, taking with her a tin cup of hot soup. She approaches the tent and hears him speaking. Odd, she thinks, and she calls his name before unzipping the door and putting her head through the sleeve. Adams sits up out of his mummy bag and fingers back strands of his matted hair, looking about the modest dwelling as if he has lost something there. Vida squeezes herself into the tent, carefully balancing the steaming soup. She settles in beside him, sees the wandering look in his eyes, a dull and vacant air to his face entirely.

"I brought soup." She holds the cup forth. "It's tomato rice."

Adams calls her a filthy name and slaps the soup out of her hand, spraying a lumpy red slop all over the bedding and walls.

"Damn you!" she says.

Adams gives her a queer sidelong glance. She backs out of the tent and calls out to Karma. "He's out of it. Totally."

Karma looks at her, hooded eyes opened wide. Doctor Reddy should have come down and been here by now. The sirdar Sherpa goes to the mess tent, retrieves the radio, comes back out to the cold open air. He presses the push-to-talk button. Vida watches his lips moving as they graze the transceiver.

"Camp One, you must read," he says. "Please, Sahibs, do you read?"

The radio erupts in a crackle of broken words.

"Need Sahib Doctor. Must come now."

"Sara, me, Wilder here," says Devin. "No Doctor Sahib."

"Doctor Reddy at the ready," Troy says. "Bringing up the rear there." Troy motions with his head as he enters camp, plants his ice axe in the snow, unclips his pack, and hefts the burden off his back.

Reddy comes up from behind. "I am pleased to see a fire," he says. "Even more pleased to see Pasang humming away busily patting chapatis." He looks over to Vida. She is holding his medical kit.

"Adams," Vida says, gesturing with her head. "In there. The tent dripping with soup inside." She hands Reddy the kit, and he climbs inside the tent, sees Adams flat on his back staring at the ceiling. Their leader's face has a greenish hue. His cheeks are fallen in, his nose and teeth unusually prominent. "You need a shave, Adams. Whiskers are not your style." Reddy does not like what he has quickly come to recognize. He looks at the man and sees water and sodium levels rising. He sees wet brain: capillary leakage, sopping white matter, flooded subarachnoid folds, an intracranial casing about to burst like a dam. Adams drools. He mumbles something about needing a drink. Reddy opens the kit and unfolds it like a tackle box, which is what the box is, and takes out of it a rubber bulb and cord attached to a band of fabric. He pushes Adams's sleeve up and wraps the cloth snug about the upper arm. He pumps the cuff up tight, opening slowly the air valve as he watches the dial wag out the numbers in a slow hiss of release. Reddy nods his head the way doctors will do, and removes the cuff. He examines the wrist burns. "Must be careful to keep all skin covered by clothing, or make sure to apply zinc at this altitude for any flesh exposed," the doctor says. "I should not need to tell you," he says. Adams looks at him, blinks, looks back to his wrists. Reddy reaches for his headlamp, takes Adams by the chin and shines the light into his eyes. He asks the patient a simple question. Adams repeats the question, his tongue thick, words slurred. The doctor shakes his head, brings forth a small vial from out of the tackle box, and with it a needle and syringe. He unwraps the syringe, uncaps the needle, and plunges it into the vial's rubber stopper. He withdraws the solution, flicks the bubbles out of the tube, and before Adams knows what's happening the doctor thrusts the needle into the thickness of his upper arm. The man doesn't flinch.

"Here, wipe your mouth," Reddy says. He hands Adams his handkerchief, and Adams does what he's told. Then the doctor sorts through the medical kit and retrieves a bottle of pills, takes a pill out, tells the patient to open his mouth, and places the tablet onto his swollen tongue. He watches Adams draw the tablet in slowly, as if it were a sacrament. Reddy hands him a flask of water. "Swallow," he says.

"I am," Adams says.

"You will be all right," Reddy says, the way that doctors like to tell you. He gathers his kit and climbs out of the tent backward on hands and knees, rising to his feet and stumbling into Troy, who stands like a sentinel before him, lean and stately and tall.

"Ah!" Reddy says.

"Ah, what?"

"Gave him a shot of dexamethasone, and a dose of nifedipine. Now we must put him back on the oxygen and monitor him carefully."

"Then we get him down. If it's what I'm thinking."

Reddy nods. "It is what you're thinking."

Greasy-looking torpedo-shaped clouds accumulate below the summit. To the west, a pea-green haze lurks over the dim chasm of the Sage's Gorge.

"That haze is the color of Adams's face," Reddy says.

A heavy boom quakes the ground. They look up to see a slab of snow fractured from the mountain's flank, careening down in a turbulent cloud.

SARA STANDS at the threshold of Adams' Rib looking out to two luminous guardian rings shouldered on either side of the plummeting sun, her frosted breath spiraling up like incense into the empyrean. She stoops to scoop up a potful of snow, unclips the snap link from the line, climbs back into the tent. "What do mock suns look like? I think that's what the halos are out there."

"Sun dogs, you mean?" Devin says.

"It means we move up the mountain," Wilder says. "I say tomorrow instead of heading down for more loads we scout up what's ahead, see if we can make the next camp higher. Take an extra tent and get set up."

"All the way up to the east ridge?" Sara says. She examines the raw cracks on her palms, wounds that look like the squinty eyes of a deity.

"We've humped more than our share up here already," Wilder says. "We'll be on the mountain until autumn at this rate. It's over a month now."

"Yes," Sara says, grinning. "It's almost my birthday."

In the morning they wake to find the moisture of their fetid breath turned to a fur of hoarfrost coating the entire inside of the tent. Wilder causes a small blizzard of it as he stumbles outside to head for the latrine edge of the crest. Sara and Devin brush the icy crystals out of their hair. They wipe the frost off the down bags and swab the rest of it from the nylon ceiling before it begins melting and dripping, turning bedding and clothing into a sodden mess. Devin opens the door flap and sticks his head out and shouts at his friend. "Hey, man, watch your step if you're not gonna hook into a line." He puts his head back inside. "Won't be needing sunglasses and zinc today," he says. Sara curls back into her sleeping bag, closes her eyes.

Wilder announces his return with a dry hacking cough

that kicks at his ribs. He pulls his smooth-soled inner boots off, parks them in the vestibule, and settles into the tent. "It's looking pretty mean out today."

"I could really use a rest day anyway," Sara says. Her belly is cramping again, but she doesn't mention it. Everyone's belly hurts up here, and people do their best not to complain.

"At this altitude, wouldn't hurt any of us to stay high and rest a day."

"C'mon, Devin, don't you wuss out on me too, man."

"No worries. I can stay here on my own," Sara says.

Devin looks at her. "No, you can't."

"Do what you gotta do," Wilder says. He starts pulling on layers of extra wool and fleece. "I'll take the other tent with me, set up Camp Two without you."

"Take a look at those clouds," Devin says.

"I see them clouds," Wilder says. "Since when are you afraid of some clouds?"

LOST IS the ability to articulate elementary words, and speech turns clumsy. Lo! Adams wants to say. But "Yo" is what he says. He stumbles about camp like a drunk. He needs help to the latrine. He will not eat. He will not drink. He does not sleep.

Mingma shakes his head, mutters his goodbyes, and sets out ahead of the rest in the predawn darkness. The air is gravid with snow as the Sherpa takes his leave of Advanced Camp, and by the time he gets down to Ridge Camp the weather has let go in a scatter of expectant flakes, a downfall that blots out the darkened shapes of every surrounding scarp and prow. He uses the brushwood they have stashed to start a fire. He will make the tea and ready the meal, be prepared for the others when they arrive. All will need fuel before heading back down the gully to return to the Sanctuary and Base Camp. He gets the fire blazing, starts melting snow. He fills insulated flasks with the heated water, melts more snow. So much snow, so little water. But the more water he melts, the more it snows; the gods, he surmises, providing a constant flowing supply for their drinking needs.

It seems too long a time has passed when finally he sees the others step through the thick pale curtain of uncertainty, the weather having changed dramatically. They are crusted in rime, bent over and beaten down like a troop of doddering soldiers. They barely discern the smoke rising from the fire within the brume of falling snow when they stagger in, the sprinkling from above having turned from thick lazy flakes into a whorling haze. Adams, in his hypoxic stupor, comes in piggybacked on Pasang's shoulders and hips in a Swiss-style seat harness fashioned out of climbing rope, the sahib's long arms and legs lolling out, like a wooden puppet attached to strings. They have stirruped his feet with loops of tubular webbing to keep them from dragging on the ground, but there was nothing they could do about his swaying arms. Pasang stumbles, utterly depleted by his human carry. He loosens the ropes from his shoulders, parks Adams in the snow, and collapses onto his back beside his sahib. "Yo!" Adams says.

The party hurries through a lunch of milky sweet tea along with peanut butter and jelly spread onto chapatis. Vida funnels bite-size lumps into Adams's mouth. Still chewing, Troy lades his pack with juniper brush and turns to head back up to Advanced Camp, where Karma fends for himself in the worsening weather. The others shoulder their loads and head down in the opposite direction to take leave of the ridge, Adams this time rag-dolled onto Mingma's back, the sahib's feet stirruped into loops of frozen rope, his head drooped to one side. Doctor Reddy takes the lead and cuts trail through the deepening drifts, Mingma and his pendulous carry right behind him, Vida and Pasang bringing up the defile. The wind squeals furiously, like tires spinning in the mud. The going is painfully slow, especially moving down through the steeper part of the gully. All cling to the fixed line, gathering to assist Mingma as he piggybacks Adams through the rifts, along the ledges, and on through the crux. When they finally make it down to the Sanctuary they find themselves floundering in a whiteout. Vida takes her glasses off to get her bearings, her corneas needled by lashing snow. Reddy points the way to the left, but Pasang shakes his head and gestures right, shouting to be heard above the wind. Mingma, still shouldering Adams, cries out that he can't go on; they must dig a trench in the snow and make shelter here for the night. The effort of bellowing out the plea leaves the Sherpa unsteady and breathless, Adams's bulk toppling them both over into the snow. They haul Mingma back up to standing, but Adams has slipped out of his harness and begins crawling away on hands and knees. "We have got to move!" Vida shouts. "We have no shovels to dig in with. We will freeze if we stop. We will die here!" They get Adams to his feet and Reddy short-ropes him, tethering him to his side with a bight of rope girth-hitched to the harnesses. He will drag him behind on the ground if need be, but Adams stays upright and staggers along.

Base Camp is very close. It has to be, they agree. They call out in unison, hoping those porters left back to tend home camp will hear them. But nothing. They call out again. Again the wind mutes their cries. They stagger on in cycloning snow, roped together, wandering in circles with the wind driving them off any course they try to keep to, the drifts beneath their feet whiffling like sheeting. No one admits to being lost, no one dares say the word, if even they could be heard, though the worry is palpable in each of their terrified hearts.

Vida is ready to scream out, giving herself over to panic. She opens her mouth and is suddenly choked by the drowning snow, and in a great fit of coughing and a breach in the mist, the red specks of the tents appear. "There!" she cries out, letting go a last burst of cough.

Two thousand feet above the others, Professor Troy moves out onto an immense blank page, and faces the storm alone. The weather obliterates landscape, abolishes sky, blots the world out entirely. Even his feet he cannot see. There is a frozen echoing in his head, as if a voice other than his were speaking inside him. A voice he knows is nothing but his crazed thoughts repeating as he grapples on. He thinks about his daughter high up on the rib of Camp I. He leans into the flogging wind and blames himself. He blames everyone else. He curses those whose foolish creed is the might of science, those convinced that human power can conquer nature. What is it but vanity? Just as his vanity has put him here, and put his daughter at risk on a blizzard-plundered cliff above. All for the sake of a name she has been named. A name that could lay claim to her life, a thought he had dismissed in the past. For didn't he reason the odds of her demise were no greater than any other life when up on a mountain? But now his conclusion seems only a denial, his logic weak. His anger takes on vigor and heat as he pushes ahead, fueling him through a lashing of ice specks stinging like sandblast. The only power now is in his doggedness, his mindedness, his drive. Ignore cold, ignore pain, this the only means of winning. His frozen lips refuse the words, but he hears the speaker speaking. Then he realizes the voice is not within, but is coming from outside, from behind. Someone follows. Troy stops, turns, lifts the goggles from his eyes. He looks into a dizzying white nothingness. He waits. He calls out. His hands and feet ache in the cold. Go on. He moves ahead. Several times he pauses to glance back, hearing the boot-steps of another, hearing a voice not his. And each time he sees the same oblivion of unbroken snowfall. He hears only the voice of a razory wind.

By the time he makes it back to Advanced Camp the tents are turned Eskimo houses of snow. He finds the sirdar Sherpa trying to knock the accumulation off the tarpaulin over the makeshift kitchen, causing slabs of it to carom off in bunches of minor avalanches. Troy shouts orders out. "Karma! No use. Loosen the guylines. Drop the poles. Tarpaulin the provisions. Weight the tarp. Plant the ice axes in." They work together quickly. Troy knocks snow off one of the tents and climbs inside. He pulls his boots off, his socks, sees his feet turned a marbled white. He kneads the few toes that remain to him. He pummels his feet. He smacks and pinches them. Karma brings a flask of hot tea to the sahib and offers to help bring life back to his numbed limbs. "Go," Troy says. "Take care of the other tent. Dig it out and get in and do your best to keep from being blown away or buried alive in it."

They huddle each in his separate tent, burrowing deep into their sleeping bags, layered in all their garb. It is hopeless trying to communicate between the two shelters, the fabric slapping furious in the wind. The gale is so strong at times Troy has to brace his back against the poles of the windward side of the tent to keep the aluminum from bending any more than it already has. He knows Karma does the same. They can only hope to God about the seaming.

There comes a pause in the night when the wind finally begins to diminish. Troy moves away from his post at the wall, the tent making a popping sound in release. He breathes easier, burrows deeper into his feather bag. The wind moves high, tearing across the upper glacier in a loud caterwauling. Sara. Dear God, Sara. Again he tries the radio, and this time a voice comes through—the words abraded and incomplete, but, yes, still a voice, a small voice, and yes, it is his Sara. "Camp One, do you read?" Troy says. "Camp One, Camp One. Please do you read? Come in, Sara. Sara?" He thumps the radio against the shell of his backpack, thwacks it again and again, but the thing is lifeless and cannot be revived. "Batteries," he says to no one listening. "Goddammit the goddamn batteries." He curses the device again, flings it. He slips back down into his down bag, cinching himself up to the chin. Closes his eyes. Hears the scratchy voice of his daughter. Tries to keep the dark thoughts away. Hold on to the voice. Troy thinks in directives, in decrees. He tells himself, yes, he will rest, but for only two hours. Two hours will be enough. Then he will pack up and start out for Camp I. The monsoon should subside tonight. The storm cannot go on much longer. He begins finally to slip off into sleep. Until the wind bucks up violently, this time creeping beneath the tent and tossing him about like a drowning man in an angry sea.

For forty-eight hours all on the mountain remain in a constant state of shoveling and scraping and digging out. For forty-eight hours, wind and snow drum at the tents, synthetic walls groan in strain, poles creak and warp at the contort. For forty-eight hours they prevail, havened in down bags, laboring to keep the snow-laden walls off their heads and their faces, staving away the weight of the downfall to keep themselves from suffocating, struggling all the while to keep their minds on happier times past or more pleasant days ahead, as the wind carries on in a satanic ear-piercing litany.

THE LIGHT was flat and weird as Wilder walked along the narrow span of Adams' Rib, making it difficult to tell what was up from what was down. The space around him seemed to expand and contract, ripple and stretch, the colorless light of land and sky become one. The rib was the singular route north that lay safe track to the upper mountain, and there could be no getting lost on it, instead only a perilous fall to the bottom if he should slip, for the crest was spectacularly exposed on both sides. He anchored one end of the rope and began to move ahead, hacking away warily at the soft snow with his ice axe, trying to find solidity before taking the next step, his balance shaky with the bulk he bore on his back. There were places where he would plant his ice axe and it would be swallowed up to the hilt, and every few yards he would strike a piece of cornice only to watch it fall into the horrible void below. He had to detour closer to the brink and the sheer cliff beneath, death only an inch or two away from the edge of his boot. He planted wands along the way, but there was no place to put in a second anchor to fix the line. He had to put his mind on his footing, to the sensation there, working to find the pressure points right under the balls of the feet, his eyes fixed on a single point ahead, like a funambulist would do it. He felt no fear, for to admit to himself that he was scared would be to admit it to his brother. He was never more conscious of his brother's presence as he was now, and this made Wilder think sharply and it made him want to carry on. He refused to look down. Forward was the only choice.

The arête tapered, becoming so narrow he considered sitting astride the ridge à cheval as if riding a hoofed animal and scooting himself across. But the technique would be painfully slow, and he did not want to freeze his hands and feet. So he sucked in a breath and let the breath out, moving lightly across the snowy high-wire, eyes fixed once again on a single spot ahead of him. And then he found himself past the crux. He planted his ice axe into solid firn, and here he drove in a dead-man and fixed the other end of the line. A strange fascination with danger drove him on.

A death wish? No, just the opposite. How can you climb a mountain if you're dead?

The boil of clouds from the valley darkened as they rose overhead, and with a shrug of the peak's shoulders they let go their keep of snow. He crossed over a rickety ice bridge that brought him to a cascade of seracs at the base of the high glacier. He maneuvered through until the slope began to open up, planting stakes and pickets along the way. The snow was falling fast and thick. He knew he could not get back across to Camp I in a whiteout.

His goggles were fogging up bad, and when he took them off to try to wipe them clean the wind blustered stinging snow into his eyes. He struggled to get the goggles back on, and then he had to take his gloves off to tie the hood of his anorak tight about his head and chin, his fingers useless in the cold. He knew he could go no farther. He was wandering in a god-damned monsoon blizzard is what was happening. He needed to find a place to bivouac quick. There was no level spot for the tent, and he carried no snow shovel. He had to use his boots to push the snow off to the side, and he flattened the ground out by stamping it down. What a breathless ordeal a simple task could be this high up. It took him a long time to level out a site with the snow bombing down and the wind lashing him. Gusts kept lifting the tent as he tried to pitch it, and he clung to the fabric to keep the thing from blowing off the mountain. He would die without it. He might even die with it.

He struggled, but finally he got the tent poles aligned and into the sleevings. He brushed the snow off his pack and tossed it into the tent to weigh the shelter down. Then he collapsed inside, his boots protruding out the door flap, the wind mewling down the slopes. His chest hurt from his cough, and his throat felt as if someone had taken a cheese grater to it. He was exhausted, wanted only to sleep. He began to doze off. Snow beat against the tent like bursts of little firecrackers. He opened his eyes, hearing his brother telling him to sit up and get your damn boots off and bring them inside before they freeze on you. Then you need to start up the stove and get snow melting. Without drinking you die, man. You die.

The hero keeps no covenant, except with death. Who said this? No answer. Wilder sat up and did what he had to do, his teeth chattering like castanets. He took the gas stove out of his pack, the small aluminum pot, the plastic bag of matches. Crawled out of the tent and filled the pot with snow. Got back inside the tent, took his boots off, lit the stove. As he did all this he talked softly. Imagine if he were without his brother's company. Imagine how lonely it would be. Lucas's very absence had brought him back close again.

The snow melted to less than a cup of water. Hardly anything. He drank it lukewarm out of the pot, and then he put his boots on and went back outside, this time taking with him a large plastic sack from out of the bottom of his backpack. He filled the sack with snow, returned to the tent, started melting more snow. He drank tepid tea, though he didn't feel thirsty. He ate bites of cheese, though he wasn't hungry. Not to sleep until you have had enough to drink and eat, he told himself, or was it his brother telling him now? Either way, he knew this was right. He drank and kept talking with Lucas and this kept him going. He talked about the words for snow, about why there's so few words for snow in English when the Eskimos are known to have so many. Yeah, but always a prefix or a suffix or a modifier or qualifier or whatever the hell you call it is attached to the root of the word. Really, they only have the root word *snow*, same as we do. So big deal, you've got your falling-snow and your slushy-snow and your fluffy-snow. And then you've got your yesterday-snow versus your tomorrow-snow, and your remembered-snow versus your forgotten-snow. Then there's your snow-with-husky-piss-in-it as opposed to your clean-snow for making the daiquiris to drink along with your horse ovaries. Wilder laughed and this got his cough going again. Don't make me laugh, man. But now there's too much snow on the tent again. This is snow-coming-at-us-from-every-direction-snow. This is snow-that-won't-stop. This is snow-a-person-might-die-in. Get out and dig, man. Melt more snow. Because that stupid piece of orgonite in your pocket isn't gonna do it for you, man. It's as useless as those ashes you carry with you. Brother, what kind of superstitious bug got into you anyway? Just go on and melt more friggin' snow.

DEVIN WAS trying to describe to her his feelings the first time he saw her. He talked about her appearing out of nowhere, described how the blossoms were coming down snowing pink all around her, and how the petals were caught in her hair like a flowery tiara or something. He told her he was carried away by her at first sight. He was still carried away, he said. Would always be. She had lifted him up and was taking him higher. "Up into the heavens," he said. Sara laughed. He hoped she laughed out of shyness and not because he sounded like any other fool trying to talk about love.

A heavy sky came down on Adams' Rib. The sky looked like it was filled with tiny white butterflies, is how Sara described it. She and Devin stayed inside and slapped the walls of the tent to keep the pileup off. All day it snowed, and they stayed nestled inside a sleeping bag. All day they made love and melted snow, made love and melted snow. They drank and they ate and they slept and they talked and they made love again. The falling snow muted all sounds but for their own. Remote avalanches came and went in fitful vibrato.

He told her of the callings he had lately, and about the man he hoped one day he might be. He had been thinking of studying engineering, either that or going into computer sciences, as this was the way the world was heading. They were launched into the eighties now, and before they knew it they'd be nearing the millennium. Imagine that. Imagine they would reach the millennium together, he said, and from there go on for years together, he and Sara, just as they would reach the summit of Mysterium together.

The snow fell harder and it was no longer enough to knock it off the tent from the inside. Every thirty or forty minutes Devin got out and took big armfuls of powder off their portable home. He brushed the flakes off his coat and shook his hat and crawled back inside, careful not to bring snow back in with him, but always there was some that got in. Sara swept as much as she could out with her gloved hands. Still their feather bags were getting wet, their clothes too. It got dark and the temperature dropped and the cold began to inflict itself. But when Reddy called up on the radio from down at Base Camp, Sara and Devin had no complaints. They told him they had enough food and plenty of snow to melt. They could barely hear through the faulty broadcast.

"We are fine," Sara said.

She handed the receiver to Devin.

"Wilder?" he said. "Left—morning—copy?"

A blast of static.

"He—down—Advanced—no?"

"No transmiss—Ad—Camp."

Loud crackle and hiss of lost words.

"—Kilo."

"—out."

"He wouldn't have tried to go up to the east ridge alone, would he?" Sara said. "He would have seen the storm coming and gone down to Advanced. Right?" She looked into Devin's eyes for an answer. She put a hand to her face.

THE INTERCELLULAR spaces of Adams's brain had returned to equilibrium down in the oxygen-saturated oasis of the Sanctuary, and he got his wits back again. His face was changed from greenish and bristled to roseate and clean-shaven, his comportment and speech returned to pedigree and idiosyncrasy, with all its oddities and quiddities. He sat with the others around the table in the mess tent taking in the faint warmth and humidity of shared breath, their tabernacle seeming luxurious with space and food and light. Outside the tent, the mountain forged weather over her cold dells and down her icy hollows and slopes. The sahibs chewed on strips of jerky, gulped wads of it down with cups of soup, followed the meal with jello wedges swallowed cold. All the while the gale howled outside. The wind gusted up in boisterous outbursts, rattling and sucking at their shelter like someone with a cudgel rustling animals out of their lair.

Mingma poured ginger tea. "For calm the stomach," he said.

Vida held on to the hot cup with both hands. She was wide-eyed and fidgety, overcome with nervous questions about death by means of freezing.

"Be aware of early signs," the doctor said. "Violent shivering, for example."

Mingma filled cups, muttering in agreement.

"Or when fingers are no longer able to lace boots or button buttons," Reddy said.

Vida stuffed her hands deep into the pockets of her parka.

"When one loses a pair of gloves because they have dropped from one's frozen claws and are blown off a cliff," Adams said. "Not a good omen."

"Frostbite, yes, but this is still in the category of mild to moderate symptoms of low body temperature," Reddy said. "More serious indicators are lack of proper attentiveness, poor decision-making, carelessness, simple remiss. For example, failure to properly tie a knot or clip into a safety harness, or deciding to abandon a knapsack rather than heft the weight of it."

"Or a veritable desire to lie down and fall into a deep slumber," said Adams. "A wish for a siwash in the snow. A symptom most serious."

Vida looked at him, still concerned about his cognitive abilities. "Siwash?"

"Siwash," he said. "To camp without a tent."

"Torpidity is a common symptom," Reddy said. "Quite common. Soon after, one enters a profound state of hypothermia."

"What then?" said Vida. A morbid interest had come over her. She wanted to hear about visions, final thoughts. She wanted to hear last words, regrets, about what spilled out of the body when all has ceased to be.

"Shivering stops," said Reddy. "Heart rate declines, as does respiratory rate, limbs begin to stiffen, the skin pales, pupils dilate. One becomes increasingly numb, fortunately, before drifting off into a peaceful oblivion."

"There may be hallucinations at the late stage," said Adams.

"Before the pumping of the ventricles stops," said Reddy.

Vida's heart took off in a run. "That avalanche sounds close."

"Not avalanche," Reddy said. "That," he said, "that is thunder." He looked toward the tent door, as if he expected someone to walk in.

"Prepare for a long night," Adams said. "I myself shall begin now." He excused himself, and rose from the table. "The Sherpas may join me in my tent, where we shall cushion one another in plump columns of down until morning. Please fill a flask with your healing gingery tea, Mingma. Pasang, you might go ahead and light the shelter and fluff things up for us as you hum us one of your tunes."

"Porters will manage all right for themselves?" Reddy said.

"Yes, Sahib." Mingma touched his chest in a customary manner.

"They come for help only before someone should die," Pasang said.

Vida looked to see if the Sherpa was joking, but saw no smile. Now she wondered about Wilder again, where was he, which camp was he at, who would be with him.

"We better start settling in, Mrs. Carson, before the thunder brings lightning with it," Reddy said. He filled a flask of tea, dug into a crate of rations and brought forth a small bottle of brandy. The wind picked up, wailing like a female in some ancient death proclaim.

Vida followed Reddy into the night, the wind doing its frightful impersonations. She could feel it working its way into her body, the cold of it, the emptiness of it. It made her feel remote from herself, as if something inside her had broken apart and slipped out when she wasn't paying attention. Lightning sheeted the sky, the ironmongery left out in the snow flaring up in a mystical violet fire. Reddy opened the tent flap. He beamed the headlamp on Vida, and she shielded her eyes. He helped her get her boots off. Then he shucked his, and they climbed into the tent and slid into their down sleeping sacks in all their wintry apparel. Vida lay back and closed her eyes to the dark underside of her eyelids. "I've never been up this high in a bad storm," she said. "And we're not as high up as the others are right now. What it must be like for them. They must be afraid," she said. "I'm afraid."

"It takes courage to admit you're afraid," said Reddy. He put a hand to her shoulder. "But not to worry, the others know to dig in and wait the storm out. They're equipped. They will be all right."

"All right," she said.

"I have an idea," he said. "You might help me complete a list I'm working on lately. A list on the use of safety pins in wilderness settings."

She raised herself up onto her elbows. "You kidding?"

"No, I am quite serious. Here, have some tea."

She sat up. "Everyone knows what to do with a safety pin."

"Ha!" Reddy put a finger into the air. "But to be truly resourceful."

Vida smiled the smile that had first caught Reddy's eyes. It pleased her to see how he again warmed to it. She felt triggered by an impulse to talk about what was, what had been between them. Take her mind away from here. But to talk about what had been would be to tell an ordinary story, a story of adultery and desire, illusion, wish, a story old as any story there is. The talk would be romantic, saccharine, cliché, for neither of them had the power of language and speech to make the tale otherwise. To speak of the intrigue, to attempt to recall the passion between them, to put a name to the feelings, would be to strip away the significance of whatever they might have had, just as it would take everything away that might still be left. And she knew that he knew this too.

"A safety pin can be used to prick the blister of sappiness," she said.

Reddy slapped at the tent walls to knock the snow free. The wind smote back at the tent. Vida's wild eye grew wilder. "Don't worry," Reddy said. He hit at the tent walls again. "I will at intervals go out and dig us out, all night long, I promise. Here, drink." He opened the bottle, sniffed, poured, took a swig. "I have sleeping pills if you wish."

"Yes, I wish," she said. She watched Reddy pilfer through his duffel, seeing the elegance in his movement and his manner that had caught her in the beginning.

"Do you ever think about your wife?" she said.

He paused, raised his head. "Yes, I think about her all the time."

"That's nice," she said. "It's a good thing." She thought to tell Reddy about her decision to leave Wilder, but didn't.

"Here, have one of these."

She opened her palm, and in it he placed a glossy red capsule. She recalled the wild raspberries she had picked and touched to Reddy's lips, already a year ago now. She wondered if he thought of this too.

"Here," he said, touching her cup with his cup. "Drink up."

She popped the capsule into her mouth, swallowed the rest of the spirits, and lay back on her back. Thunder racketed out in the wild beyond in a shattering-of-metal sound. Vida felt the heave and quake of it in the ramparts of her heart. She pulled the hood of the down bag over her head. She waited for sleep to take her.

AS SOON as the sun breaks through the clouds Devin takes his binoculars out and scans the base of the north flank. Right away he spots it; the yellow tent set below a wall of icy spires. He puts all his layers on, packs his pack up, steps into his boots, and crawls out of the tent. He laces the gaiters, grabs the ice axe. He tells Sara to stay put where she is. "Unless someone should come up to get you," he says. She nods, squinting in the radiant light, her head poking through the folds of the opening. She imagines herself to be Eve born to the world today. *J'arrive!*

Mysterium shines like an iridescent pearl. All about her an ocean of snowpeaks swell up like foamy breakers. A gentle wind lifts layers of icy spicules that feather off into the air, air that is deathly close to Devin's feet. He looks out along the long white plume, seeing not a single boot track. Then out ahead the first wand beckons. He wades into knee-deep snow until he is just past the wand, and here he plumbs a hand into the depths of the powdery drift until his thumb snags the buried line. "Good going, Wilder."

He clips into the rope and stands tall, hammered by a sudden happiness he can barely explain. Something about the day, the beauty of it, the enormity of it, has to be, and just the quality of the light, the incredible light all about him, standing alone where he is in this incredible otherworldly light, with the girl he loves so very much safe and waiting for him behind, and a friend in need of him ahead. He is overwhelmed with a sense of belonging, belonging to a place that fits to the person he is. Belonging to a place, and belonging to someone he chose and who chose him, someone not his mother or his father, though he felt he never really belonged to his father, for the simple reason that his father had failed to claim him. He suddenly feels pity for the old, lonely man. Devin knows that he now belongs to something greater, something more sovereign. He feels a delicious freedom, wherever it comes from, whatever, whoever, place or woman or both, mixed in with it too the euphoria of altitude.

He slides his carabiner along the static line and trods the arête in the fresh downfall, avoiding the horrifying cornices, breaking trail, troughing a straight line through the snow, packing it down solid beneath his feet. The way back will be easier, and crossed enough times the crest will become a good firm sidewalk to have to travel over, even if it's a mighty narrow one.

He moves along cautiously, until he is off the rib and onto the base of the glacier. The snow is the texture of styrofoam, bunging up his crampons, and a thick mist begins to settle in, distorting breath and width and distance. He collides with a hummock he takes for a hollow and is working to get his bearings when the earth is suddenly giving way beneath him, sucking him in like quicksand, restraining him up to the waist. He flails his arms about, but the snow drawing him in is like the jaws of a giant fish. And like that, he is swallowed.

People say such a thing will happen in slow motion, but there is nothing drawn out about the fall. It is more like being momentarily outside the body; Devin watching himself plunging into the depths of the crevasse. He was up there, and now he is down here, his consciousness not caught up to the action. He realizes his backpack, wedged into the breach, has stopped him from plummeting into the endless darkness beneath him.

His feet hang into the fathomless cavity. His ice axe dangles from the sling on his wrist. He is buried in a deathly hush, in the coldest darkness he has ever known. He cries Sara's name.

He imagines her outside the tent melting snow for tea, antici-
pating his return, and he feels overcome by a profound regret at
missing the tea and the warmth that is waiting for him, missing all and everything more that is Sara and the life to be had
with her. He feels foolish, punished. He thinks of his mother.
He wonders, why me again?

He touches the pouch of his anorak, reaches into it gingerly
as a thief picking someone's pocket, withdraws his headlamp.
He thumbs a switch and lights up sea-green walls of ice. An
ominous tinkling of frozen splintering drops into the depths
below. That this is it, the end of his story, that he will be held
forever in this frigid prison is a thought that skitters through
his mind like a tiny mouse frantic to get out. He realizes he has
lost his hat, and the sweat of his terror has frozen his hair into
a helmet. Fright needles along his spine, bores the cold deeper
into his bones. He screams out a loud help, a drawn-out wail
for as long as his lungs will hold. But his cry is absorbed by
walls of solid ice; soundless as that in a terrible dream. He looks
up to the silent sky hole of light overhead. How far away, he
can't really tell. What does it matter? There is only one thing to
think about—how to move up and get out. He shines the headlamp over the chined walls, sees a narrow shelf above, an edge
he could pinch with his fingers, and there, up there near a ledge
along the wall, a place he could get a purchase on with the stick
of his crampons. He has to stay calm. He has to think lightness
into his body. He has to know that he will get out. He sees
himself doing it. He takes his gloves off, pouches them in his
anorak. He lets the ice axe hang loose from the strap on his wrist
as he gropes at the narrow chinks in the wall and inches himself
up, fingers crimped, feet planted flat, his back bowed like a cat.
He manages to get his legs into a V, spiking his crampons into
opposing walls, waggling his body back and forth, pulling up

with his arms, his metal footwear like lobster claws barbed into the ice.

The ledge is near his face now, and he raises his leg high enough to get his foot onto the thin platform, pushing off and muscling his entire body up, drawing nearer to the opening. He reaches up to the lip of the fissure, fixing a knee out on the edge of it, using his arms to drag himself out of the hatchway, and like this, he pulls himself up over the verge and on out of the crevasse. Daylight pours down over his head like a mother's kisses.

THE SILENCE outside is immense. She has never known such pure quiet, the mountain softened and muted by new-fallen snow. She would listen for the voice of her mother in the wind, if there were any wind at all to hear. But she feels her mother's presence all about in the caress of weather gowned down upon the mountain. Sara lies listening to her heart pulsing through the fleecing of her makeshift pillow. She senses the other heart inside her beating too. A tiny heart, just a translucent sac of throbbing tissue, a pink sheathed bud, yet to be looping and roomed, but a heart it is.

She would tell Devin on their way down the mountain, adding to their rejoice at having made it to the summit together, happiness compounding happiness to come. One thing at a time. Then they would tell her father. "A grandfather, can you imagine?" she will say. She sees a look on his face.

She puts her head outside the tent, inhaling the day like a vapor. She surveys the terrain to see how far Devin has gotten along the crest, but a thick mist has settled. It is impossible now to tell mountain from sky. An elemental light filters in through the tent walls, hollowing out the amnion space that contains her.

She takes the pot from the stove, holds it out the tent flap, and fills it with snow. She lights the stove in the vestibule, waits for the water to heat, warming her hands on the warm flesh of her abdomen. Then she takes out of her backpack the small sketchpad, opens it to a sheet white and blank as that which circumscribes the day outside.

I am Eve, day one.

What do I see?

How might I tell you?

She begins to fill the page, conjuring images cached within memory. She envisions the mountain, the massif that enfolds her. She draws the nose-like buttress, sketches out the sloping shoulders, penciling in the earthy ribs and spines, the nipples of rocks, the icy teeth and clefts, the tongues and lobes and toe slopes, the fingers, the thumbs. She skulls a dome of cold sky above. She fosters the drawing until her fingers begin to grow cold and numb, until she has to stop and massage her hands to bring them to life again. She puts her mittens back on and studies the lifeless sketch she has made, the lines seeming but a heap of unimportant particulars, a meager attempt to portray the mountain as it most certainly is: an ideal of the purely vertical, in all its strangeness, in all its wondrous is-ness and significance. How to bring forth such meaning? How to escape the rut of what is ordinarily seen? Eve, day one, would not be working from any memory. So, you are no Eve. She believes she may be learning a little humility.

She warms her hands on a cup of tea. She will pick the pencils up, try again, even if the goal seems unachievable, not because of any technique lacking. She knows the wonder of what she wishes to depict belongs solely to another order, a realm beyond that only the rare artist might capture and achieve. Just as it is impossible to conquer a mountain by simply standing at the top of it, so she understands that the mystery of what might be seen cannot so easily be gotten by any kind of rendering.

Maybe impossible, but always it is necessary to try, for only in the trying is one carried away into the wilderness of the unfathomable, and in this way drawn closer to the all-ness of the very thing itself.

She could never explain to anyone these conclusions of hers very well, explain how the whole of what mattered was to see and to speak what truly is, or try to anyway, if only to keep realizing the falsity of the line or the shape or the word conceived. Try to say what can't be said. Only by knowing what is false can anyone get closer to the truth. This she would say most certainly.

DEVIN CARVES a path through the deep snow by porpoising himself through it, finning himself up and forward with his arms, spouting steam from his mouth as he moves along. Wilder doesn't hear anyone coming, thinking it might be a hallucination when he looks out and sees someone appear through the mist. But, no, it's not an illusion, it's Devin he sees, though the name he shouts out is not his friend's name, but his brother's. "Lucas!" Wilder tugs his boots on, climbs out of the tent, heads over to Devin, who lies toppled down and is struggling to right himself.

"God, you made it," Wilder says, gasping for air, still weak from the night's ordeal.

"Never so cold," Devin says, his frozen lips barely moving.

"Get up, man. You look pathetic." Wilder offers a hand.

"Yeah, you too."

Wilder's laugh is like broken glass. "Twenty-two thousand feet is supposed to be cold."

Inside the tent Wilder primes the stove, puts a match to the gas. The flame erupts in a welcoming whoosh of reception. "We rest tonight," Wilder says. "Start out early tomorrow."

"Know what I realized at some ridiculous point today?"

"What's it you realized?"

"I came here to impress my father by making the summit."

"No, man, you came here to be with Sara."

"But I still want to prove to my father I can get to the top," Devin says. "No, not prove to him. Beat him. I want to beat him to the summit."

"So what? Old story. You should want to beat him. Here, drink." He fills Devin's cup.

Devin swallows the tea down.

"I have nothing left here to eat," Wilder says.

"Look in my pack."

"Where at?"

"Deep in the bottom there."

Devin leans back, watching his friend rummaging through the backpack. "Ever fall into a crevasse, man?" he says.

PASANG IS roaring in horror even before Reddy has inserted the pliers and vised the molar, but when the doctor gives a hard yank the Sherpa's cries are extracted as fast and final as the tooth is. Vida holds the cup out, and Reddy releases the pincer's grip, the lump of blackened enamel and pulp dropping into the tin with a dull clunk. He pushes a wad of gauze into the Sherpa's mouth. "Bite down," Reddy says. "Keep biting down."

Pasang holds on to his cheek, looks at the doctor suspiciously.

"And do not be sprinkling any more holy rice about," Reddy says. "You are instead to take these pills as directed, and please be done with all the other hooey and such." He hands Pasang two midnight-blue capsules. Now the Sherpa smiles, knowing there is commerce in the palm of his hand.

. . .

ADAMS SITS in the mess tent drinking black tea, writing a letter to his wife. Likely there will be no mail carried down before the expedition leaves, as the few porters remaining are needed for the final haul out. So he will deliver the missive by hand, his testimony meaning no less.

Friday, August 15, 1981

The Sanctuary

My Dearest Hillary,

After 48 horrible hours a severe monsoon storm has finally ceased, and I have since recovered from a most serious case of cerebral edema. Fortunately, my dear, you were not here to worry about me nor see me in the asinine state I was in. Never have I felt more thwarted at having a word in mind, only then to find myself completely unable to bring it forth and release the word from my lips. What a slathering fool I must have appeared. What a fool I had become! I was fed and dressed and cared for like a child. I was hauled about like a load of cargo. I had wits enough to sense the humiliation of my condition, though I was too helpless to do much of anything about it. On the descent my mind and body came to, as it were, though we were by then in the throes of a blizzard, the mountain doing her utmost to shrug all of us off her slopes. Alas, we each endured and shall go on without further ado.

Now at Base Camp I am settled in and breathing voluptuously saturated air that seems teeming with oxygen compared to the heights of the upper camps. My mind is sharp again, my body in tune, and I am truly grateful to be alive and can think only of renewing my fidelity with you, my dearest Hillary. My friend Hilman once claimed the reward of returning from a dangerous climb was the acute awareness of the privilege one had at being allowed to live. Surely, the man was right. Never again should I wander away without you by my side, or shall I say, let you wander away from mine.

There is no need, nor any desire left in me, to stand once again at the summit. What has led me to the realization so late in this game, I intend to soon commit to paper: more of that and later. In any case, my plan now is to abide at Base Camp with Mingma Sherpa and several remaining porters until other party members have achieved their goal of the summit and are returned. Doctor Reddy and Pasang Sherpa have just an hour ago left for Advanced Camp, where they intend to join Professor Troy and Karma Sherpa. From there they make their way up the mountain to join the others: Sara Troy, Devin Reddy, and Wilder Carson, the three now camped at over 21,000 feet and moving higher. Mrs. Carson remains here at Base Camp with Mingma and myself.

The sky is back to a beautiful high-altitude blue, and Mount Sarasvati, as if ashamed of her wayward ways these past days, sits hidden in a delicate mist. May she henceforth comport herself and remain benevolently subdued.

Until soon, my darling, when you shall be once again in my arms!

Your devoted and most uxorious husband,
Ad

WHEN REDDY and Pasang arrive to Advanced they find the camp silent and deserted, the shelters sagged by bent poles and slacked by guylines, tent flaps zipped shut. The fire is cold, the radio without batteries. They spot a note tacked with a sky-hook to a food crate: *Left for Camp I. Bring up more rope along with provisions—S.T.*

Reddy and Pasang search through cartons and barrels,

finding no coils or lines of any length or width. They inspect the entire camp, but still nothing.

"No rope, Sahib."

"What do you mean, no hope?"

"No, Sahib. I say no rope. No rope."

Reddy looks at him.

The next morning the two shoulder their carries and start the hump to Camp I, the sky like frosted glass. They are thick with clothing and fully armored, their faces greased and masked, heads hooded and capped, eyes goggled and wide. They move through the phantasmal three-dimensional terrain like alien explorers on a distant planet. Their loads are heavy, the steep exhausting. They chuff and gasp for breath, lungs sucking at the paltry air, cold suffusing through their boots. They stop to drink but move on quickly before their sweat begins to freeze. The water in their guts swings and slushes about as in buckets. The frozen river of ice below their feet groans and creaks.

They cache their loads at the roping-up place, gathering rations enough and gear enough for the next several days, re-packing their backpacks, clipping into the fixed line to begin their ascent up the steep rib. Reddy takes the lead, and one at a time they jumar up the first pitch. They make the traverse past the rampart of daggered ice, and from here move up and over to the next stretch of vertical. Pasang fixes his stance and waits for the sahib to gain the rim of the crest. Reddy dusts the fresh snow off each hold as he moves along, sending down frosty palls so that Pasang must lower his head to shield his eyes. Reddy reaches up and grabs hold of a large rock, using it for support to haul himself up, when the bowling-ball-size boulder waggles loose. Reddy tries to push it back into the wall, but the rock is heavy and flexes his hand back and tweens free in release. He calls out but the Sherpa looks up just at the moment he should not, and any reaction at all is too late now as the boulder thwacks the man in the chest with a force that knocks the wind out of him completely, throwing him off his feet and straight off the cliff of Adams' Rib. Reddy looks down, sees Pasang hanging twirled at the end of the rope like bait dangling at the end of a line, swinging out into an ocean of space. The Sherpa rights himself and climbs back up the rope, skating and falling, hanging suspended again, then another attempt only to skate and fall and sway, until finally he gets a decent grip and scrabbles his way back up the slippery ice, his life all the while reliant on a tiny ice screw twisted into the skin of a mountain too easily piqued.

When the two are up and over the verge at the top of the rib they find Camp I empty and soundless as a grave. Sara and Troy have gone up the mountain, and Karma has left to descend back to base. But Reddy locates a radio with working batteries inside the otherwise empty tent.

Pasang, bruised and sore, says he will go on no farther. "I am finish," he says. "We have make mountain angry."

"Do not be foolish, Pasang. A mountain has no feelings of any kind."

"There has been jiggy-jiggy for not-married in Sanctuary."

"What do you mean jiggy-jiggy?" Reddy says.

The Sherpa makes a circle with thumb and finger, thrusting a finger of the other hand in and out of the hole. "You and the Memsahib Missus."

"Stop that with your hands."

"I stay here," he says. Pasang crosses his arms over his chest and looks out toward the Sanctuary. He shakes his head. "You allow no more holy rice. You allow no I am sorry to Sarasvati."

Reddy lifts his arms, lets them slap to his sides. "I give up."

"I go home," Pasang says.

"Tomorrow very early we go down to the base of the rib and bring up more loads from the cache," Reddy says. "Stay here if you wish. Go back if you wish. But I will be moving on." He shucks his boots off and climbs into the tent. "The gods," he says. He heaves a breath.

SARA FOLLOWED her father in a balancing act along the ridge, the two umbilicaled to the rope with carabiners, their angular shadows pitched off over the brink of the slope. Troy hacked out tread with his ice axe, and she lengthened her stride to fit the cuts. They walked uplifted with a slight bend in the knees to steady the weight of their shouldered cargo, eyes fixed on each footfall ahead, any fear veered toward the augment of target and heed. Ice axes were leashed to their wrists. Their crampons chewed at the snow.

They breathed and stepped and breathed and stepped, sliding their snap links along the static line. After nearly a mile they came to the rib's terminus, and here they unclipped from the rope and with a leap each launched off the farthermost tip and clambered out onto a high lobe of glacial plateau. They stood amid a throng of tall columns of hoodoo-shaped ice, where deep blue ravines beneath ran akin to the pinnacled ridge. Tendons and swells were embellished and hollowed into snow, and all the sharp edges of the milky landscape were filed away to female by downfall and wind. Mysterium glimmered like a mirror above, capturing every image cast upon her, yet offering no semblance or facade, no persona or clone, no similitude or guise in requite or give otherwise. The only smell was the smell of the cold.

Sara took a mitten off and held a hand out to take the

water bottle from her father, the light glowing through the translucent flesh of her fingers. Her gums showed pink when she smiled. Her nose dripped in the chill. They passed the bottle back and forth and drank, drank until the water was gone and their bellies were swelled. Troy took the camera out of his backpack, and detached it from the leather casing. He stood and looked about, casting his glance far and wide. The sky was a jeweled blue, and wispy cirrus halo'd the sun in a parry of light waves and prism. Light ricocheted sparks off the slope.

"Incredible," he said. "Just incredible. In all my years of climbing, I have seen nothing like this. So savage and superb the mountain is." He turned to face Sara, and she saw herself framed by Mysterium in the mirrored lenses of her father's glacier glasses.

"I feel I belong here," she said. Her voice cracked with sentiment.

"Hypoxic raptures," her father said. "Buck up a bit. But hold that smile," he said. With a click he shuttered the instant in.

What she feels she does not say. She does not say that the mountain is her true and rightful place, just as she does not say that the mountain has title to her as well. The possessed and the possessor, the seer and the spectacle, the subject and the object; are they not but counterpoint, mirrored images of equal value and force, at one level, one and the same? So her father would say if he had spoken the thoughts he had taught her.

Sweat began to freeze into the weave of their underclothing, and goosebumps erupted across their flesh like a sting of pelleting ice. Troy packed up camera and water bottle and strapped himself back into his backpack. They were turned to head up the incline when they heard the loud fracture. They planted their axes and looked back to see a windslab big as a warehouse break from the slope in a lusty pneumatic whump. They watched it slide off into the steep gully below, shivering with laughter as the spectacle unfolded, feeling hysterically joyful, favored and out of danger.

They continued up the high skyline rise, drifts of wind trimming away thin layers of snow from the earth like peeling skin. The icy water of melt channels surged beneath their feet the way blood runs through veins, and strands of waving ice dust blew off from the summit. The universal beauty, the wise silence, the mountain Mysterium, all this Sara took in as the simulacrum of her mother. The mountain was her mother's calmness, her stillness, her fortitude. The skyline ridge was the shape and texture of her mother's shoulder, a shoulder Sara had so often rested her head on. Sweeps of avalanche that ruptured from the cliffs were like instances of her mother's temperament, the tremble and rumble of them like her belly laugh, and all the surrounding whiteness held the goodness and certainty of her mother's intent.

Mother.

Amanda.

Mysterium.

Time past rests in memory.

Memory rests in flesh.

Flesh rests in earth.

Mysterium.

Sarasvati.

Bestowed this name, bestowed this mountain, bestowed this life. "Mother," she said. The wind voiced aeolian, in aria, in hymn.

Through me the way to the top of the mountain.

Through me the way to an infinite paradise.
Through me the way to the eternal One.

"Father," she said.

Sara again saw herself framed in the mirrors of Troy's glacier glasses. She had never felt more complete, never happier than now. Nearly twenty years ago, a mountain had taken the breath of her mother away, had broken her bones, ruptured her lungs and her heart, soaked up her blood. And now a mountain poured forth a milky snowiness and breathed her mother back again, the wind bursting from ribs and rolling off shoulders, the wind intoning in song. Did her father feel this too?

Troy let his daughter take the lead as they moved up toward the scarp to Camp II, their footprints necklacing the slope like a string of pearls in their wake. They made their way through a chaos of seracs, and then on into a maze of ledges that zigzagged up the mountain, the snow glittering like tinsel in the sun. Little snowspouts gusted up around them, dervishing off into the blue. An outburst of current stirred up a whopping bolus of white powder, and in an instant Sara was lost completely within it as if effaced from the earth. Troy looked at the nothingness ahead of him, standing fixed into position, jaw hung loose with sucked-in breath, stunned in wonderment, waiting for his body to cue the next move. He took his glacier glasses off but the glare of the sun pierced like an ice pick, and he had to put them back on before he was blinded. He stood reeling within the incomprehensible, trying to right his sight, ready to cry his daughter's name out, afraid to look down into the depths for what he might see. God, how can this be? She was gone. His breath caught, all his body suddenly numbed. And then in the dazzling luminosity she appeared. She was covered completely in a glint of white crystals, her shimmering backpack pinioned up high behind her shoulders, her smile radiant as all the light that ever was and all the light that could ever be. He gazed at his daughter in wonder, aware of the miracle of her existence, aware of the miracle of his. Oh, how we live in the flicker.

"Father," she said. "What is it?"

"I don't know," he said. "Just the heights. The altitude playing its tricks."

He followed her on through a wintry desertscape, a corrugated sweep of sastrugi, and up they moved onto a snowfield shellac'd and meringue'd with flanks snow-cupped and duned. When the path became too deep Troy took over leading again, breaking new trails through a steepening ramp of waist-deep sugary cumulate. After hours of laborious swimming and kicking, nearly suffocated in altitude and sun, they reached the top of the east ridge and arrived to Camp II, where here they would need to rest and eat and hope to sleep a most delicious sleep, continuing on into the magic that would be there for them the next day.

STILL, WE do not act recklessly, as fear is intrinsic in the will to exist. In this way, nature preserves her species. Yet when a person is able to overcome fear and is possessed with a wave of courage, is it not a case of nature not only preserving, but enhancing her species? For courage, with its surge and outpour of blood from the heart to the arteries, propels one to act boldly, making adventure and conquest possible. These are the men and women whose actions lead the human race, whether in the world of politics or philosophy or exploration. Others, checked by fear, with constitutions more timid or feeble, their blood pooled in the veins, remain ordinary spectators, mere bystanders with cold hands.

. . .

IT IS still the majestic Mysterium he looks up to, but Virgil Adams realizes he no longer sees with the same eyes. How to describe the feeling of desire that in the past so encompassed him? He had once looked up to the mountain with an over-whelming yearning, enticed by the beauty and splendor of what seemed so very far from his reach. It was a yearning that had come to him as a boy when playing in a woods or splash-ing about in the ocean: he could not get enough of the very thing that so immersed him. It was a hunger not to be sated, a desire for something he could not get at and yet he so desper-ately wished to have, more so, overwhelmingly needed. But no matter how far he walked into the forest, or how vigorously he swam in the sea, he could never be close enough to the object at hand. He could not grasp the very thing and make it stay. He could not swallow it and keep it inside him. He would feel the craving for its illimitable beauty in the pit of his stomach, like an ache, or feel it deep in his groin, like a lust, and some-times the sensation moved high into his chest, leaving him wanting and breathless and strangely elated. For the woods and the waters and the peaks were perpetually a forelooking, for-ever a beyond, always an elsewhere though he be held in the very midst of it. What in him had changed?

Twenty-five years ago, he had stood with Hilman at the top of Mount Mysterium trying to take the moment in, so potent the moment was. The experience had been almost too much for the senses. One feeling gave way to another as he beheld the infinite allure of the world in front of him, a perfec-tion and beauty it seemed he finally had come to possess. The mountain had been penetrated. They could walk no higher. They had not so simply, yet somehow, yes, simply: they had arrived. Then all logic was toppled. Like a flip of the coin, an emotional antipodal, their overwhelming joy turned in an instant to the deepest regret. And though he and Hilman later spoke of it, they could not say from where the remorse really came. Perhaps it was hunger and fatigue, as well as the heights and the light-headedness, so they agreed. They allowed any tears to freeze and so desist, and without further delay, they started back down the mountain.

Adams gazes up at Mysterium's summit, he and Hilman since disappeared from it as if what had happened never had been, their feat turned to no more than story, now but a piece of imbued history. He sees no longer a paradise, as he had in his youth. The mountain Sarasvati was heaven for him when he first pursued her. Yet once she accepted him, once he had had her and was betrothed to her, the maiden had thereby lost her charm. For how could she remain heaven if she had stooped so low as to hold him?

The understanding comes over him like a weightlessness.

"Hilman," he says, "you bet, my man, I have got it."

SARA STUMBLES into Camp II behind her father, pulling mittens off with her teeth. She unleashes her wrist from the wrist-sling and lets the ice axe drop with a *thunk* to the snow. Then she unstraps the crampons and kicks them free of her boots, shucks her backpack off, climbs into the tent, and plunges into sleep.

The others remain outside in the unfolding crepuscular light, collecting snow for the stove. They pass around a pair of binoculars as water heats in the pot, each man studying the headwall of rock cliff that fortresses the summit. They search for possible routes upon a rimy crag of pure vertical, a face cracked by overhangs and ossicles of rock; at the buttress's top a skullcap of snow. Devin aims a finger toward a cleaver that spikes sharply out of the névé just at the halfway point, and above this Wilder sights a draw, the long glazed leg of a pathway that leads to the base of an arachnoid mass of perpetual ice and snow. They can only hope for a ledge below the spidery growth that will allow for a traverse, if they are to find a decent ledge there at all. Troy glasses the aprons of ice, the blocks of rock, siting a number of exit cracks higher up that lead to the smooth snowfield that tonsures the bulwark. All three agree that breaching the rampart isn't going to be easy.

So, who ever said it was going to be easy?

In any case, no one is expecting a promenade.

That night, in preparatory drudgery, the foursome gathers rope and webbing, pitons and hammers, extra tent and poles. They melt water for water bottles. They sort through clothing, untangle harnesses, rig safety tethers, adjust crampons. In the morning they will pack in the food and the water and the extra garb. The plan is to be off by daybreak.

It is a long and miserable night for everyone. They are four adults with backpacks packed into a three-man tent, pillared together in columns of down with most of their clothing on. It is the most bone-chilling cold they have so far encountered, but at the very least they need not put boots at the bottom of their sleeping sacks as they usually do, so tightly are they jammed inside the tent. The boots are tucked into the tight spaces between their feather bags where the leather will remain in a state of defrost. But lug soles protrude into hip bones and collarbones, leather shanks poke into tailbones and ribs. Wilder adds to the jabs and spurs with his constant cough, a brassy hacking that pains the others the whole night long. There is a muttering and babble of cursing until dawn, wind thrashing at the tent, spindrift grating like sandpaper against the soft walls. Any sleep is at best spasmodic and modicum, and when it comes at all it carries no more than pieces of broken dreams.

Devin is amazed to find his mother in his arms, all the way up here near the top of the mountain and in the middle of the night. His mother is light as snow. She is hard and cold as ice. Her bones jut out like cleavered rock. Her skin is ash-colored and fissured. Only her eyes are alive, dark wet stones, eyes that prod, eyes that tell him once more to give her more, please give her all of it again. No, there is no more medicine left, he has given it all. And she went to sleep already, didn't she? Finally. Such a deep and final sleep. No, Mother, please do not, please do not plead. But his father is too selfish to do it, too much a coward, isn't he, a man too much in need? Yes, Maggie knows this, you can see it in her imploring eyes. But a person should only have to die once, and Devin cannot do it again. Now he is doing the pleading, but only a pitiful whining comes out of him. It hurts to hold on to her, so sharp and cold are her bones, but he knows not to let go.

It is Wilder who elbows Devin in the ribs and brings him back out of his altitudinous delirium. Or maybe it is a hard boot sole he has rolled into that wakes him, an irritating rubber welt along the backbone. Whatever it is that breaks the dream, he is left in a cold sweat, with the wind keening into the night like a despairing she-demon.

AT FIRST LIGHT they begin the dismal task of melting snow and fixing breakfast in a cramped tent. Tempers reach a boiling point that the water never does, as people struggle to find a lost sock or a glove, only for someone to knock a pot of almost-hot water off the stove and drench the down coats and bags.

There are arguments about space enough, sugar enough, patience enough, manners enough.

"Enough," Sara says. She remains tucked deep into her sleeping bag hoarding warmth, doing her best to stay out of the chaos. She is dressed for the climb since last night, wearing her mother's emerald-colored sweater and the kata around her neck. But she is so drained from the day before that she will not sit up to take breakfast or drink anything. Devin tries to coax her into activity, but she doesn't respond to his cajoles. He hears himself pleading, as he did in the dream. He hears the wailing of the banshee. And then he sees that something is not right.

"I'm staying here with Sara," he says. "We'll take it easy today, go up the buttress and join you guys tomorrow." Devin looks up at Wilder. "You need to get a move on, friend."

Troy puts a hand to his daughter's cheek. "I would love to have you at my side," he says. "But you're tired, I can see. You'll be better with a day's rest."

Troy and Wilder know they have to set out while the weather is good, tackle the buttress, fix the ropes, and install Camp III a thousand feet above, the last establishment on the mountain. No, they are neither one the companion of either's choosing, but they shoulder their burdens and their ropes and pair up.

They look like soldiers strapped with ammo, so racked are they with hardware. The backpacks are heavy, and it is bitter cold. Only cold and howl and snow all around. Rasp and plume of breath. The light paling the sky, illuminating a bald and colorless topography. A wind that staggers. Both know a gale any stronger would send them sailing off to either side of the cliff, down into the darkness of the depths below. To their left the southeast face slips away, disappearing into a murky gray foramen; the northeast flank on the right plummets into an appalling nothing. The knee-deep snow shields them from the temper of Zephyrus as they posthole along, but with heavy loads the labor of breaking trail takes every bit of muscle and heave they can muster. As they near the buttress, the abutment grows so hulking they cannot see the towering summit behind it. It begins to snow. They slog on, stooped and paled like elderly men, their eyebrows and whiskers hoared thick with ice. The wind gusts up and ghosts the snow from their outerclothes, and bodies of vaporous dust spiral out into the gloom. They walk a cold line between heaven and hell, feeling small and armored and insignificant. At midday they arrive to the base of the craggy stanchion. The sun is shrouded in cloud.

Wilder hefts his backpack off, takes from out of it a length of tubular webbing, and with the webbing he swamis himself about the waist. He ties the belt off with a water knot, widens his stance to plant himself firm to the frozen ground. Troy takes hold of the belay line and starts up the bulwark of quartzite and ice, brushing sugared snow off every blocky foothold and handhold, moving fastidiously, placing ice screws and thin blades along the way. Wilder stands shivering, scrutinizing Troy ascending in the steady and classic manner that he does. People climb differently these days, with guys carrying less weight and now practically running up cliff faces. How much more quickly this day would go if Devin were his partner instead, the two friends having trained for speed, their style modern and their method sleek, knowing swiftness to be a necessity on any threatening precipice.

"Slack!" Troy calls down.

The command snaps Wilder back to the here where he is. He pays out more of the rope and watches the professor muscle his way up a chimney, jamming and manteling with his hands, bridging his feet against the ravine's pursed walls, moving without falter or pause. The climbing is demanding and thin, and though the professor is not fast, Wilder cannot help but admire the fluid movement of his performance on this arctic stage. The man's a tiger, he hears his brother Lucas say. A real tough guy, right? Like you, man. Wilder shivers in the cold. A heavy mist settles in from above, and he sees Troy disappear up into the gray haze, becoming just a clinking of ironmongery as he moves higher up, a ghost hauling its chains.

"Climb!"

Wilder moves at the decree. He fixes the jumars and starts up to join Troy, who waits anchored to a ledge. Troy puts his gloves back on and claps his hands together furiously to bring heat, stomping his frozen feet as he waits for Wilder to ascend. It is very cold, and every halt and post a belayer takes is all the colder in the waiting.

They find a boot-width ledge below the névé'd mass they had spotted from below in their binoculars. One at a time they move along hugging the wall, the grainy quartzite bulging rudely out. They lean back and kick steps into the firn and inch their way sideways along the buttress, clinging to flakes in the rock above, the weight of the loads on their shoulders bowing them perilously backward, barrages of spindrift pouring down over them like frosty talcum from above. Past the ledge, Troy moves up an ice-throttled crack, his freezing hands gone nearly numb as he crimps and jams his way up, the teeth of his crampons holding only at the foremost toe points. He grabs the hammer from his sling, drives a bong into the rock, clips a carabiner in, an etrier, and then crampons up to the next step. He sets his stance and once again blows life back into his hands, feeling a grateful tingle and ache as he waits for Wilder to meet up with him again.

A cloud pregnant with malice frees itself from Mysterium's summit and snags at the top of the buttress, peening the air with icy spicules. They are hungry and thirsty, but there is no perch wide enough to sit or plant themselves on now. They have to keep moving, for not to be moving is to be freezing, and to be freezing is to be dying. It is better to fall off a mountain than to freeze on a mountain, so Troy has always believed.

They press on, the buttress never letting up, the weather determined to hunt them down. Despite the hardship, despite the stone slides and snow spray the mountain spites on them, the two move as one, rope length by rope length, steadily gaining altitude, automatons on remote control, both white as spooks and crusted with ice, caught in a blinding meteor of snow.

One last steep pitch of icy rime-covered rock brings them to the rim of the vertical wall where the slope crests off onto an airy snowfield higher up. Troy struggles desperately on this last maneuver, grappling to get a hold of something that isn't powdery soft and falling away. Nothing offers a decent grip to pull up with. The wind whips at him, and snowdrift finds its way into every opening and crease of his clothing. He feels himself beside himself in the struggle, anguished, finished before the finish. He hasn't strength left enough to brush the doomed thoughts away, just as he no longer bothers to brush the snow off his face. There is nothing left in him. He is done in. How can it be? Wilder's calls drift up, words erased by wind. So close. Just rest a minute and gather strength. Stand here a minute and sleep. How wonderful to sleep. Maybe a deathly freezing is not so bad at all.

A loud crack of avalanche sparks like electricity that surges through Troy's body, head to toes. With a burst of whatever it is left inside him he reaches up and feels the chunk of rock that had so cluded him. He tests it, finds it does not mock with any give. Carapaced with equipment, he hefts himself up and swings a leg high, his hands frozen to claws. Like a pincered crustacean he crawls up and over the brink, splayed out prostrate in an ocean of snow.

Wilder starts up the last pitch before the rim, and as he ascends he sees through the flurries the rope stretched across a knife-edge section of rock. He watches the rope stretch and fray over the saw of rock as he moves along, trying with all his might to ease his weight off the line, thinking what a horrible lousy joke, thinking what a spiteful bitch of a mountain this is, thinking all this effort, all this distance, thinking crazy and angry and banal thoughts and all without a moment to be afraid. Then he is up and over the lip and onto the crest, collapsed into the snow next to Troy, thinking holy Christ they have made it.

The cold bites like a ferocious animal. They labor to their feet and push on, bowed over and pathetically slow, paddling through the snow as the powder deepens. They continue up the incline searching for a site wide and level enough to accommodate the tent, finding nothing. What to do? Where to go? Exhausted, they retreat back to the buttress's edge, where they find the depressions their bodies had left in the snow. They chuck their backpacks, reach in for the mess tins, and with cups and plates and hands and feet they begin to level out a space all around. They have come to an altitude of more than seven thousand meters, twenty-four thousand feet, and every one of their efforts threatens to put them over the limit. Their lungs rasp in a metered need for a decently sated breath, their hearts pound like kettledrums. Wilder coughs his hacking cough, feeling the splintering in his ribs.

The fabric whips and luffs. Their frozen hands are clumsy

as clubs as they pole and stake and tame the tent into place. They are dredged in white, featureless creatures swallowed up in the terrain. Clouds slink down the mountain and settle in at the base of the buttress, cloaking everything over. The sun casts a cataracted eye.

They camp at the mountain's throat. After they radio down to Camp II they begin to melt snow. They drink potfuls of warm tea and dine on tinned chicken spread and cold hard candy bars. They discuss the summit, which route to choose. Troy says he wishes to take the most elegant course, traversing the face of the east peak to its top, then getting onto the saddle between it and the main summit, and following this line straight up to Mysterium's apex. But Wilder argues for avoiding the face of the east peak and taking the couloir behind the peak that joins right up to the saddle, in case they're short of rope. Then from there follow the saddle to the main summit.

"The couloir is likely an avalanche trap," Troy says.

"Your way is longer, and more exposed."

"The others will bring up more rope."

"What if the others don't come up?"

"Then we manage the route without it," says Troy.

"In that case no need to take the same line to the top."

"No need, I suppose." Troy pulls the thermos from his pack, pours a capful of tea, offers it to Wilder.

Wilder wags a hand at the offering. "Thanks anyway."

"You had the worst of it today," Troy says. "I kicked a mess of ice and rock down on your head with every one of my boot-steps, not to mention the near miss of the teeth of my crampons aimed right at your face when I slipped. You handled it like a pro."

"I don't need pats on the back." He works to stifle a cough.

"Have it your way." Troy swallows the capful of tea down.

Wilder lets out a rhonchus cough. "Listen," he says. "There's a frazzled piece of rope on the last pitch before the snowfield."

"Will it hold a rappel?"

"I don't know. I could see the white core showing through."

"So we'll have to double the rope."

"With what?"

"The others will bring up another rope and we'll double it."

"What if they don't?"

"Then we'll fix it on the way down. There's a trick."

Wilder fidgets with a glove. "You should know that I'm why we won't have enough rope." He slaps the glove to a knee.

"You're why what?"

"Devin and I thought to lighten the loads up in Delhi."

Troy looks at him. "I don't want to hear this."

"I know Devin won't have any more rope to bring up."

Troy grabs the glove out of Wilder's hand, tosses it against the wall of the tent.

"If we had moved up this mountain faster," Wilder says.

"You've said enough," Troy says. He lies back, closes his eyes.

"What's your trick to fix the rope?"

Troy rolls to his side, facing away.

Wilder switches off his headlamp and zips himself up to the chin. They sleep, or try to sleep, drowsing in and out of an uneven alpha state, a kind of twilight condition between wakefulness and slumber. Even exhaustion does not adjourn consciousness. Call this spell of hours repose. Call it rest. Call it drift. Drift at an altitude hostile to human life, to any life. Their warm breath crystallizes the opening of their sleeping bags with hoarfrost. Their bodies hum on in a state of rapid decay brought on by a paucity of oxygen, organs in a phase of early mottle and rot, blood darkened and sludged, their dreams veered and halted cold in the unlivable kingdom in which they hope now to sleep.

THE NEW-FALLEN snow had covered over the icy walk along the crest of Adams' Rib. Reddy needed the static line so he could clip in, and digging the rope out of the deep snow there was punishing work. He could have returned to Advanced Camp and demanded that Pasang assist him, but if he did he would have been faced with the task of having to furnish some sort of apology to this man of vassaled allegiance. For Reddy knew he had wounded the Sherpa by calling him a fool—what's more, an aboriginal fool—and by doing so had no doubt trod on the man's self-respect. Reddy knew himself incapable of telling the man he was sorry, even though as a physician he had repeated these words over and again to patients and to their loved ones; words spoken in ritual, words said out of training and custom, or perhaps words of vanity meant for himself in his regret at having failed at a task that should have brought him success. But when the utterance is of most account and truly needs to be said, the words catch in the doctor's throat like fish bones.

He is a proud man; too proud, he would admit. Of the seven deadly sins, pride would be his, most certainly. He is hard on himself, you might say. He has no doubt been hard on his son, anyone would say. He has pushed Devin, accused him of ineptitude, of carelessness and foolishness. The doctor feels helpless to control the outbursts and curses; his faults of temperament, his littleness of mind, perhaps his soul, a soul that cannot be mastered. The flaws and defects in him are now too deeply hewn. He knows he suffers from his own battery when he attacks Devin, a regret he feels after belittling him. And always there is the great remorse from never having been able to love his son enough.

Reddy looked up. Mysterium's pyramid summit was radiantly still, crystalline, without hint of a plume. The air was so transparent it seemed he was just an hour's reach of the mountain's crown. He turned and moved on, his detour of reverie dissolving, though not his regret. He slid the carabiner along the frozen rope.

When the doctor arrived to Camp II he found his son sitting half-in and half-out of the tent, scrutinizing the buttress through the binoculars. Devin glanced his father's way, then he put his eyes back to the glass and the two dark specks spidering upward, watching the higher dark speck vanish into a cloud. The curtain of mist sunk farther down the face of the headwall, and Devin saw the second man disappear; both climbers severed now from the ordeals of the world below.

"How far have they gotten?" Reddy said.

"Over halfway up the buttress already."

"And Sara?"

"Trying to sleep. Her belly hurts her."

Reddy unstrapped his crampons and worked his boots off and crawled inside the tent. Devin moved to follow.

"Where is the pain?" the doctor said.

Sara put a hand to her lower abdomen. "Down here."

"Let's hope it's not your appendix."

"My appendix I've already had out."

"Maybe just inflamed lymph nodes then? Let's examine you." Reddy rubbed his hands together to bring heat, reached beneath layers of wool and down and found the soft flesh of her belly. He pressed gently. She winced.

"She's been dizzy," Devin said. "And she hasn't eaten since

yesterday. When I did get her to eat, it was hardly anything. She vomited. Even liquids she vomited."

"You haven't been drinking, Sara?"

"Can't," she said. "Try, but I can't."

"You are feverish." He took his hand from her cheek and put it to the flesh of her neck, then to her stomach again. "Very feverish."

"It's like bad cramps is what I'm having."

"When did you last have your period, Sara?" Reddy said.

"Before we left home. Only once some spots of blood since."

Reddy opened his backpack and reached into the depths of it, pulled out a canvas medicine pouch. He sorted through the contents of the pouch, brought forth a blister packet of tablets, pressed a tiny tablet through the aluminum seal. "Put this under your tongue," he said. "Let it dissolve. In a short while you should be able to start taking liquids again. And then I will give you a pill for the pain." Sara took the pill, lay back, and closed her eyes. Ice flakes brushed over the skin of the tent, making a soft swishing sound, as if a hand were tenderly stroking it. Devin stretched out beside Sara and put his arms around her. Reddy prepared for an early start the next day, repacking his pack, sorting gear. When Sara fell asleep, father and son were silent, switching their headlamps on as the darkness came on. They started the chore of melting snow and concocting an evening meal. The radio erupted in a pronouncement that ruptured the silence.

Devin grabbed the radio. "Camp Two hearing you loud and clear."

"We made it up the buttress."

"Friggin' knew you guys would do it."

"Camp Three established."

Devin handed the radio to Sara. "Hooray," she said, her voice sounding more feeble than she meant it to be.

"How's my Sara?"

"Fine. Planning to be up there tomorrow with you."

Reddy took the radio. "How is Camp Three?"

"We're perched on the northeast edge. How is Sara?"

"Smiling as usual. Not to worry. How was the buttress?"

"Terrible."

"Will the rest of us manage it?"

"Bring up extra rope," Troy said.

Father and son exchanged glances.

"Glad you're with my girl, Reddy. She'll listen to you. If you don't think she's strong enough for the buttress, tell her not to come up."

"The summit is not everything," Reddy said.

"Right now I cannot Oscar Kilo that."

"Over and out then, my friend." Reddy switched off.

Sara sat up. "I think the pain will go away. It has before."

"How long have you had this pain?"

"Started as a dull ache, and off and on cramping. It changes."

"Do you think you might be pregnant?" said Reddy.

She looked at Devin. Her smile was her answer.

"Sara," he said. He touched her head.

"I'm feeling better already. The pain medicine is helping."

The doctor did not tell her what he was afraid of.

"Tomorrow's my birthday," she said.

She smiled, showing snowy white teeth, a smile too soon dissolving.

HOW TO describe the most beautiful day of one's life.

Start with the light. Start with the sun rising across a sea of nameless peaks. Peaks that color and oscillate in illimitable distance.

Tell of the light. The sublime light. A radiant, delicate light. Elemental. Colorless. Odorless. Rare and arid and cold.

Try to describe.

Mysterium, the primordial mound of earth they are perched on.

You must tell of it.

Her pageantry. Her display. Her wintry polish of snowy masonry within a summer domain. Her palace filled with alabaster pillars. Paled corridors, circlets and vales. A keep of wind-scoured watchtowers. Escarpments corniced in velvety drapes.

Sara would recall it all, tell it all and always.

She had gone outside, overwhelmed by the spectacle of her morning surroundings. She was squatted down onto her haunches taking every bit of the magnificence in, but in an instant was overcome by a stabbing pain. A different pain. She went back to the tent on hands and knees, crawled in, and settled deep into the sleeping bag again. She wanted to tell Devin what she had seen, but was muted by the pain. She would hold it inside until it burst from her, the experience she could not now describe.

"Don't speak," Devin said. He felt a chill, a strange vibe in the ether.

The doctor radio'd up to Troy. He thought it best to let Sara rest another day. Then tomorrow she needed to start down the mountain. She could not remain at this vicious altitude. Troy and Wilder should go ahead to the summit. Get back down here. Accompany your daughter back to Base Camp.

Troy agreed. "Tell Sara we go up today in honor of her birthday."

"She says this is the best gift you can give her," Reddy said.

. . .

UP THE slope a crusader will go until arriving to the pinnacle of the ziggurat, a tower of Babel where there is a name to be made for oneself, believing that once to the summit nothing will again be out of reach. So the mountain becomes an emblem of the ceaseless effort to raise oneself higher, to work a pitch above the last height achieved. But when the last step has been taken, and the zenith reached, he or she finds that it is not the end, not in the least. For the end brings only another beginning. And once again, step-by-step, a person is left to scale the mysterious ladder: the lure that forever shines, a light which leads to the next redeemer. The past is swallowed and forgotten, the coming and becoming is all in the All, the journey a never-ending procession.

SHE SAID, "I'm going to die." And Sarasvati Troy closed her eyes and did. In an instant her face became a testimonial of stillness and peace. But Devin and Reddy would have none of it, this stillness, this peace.

Devin took hold of Sara's shoulders and began to shake her violently. He shouted her name, shouted again and again, but she would not wake up. He put his lips to her lips and blew air into her shrunken lungs. Her chest rose and it fell as he breathed for her, rose and fell, rose and fell; his father pressing down on her breastbone to a silent and metered count. Twenty minutes, thirty minutes, forty or ninety, who knows? Devin knows it was daytime, but he felt it like the longest night of his life, a night that continued to be night, would never stop being night. The world was dark and impalpable. Her lips turned so very cold. Reddy, exhausted, ceased to prod her heart. He shook his head slowly. "Stop," he said.

The wind made the sound of a long and horrible no.

Devin called her to come back. Please come back. He tugged at her clothes, he pulled at her fingers, he pulled at her hair, but she stayed lax as a cloth doll. He slapped at her cold swollen face. He shouted her name. He slapped again and harder, and then his father pulled him away from her. Devin curled into himself, buried his face in his arms. He rubbed at his head. He balled his fists and rubbed at his eyes and he bawled like a child. He wept for Sara and he wept for Sara's father and he wept for himself and he wept for everyone else, wept at her missing out on a world so brimful and significant, wept for the world entirely and now so cold and without her. His cries rustled the tent and rushed out through the door flap, went pouring out across every kettle and drumlin, every dale and fell, through valleys and coulees, through fosse and kame. It surged up into gutters and chimneys and ravines, the way blood runs through the veins, loosening footwalls and breaking cornices free, before it went seeping into the folds and the cleavers of all the sentinel peaks. The sobbing was caught up in a burst of wind and was swept up to Mysterium's tremoring heights, where Sara's father would stand at the summit and feel it like the deepest quiver and chill, as if someone had just stepped across his grave. He would grow weightless, feel himself lifted up and into the expanse, all the sorrow from below moved past and out into the vastness of the swirl and the pulse beyond, in boundless time and boundless space, a lament become requiem.

ON AUGUST 17, twenty-five years to the day after the first successful ascent of Mount Sarasvati, Stuart M. Troy and Walter "Wilder" Carson exit the tent to make their way up to the summit, intending to stand in the vanished footprints of Adams and Hilman. They set out confident of good weather ahead, the firmament so clotted and awash with planets and galaxies that it seems some great hand has tried to scrub the great soffit of all its darkness. Over the distant plateaus of Tibet silhou-ettes of cumulus dendrite the horizon with a spread of red ves-sels, the storm moving farther away and off into China. They walk without headlamps needed to beam the way, the slopes polished bright in the light of full moon. Vortices of wind lift sheets of the crusty covering. The air is deathly thin, less than a sigh beside the sea.

Their packs are packed with bottles of water, bars of choc-olate, altimeters and cameras, an added pair of socks for each; the colorful bandanna a daughter's bestowal, the extra weight a brother's remains. They wear all the clothing they have brought along. Their boots are stiff as wood blocks, their gaiters rigid tubes in the freeze. The cold eats at their feet. It gnaws at their faces. They pause to rest and take more breath, stomping about in place, working to keep blood moving.

They continue up along the dark verge, the crusty snow turning soft and deep to the waist, taking turns at the labor of breaking tracks in the bottomless stuff they walk across. They have said nothing since leaving the tent, and when they stop to swap places no talk is traded between them. Together they move on, aimed in common enterprise, lost and separate in thought, their wakened lives seeming brinked on dream, as dream is carried into wakening.

Three hours later they arrive to the base of the east summit. Light begins to pale the sky, revealing a dramatic curvature of earth. Snowdrift banners off the top of the main summit above, a corona seeming within arm's reach, but both know the moun-tain's deceptions.

Wilder is the first to break the silence between them. "No two people climb at the same rhythm. Trying only interferes with a person's energy flow," he says. "We all know this. And I'm for taking the quicker route."

"You don't know what you'll find there," Troy says.

"Your way, neither do you," Wilder says.

Troy laughs a raspy laugh. "We will see," he says. He extends a hand and Wilder reaches out and does the same, knocking each a gloved fist one to the other. Then Wilder turns away and plods on, white as a waxen effigy. Troy watches him until he rounds a bollard of rock, and then he is gone.

Once he knows he is out of sight, Wilder stops to rest and catch his breath. It hurts to breathe now. He thinks the coughing has torn cartilage, probably even splintered some ribs. He staggers forward, stopping to take breath after every five steps of the way. How easy it would be to die of exhaustion. Death the only covenant, he hears his brother say. It is a fight not to give in. Breathing takes every bit of effort, especially effort to think. He lifts his head and looks out to sky turned a soft glowing blue, the blue of a great cosmic energy. It is a sight that revives him. He breathes, seeing he is filled with this intangible, immeasurable, life-giving energy and blue light. Volts of impulse like an electric current course through his body. He pushes forward, fracturing the blockages. He knows he must pace himself evenly. He reminds himself to drink.

He stops, takes his backpack off, and sets it at his feet on the slope. The air tastes harsh, tastes of emptiness, tastes of need. The pyramid ahead looks small and flattened. Surreal. He takes off his gloves and opens his pack and takes the water bottle out. He unscrews the lid, puts the rim to his lips, and tips his head back to drink. So much effort even in this. He swallows, pauses for breath, choking for breath, and now he is coughing violently again, his throat and lungs burning as though he were spewing fire, his ribs ripping apart in pain. He works to tame the cough. He drops the lid of the water bottle, and as he bends to reach for it he drops his gloves to the snow. He falls to his knees, struggles for the gloves, but they are lifted by a gust of wind. He crawls forward and reaches and again the wind gusts them up, as if someone were playing a trick, and then he lunges and traps them under the length of his body. He rests a minute, feeling a moment of relief. He rises to his feet, gloves back in hand, and as he is putting them on he sees the backpack moving away from him. He thrusts his arms out as the thing goes sliding away down the cliff. And then it is gone. His arms are held out stiff, still waiting to take hold of it as he watches the pack that carries his brother's ashes go sailing off the steep pitch, tumbling out into the nothingness. The howling is a sound that comes from him, though he hears it as the wind. He brings his hands to his head and looks down into the emptiness, into the great yawning hole below, the echoing wailing pumped through his blood, frozen into his bones.

HER LIPS were cold as metal when he touched them, her face changed to porcelain, pale and bluish, translucent. She was beautifully serene. He had never seen a face so serene, like a fairy-tale queen in slumber she was. She had a look of just-about-to-smile on her face. He put his lips to her cold lips. He tied the knitted strings of her wool cap beneath her chin and he kissed her again. Then he entombed her into the sleeping bag, the zipper sounding an unbearable moan in the closing.

His father helped him carry her body out of the tent. They had no rope to secure it to the slope with, so they wrapped loops of tubular webbing around the down bag at the head and the feet. They used their ice axes to stake the slings into the snow, anchoring the bag into place. They would not move her until her father returned from the summit. Reddy would have to tell him. Troy would radio once he was arrived back to Camp III, and then Reddy would speak the words to him. He would say, "I am sorry. I have some bad news," he would say. He thought of all the times he had uttered these words in the past, words engraved into the seams of his brain having been so often repeated. How could he say the same to his friend?

Reddy tried to break his son out of the frozen silence between them. Devin remained curled on his side in his sleeping bag facing the wall of the tent, listening to the wind cry out like a woman giving birth. Finally the wind settled, and the stillness about them grew immense and horrible.

"I am sorry," his father said. The words burned like dry ice in the throat. They scalded his lips. He crawled out of the tent and left his son alone. The sun was hot and brilliant, pouring its light upon the lonely and colorless slopes. Mysterium rose merciless, remorseless, cold. He looked to the summit, where Troy might have by this time made his hard-won appearance. Why not climb up and meet his friend at Camp III? It would be better to be with Troy when he said to him what he had to say. If he left now he could make it up the buttress before nightfall. He turned back to the tent to gather his gear, and he saw that Sara's sleeping bag was gone. He stood for a moment, bewildered into position. Then he rushed forward to see the depression the body had left in the snow. But no, no body. No stakes, no webbing, no anything. He turned and surveyed the wintry emptiness around him. He called his son's name out. He called again. He put his head inside the tent, his son lying there quiet and alone. Reddy got up and looked around again. His eyeballs constricted in the cold. He blinked, frozen in pose, lips parted and hardened as if shaped by the word *how*. How does a person simply vanish? This, a question not the first time asked of himself.

. . .

TROY TOILS on in silence, in the deathly hush of nothingness. The spell of vitality he felt at the start of the day has melted away. In this vertical desert of ice he is small, he is helpless, he is alone. Something near despair hovers in the vastness above. Not a sound other than what is inside him, the churn and throb and pant of a man subjugate to something beyond. He leans into the wind and presses on, every boot track he leaves in the snow an imprint of will. He sees himself writing scroll across the face of the mountain. Indelible. Not to be forgotten.

He walks over the frozen dunes with arms hung loose at his sides, his head lowered, his eyes set upon the patterns the wind has glyphed in the snow. Like the writing of the ancients. Messages left for him to decipher. He looks up only occasionally to the pyramid, the zenith appearing at times to be rearing closer to him; at other times it is grown farther away than it has ever been. He does not look behind him, does not see the dark speck that Wilder has become on his retreat back to Camp III.

He has the sensation of moving under water in slow motion. He has lost his sense of distance; no longer has he any idea of time. There is a certain derangement necessary in the going on. Yes, he knows this. He climbs as one possessed, borne aloft by some unexplainable impetus. A quest of transcendence. No more feelings. No reason. Only striving. Step, rest, take breath, take breath, take breath. Breath that fills him up again to step. Then step again, rest again, breath again. The snow is floury and deep, the going agony. He falls to his knees and slumps forward onto his ice axe, settles his head on his hands at the adze. He is thinking about how long he can go on when he is startled to his feet. A voice. He looks up, scans his whereabouts. No one. Ha! It is only the sound of himself again. He sees an easier line to take. Up and over to the right. Up and out of the trough. He traverses into harder and grainier snow, the pitch turning steep as a church roof, but his boots sink in only up to the ankle now. Clouds pulse in the distance. He has again the feeling there is someone walking behind him. His breath is like the voice of someone other. His footfalls like the words of another.

Lack of needed oxygen in the blood; a body and mind in rapid decay.

He does not believe in ghosts.

He walks in a swelling mist, crystals twisting past in bodily shapes. Beside him, enormous torsos of cornices. The way begins to plane out. A most hollowed experience. Yes. He belongs no longer to the world below. The clouds break apart like a cracked egg, spilling out a yolk of sun, spilling out life all about him. The air is revealed in a rare transparency, the landscape the quintessence of purity. The crust of icy diamonds he walks upon ring like chimes beneath his feet. How to describe the wonder of this? Wind silent. Air of glass. The sun touching him like love. Above him nothing but sky. Man is not meant to be here. Yet he stands here. He stands at the top with the cruel and beautiful Mysterium beneath his feet.

And then he sees it. The white bird winging across the vastness before him. Boreal, accidental, rapturous. Cryptic, with quills of snow. Moving without sound into the silence. Fading into shadow until it is gone from sight.

WHAT, THEN, *is the impulse, the* thymos, *the voluntary pathos that drives the seeker? Is the striving in a climber, in each man or woman alive, as with every animal, not the same as that within any force of nature? The contest of existence, the noumenal force we are born to, the thing in and of itself, this, life's essence which a human is but a mirror to, just as the moon is a mirror to the sun.*

Birth and death belong to this essence, the natura naturans, *the* mysterium tremendum *propelling all into being. Even in the presence of quietus, we need not fear being cleaved from the unity and eternity of nature. Thus death cannot be seen as an end, but only as part of an entirety. Nothing divine dies.*

EPILOGUE

Five years after the death of Sarasvati Troy, the Indian Army sent seven men from their parachute regiment to make a lustrum attempt of Mysterium's east and main summit. After their success, the soldiers down-climbed to a high-altitude plateau between the two peaks, where here they placed a pile of memorial stones for the girl who had been christened with the bliss-giving goddess's name. They camped that night near their shrine of cairns under a veil of rainbow-colored cloud, a nimbus halo'ing a golden full moon. One of the men, arm raised and hand outspread, entombed the moon finger to thumb so to frame the colorful aureole.

The next day, in gloriously brilliant sunshine, the troop began its descent through a steep pass of new-fallen snow, where here they were swept away to their breath-taking end.

A NOTE ABOUT THE AUTHOR

Susan Froderberg was born in Washington State and grew up hiking and climbing in the Olympic Mountains and the Cascades. She worked as a critical care nurse in Seattle before moving east to study medical ethics and philosophy at Columbia University, where she received her PhD. *Mysterium* is her second novel.

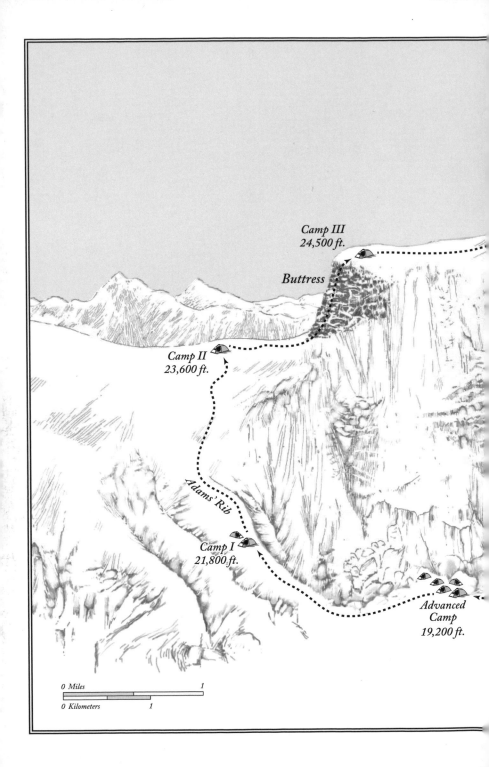

Camp III
24,500 ft.

Buttress

Camp II
23,600 ft.

Adams' Rib

Camp I
21,800 ft.

Advanced
Camp
19,200 ft.

0 Miles   1

0 Kilometers   1